A CURSE
OF
FEATHERS
AND
FIRE

Emma Bradley

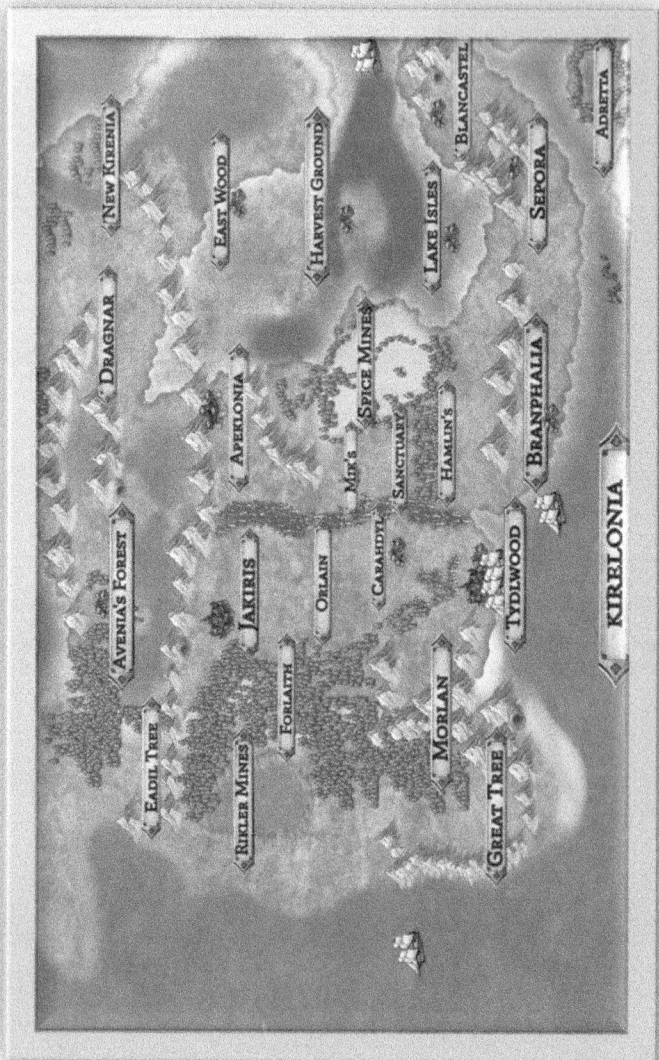

DEDICATION

For all of us who grew up reading fantasy
living in our own heads
and wishing for a place to belong,
somewhere that truly felt like home

Welcome to Kirelonia

ISBN: 978-1-915909-28-2

CHAPTER ONE

'One bird, two birds, three birds craw, jagged
wings bring death to the door'

When the dark shadows passed over a small settlement deep in the heart of the Kirelonian eastlands, the folk patted their chests twice. Once to guard their own hearts and again to protect those around them.

Sat in the open doorway of the settlement's candle shop drenched in the dazzling white light from the sun, Neri lifted her head to watch the dark blot soaring high above, three crawbirds flying to form a jagged line with their ridged ashy wings.

Ignoring the superstition that the locals clung to, she swiped the blade in her hand across a cylinder of wax with deft flicks. The folk of the settlement didn't regard her as one of them despite her spending a whole winterspan of seasons among them, but she was useful and times were hard.

She lifted her head and checked the nearest windowsill but the dish of seed she'd left out for the birds was still half full. Large or small, smooth-winged or jagged, she wouldn't let silly child-tales stop her from doing what she had done since she was old enough to walk.

"-Restrictions. Fluff and dander, that's all it is. I'd like to see them do an honest day's work!"

Neri smiled to hear Lorilee's voice and looked across the cracked dirt of the lane outside. Lorilee was a great friend of Hamlin, the old man who owned the candle shop, and she often came by to chat. Hamlin insisted Lorilee was seen as something of a soothsayer by some and a cranky baggage by most. No doubt she was harping on about the latest commandment by the local patrols, but it was dangerous to speak ill of the Governance in public.

"I don't care if they do hear me!" Lorilee's voice rose. "Let them! What are they going to-"

A bumping noise echoed over the last of her words, the rhythmic *thud-thud-thud* of cartwheels cutting Lorilee's vitriol stone dead.

Chills rippled over Neri's arms and legs, her instincts roiling at that familiar sound. Scanning the lane, she clenched her fist around her blade, the urge to run pounding. Along the lane folk dashed into whichever dwelling was nearest. Unless you had no heart and even less sense, you accommodated anyone who needed shelter when a Governance patrol went by. Better to shelter someone you hated than face their family afterwards if you didn't.

The cartwheels grew louder, accompanied by the stomping of boots. Neri inched to her feet in the doorway of the shop as they came into view, six patrol members cloaked in dark grey with two horses pulling a warped wooden cage on a cart.

"What's this then?" Lorilee demanded, apparently determined to go down swinging. "Come to drag us all off have you? Where'd you get your favours then? Hmm? What- get your hands off me!"

Neri took a step forward, her foot scudding past the sanctuary of the doorframe and into the fierce sunslight. She froze, hovering on the boundary between the decency of stepping in and fear of them targeting her next.

Memories of those boot-stamps had echoed outside her family's dwelling shortly after her mama died. First her mama, then her gramma had disappeared, turning up dead a few days later.

Neri flinched as a pressure landed on her shoulder. Even as she whirled around to find Hamlin right behind her, she had her hand up to strike, her other arm sturdy with the carving blade ready for a second attack. Lorilee's strident protests had turned frantic, filling the air with indignance mingled with pleading.

"Nothing we can do," Hamlin said, his tone quiet.

Neri barely had a second to struggle as he pulled her inside and shut the shop door, let alone argue.

"We can't leave her to them!" she insisted.

Hamlin rubbed a hand over his tired, wrinkled face.

"Lorilee knew the risks and she made her choice. Getting involved now will do no good for you and it won't help her either."

Every nerve fired with the urge to rush out there, to protest, to do *something,* anything. But Neri stayed behind the door as the stamping started again and the rumble of the cart followed it along the lane with Lorilee's protests fading fast.

The moment the sounds died away, Hamlin patted Neri's shoulder and let her go.

"You're too young to spoil her life for the sake of opinion," he said.

He stood silent for a long moment before swinging the door open again, letting in the sunlight. Only the silence outside gave a reminder of what had happened.

Neri watched him walk slowly to the door at the back of the shop that led to the candle vats, then she dropped back down to sit in the doorway.

Hamlin was right but it didn't make it any less awful. Lorilee was harmless but the Governance didn't care.

Any sense of individuality, any sign of pertinent thought, and there they are with their stupid boots, stamping stamping stamping.

She inhaled a sharp breath to quell the urge to scream and picked up a candle from her basket, hacking at it with savage fingers. Anyone expecting Lorilee to return was a fool, and nobody would dare to as much as mutter about it either. Folk desperate enough would run straight to the grey-cloaks and tattle. Maybe in the deep of night they whispered to those they trusted, but otherwise Lorilee was no longer a part of their settlement and folk would plod on regardless.

Neri had found it strange at first, living in such a small community where everyone clung to the smiles, nods and pleases that were reminiscent of an older, safer time. But the Governance continued to reach its devious fingers further through the realm, until their silver and red banner hung from every garden wall, inn window and mail-post, and the sound of horns bellowed a curfew every evening without fail.

But it was still better than rumours of what happened in the westlands beyond the supposedly cursed forest.

Neri dropped her candle and blade into the wicker basket at her side, starting in surprise as a shadow fell over her legs. She knew most folk who came for candles, but the newcomer who towered over her didn't look like a local, tall and shadowed against the suns with the hood of their cloak shrouding their face.

A quick glance into the shop and Hamlin was right there as if he'd sensed her uneasiness. More likely he'd heard the stranger arriving, but he seemed to have an unerring knack of appearing wherever and whenever he was needed.

"Come, be welcome." Hamlin beckoned. "It has been more than mere days since we talked."

The figure lurking in the doorway glanced down, and Neri narrowed her eyes in reply. Despite her hostilities, the stranger stepped clean over her legs as if they were sleeping kittens and strode into the middle of the room.

Strong, pale fingers pushed down the hood, an odd choice in such sweltering weather. Harsh wisps of auburn beard made the young man beneath look grisly, with dark, sunken eyes that aged him, but he couldn't be much older than her nineteen winters young or twenty, the rest of his face youthful enough behind flicks of auburn hair. Neri assessed him as his gaze drifted back to her.

With an outstretched arm and no word of introduction, Hamlin invited his guest through the door at the back of the shop, following him through and shutting the door behind them.

Neri clambered to her feet, snagging the candle basket on her way to the shop's counter.

Shouldn't pry really.

Hamlin had taken her in after her mama's death but they didn't encroach on each other's past or personal space. Still, the shop had become her home over the past year. Since running away from the cesspit the settlement she'd grown up in had become, Neri hid herself away with Hamlin.

The shop became her sanctuary with its routine customers coming to trade for candles and the quiet bubble and crackle of the wax being melted in the vats. She knew the smooth brush of every warped wooden shelf on the walls and the placement of each wicker basket full of colourful candles. Most of the floor space was left empty, but often she would sit in the shop doorway and watch the lane. Sometimes Governance patrols would go by and she would duck inside, but more often than not it was just folk going about their business, as if the civilisation they knew wasn't collapsing around them.

She stopped at the counter and looked down at a mass of black fur, her frown softening as Dog lifted his shaggy black head and panted over her ankles. Stuck until Hamlin and his mysterious guest reappeared, she pushed her hand into the pocket of her faded blue shorts. Her fingers skimmed the dimpled surface of the small token there.

Today was her birthday, but she had nobody left now who might remember.

I've been here almost a winterspan. There can't be any harm in wearing it for today.

She pulled the token out of her pocket and stared at it. The dark grey stone sat on her palm, a flat piece of rock chiselled into the shape of a curved feather. All children were gifted their own token when they were born, each surface flecked with glimmering facets of pale gold and silver that caught the light and created prisms in all the colours of the rainbow. Each token had a different image carved on it, but Neri didn't know the meaning of the feather on hers.

Ignoring her mama's warnings from long ago that folk shouldn't see her with it, Neri let the token drop on the end of its delicate silver chain and clasped it around her neck.

Mama might not be here anymore, but I still have this to remind me of her.

She clenched her fist around the token. In the days before the Governance took power over the eastlands, she could have gone to the academy like she'd dreamed of in younger years. But the moment the elite seized power and overturned the traditional ways in favour of control, the land went to ruin fast. If it weren't for them and their restrictions, her mama might have had access to a healer, might have survived.

Neri shook the more morbid memories away. Survival was the goal for most folk now and Hamlin giving her a place to stay was a blessing. She couldn't risk returning to the settlement she'd grown up in or to Apeklonia, the vast settlement she'd been born in hadn't been her home since she was barely able to crawl. Anger and grief turned her mind sour, like withering blooms rooted in poisoned soil.

One day I will make them pay for what they've done, what they've taken from me.

A low hum reached her ears. She cast a glance sideways toward the door to the vats, knowing the catch was broken and the door sometimes drifted open by accident. It stood ajar and the voices floated out from within.

"Never mind that, it'll keep for now. What news do you have for me?" Hamlin asked.

"We haven't found much." The stranger's voice was low, secretive. "Moonshine's hunting in the south but we're coming up against obstacles. This latest threat from the Governance will likely force most of us into hiding for good now."

Neri left the counter and inched toward the vats, prepared to flee across to the shop door at the first sign of movement.

A long moment of silence passed. She took a careful step back.

"I may need you to take care of my effects soon," Hamlin continued. "You'll do the right thing?"

Neri frowned. Hamlin having his 'effects' taken care of sounded scarily final.

The stranger huffed. "You're asking me? Why?"

"I trust you, Niall. You think someone like Finn would be a better choice? I wouldn't ask otherwise."

The stranger, Niall, said nothing for a long moment.

"Fair point. Finn is on the move anyway, so you're stuck with me."

"Are you sleeping out still?"

"Not anymore."

"You're at the sanctuary?"

"Yes, for now."

Niall didn't seem inclined to give much away. That at least Neri could relate to, but the mention of sanctuaries drew her attention.

Some kind of resistance? She'd heard rumblings of course, but never anything this blatant.

A scuffling sounded from the lane outside and she whirled around. A young girl hovered in the doorway. Her fingers clung onto the doorframe like claws and unruly blonde curls spilled over her skeletal shoulders.

"Hello." Neri smiled. "Are you okay?"

The girl didn't answer, one foot braced to run.

"Hungry?" she asked again.

The girl nodded and looked at her feet, but not before Neri saw the hint of shame in her eyes. Neri kept her footsteps steady and her stance unthreatening as she went across to her pack. It was an old one, sewn from a sacking pouch used for carrying grain or fruit, but it had served her well so far. The straps were crusted with grime and the rope looked like it might break again soon, but she had kept it useable for the last few winterspans and didn't plan to lose it now. Inside she still had two packets of grain that could be softened with water and some boiled resin sweets that would probably have survived the land's ending. She rescued the bag from underneath Dog's head and

9

approached the girl.

"Here, take these." She handed over the lot. "I can get more if I need to."

The small parcels neatly wrapped in fabric barely fit into the girl's arms but Neri refused to take the vehement head shaking for an answer.

"He feeds me well here and I can gather more. All I want in return is one of those flower crowns you have in your hair. My fingers are so clumsy and I can't make them anywhere near as well as you. It's not often we get to have pretty things anymore."

She lied easily, her fingers still more than nimble enough from the precision of candle carving. The girl's flower crown of dusky blue blooms had seen better days, but the offer would be refused unless some kind of trade was agreed on.

The girl bowed her head, arms shaking. The submission was a serious sign of trust, for they both knew Neri could well be capable of doing anything to her, three times her height and much stronger. With the lightest touch she could manage, Neri plucked the browning flowers from the girl's hair and stepped back.

"There you go. Will you be able to get home safely, is it far? I don't want anyone to try taking that lot from you."

The girl nodded, a tiny smile flicking at the corner of her mouth.

"I can hide better than most," she whispered. "Thank you."

Just like that, she was gone. Neri sighed, her shoulders sagging. Helping others wasn't something folk did anymore, not unless there was some trade-off in it for them. From what she'd seen the sheer act of survival had killed off a lot of the communal spirit she remembered from younger years.

"That was kind." Hamlin's voice made her jump. "She's been hanging around and darting away whenever I go near. If she'd asked me for food or candles, I'd have given them to her freely. I even thought about leaving a box outside but it'd only get taken by some chancer or one of the Governance patrols."

Neri shrugged. She got the feeling that Hamlin was as harmless as he seemed, but mistrust was a hard habit to break.

In the silence that drifted down around them, Hamlin looked from her to the mysterious Niall, who so far hadn't said a word or made any movement to leave.

"I have some wine behind the counter," Hamlin said, his eyes widening with hope. "I was saving it for a special occasion, but when do I get to have two friends around these days?"

Neri frowned, curious about the wine. Such a luxury was hard to get without proper coin or trade, unless you had the ability to make it from scratch at home but even then, the berry bushes seemed to be growing less and less every winterspan. As Hamlin unearthed a dusty, black drinking pouch from beneath the counter, she tried to keep her expression neutral. The pouch hadn't been there two days ago when she'd tidied. Either Hamlin had been expecting Niall's arrival, or he thought this occasion might be the last chance he had to drink it.

As Hamlin poured into wooden cups, Neri eyed the lane. The suns were finally beginning to drift behind the rooftops which meant the mysterious Niall either lived close by or he would be risking a lot by being out after curfew.

None of my business. If something is changing though, I'll need to replace that food I gave the girl and be ready to move on.

Hamlin held out a cup to her with a generous splash of fruity-smelling purple wine inside and Neri took it without argument.

"Thank you."

Unaccustomed to drinking wine, the acidic flavour made her cheeks twinge and her throat seize.

"Niall?" Hamlin held up a cup already poured.

Niall shook his head and swept toward the doorway before Neri could step clear of it. A waft of something whirled through her nostrils, a sweetness like short-night spice. She savoured the swoop in her stomach for a split second and the zing of childhood memories the scent conjured.

As Niall shot one final glance at her with dark brown eyes and darted away, Neri stared after him. He had his hood up again as he strode down the lane then he was gone, out of sight as if he blended right into the lengthening shadows.

Neri eyed the Governance's banner hanging tall and wide at the far end of the lane, silver splashed with red. She stuck her tongue out at it, wishing she could take a blade or a match to it instead.

Hamlin sighed. "I think it's time to shut up shop."

Neri turned the sign to 'Closed' but kept the door open. When the curfew patrols arrived as they did every evening, ringing their bells to chase folk into their dwellings, she'd have to close and lock it. But until then Hamlin seemed happy to indulge her need for the outside world.

"Neri?" He hovered at the bottom of the steps that led up to his dwelling above the shop. "If anything should happen to me, you can trust Niall. I don't say it to worry you, but you can rely on him as you can me."

The memory of his earlier words danced into her mind, about Niall taking care of his effects.

"Why would anything happen to you?"

Hamlin smiled, but Neri couldn't be sure if she was imagining the wistfulness in the one-sided press of his mouth.

"Consider it old man's folly," he reassured her. "I just want you to know you can be safe."

The loud blaring of the Governance horns tore through the otherwise silent street and Neri moved to shut the door. She wasn't even sure she should stay another night if Hamlin kept saying alarming things, but she couldn't be caught outside after curfew without a good reason. She locked the door and turned to resume her questioning.

"Huh," she muttered.

Hamlin had disappeared and the door at the top of the stairs was shut, a clear sign that she'd get nothing further from him now. Uneasy, she retreated to her blankets which hid her well behind the counter at night. She would question him in the morning.

With her eyes shut tight, she decided that for one night she would avoid the nightmares that plagued her. Each bedtime she vowed the same thing when waiting for sleep, but always the spirits and spectres from her past swirled through her mind, dragging her down.

It seemed like only moments had passed when she woke again, the faint swirl of memories still clinging. She reassured herself with panicked panting that it was only a dream, but the sounds lingered. She sat up, her clammy skin chilling through to the bone. Shouting voices and banging doors out echoed out in the lane along with that tell-tale stamping that sent revulsion searing through Neri's veins.

The Governance had returned.

CHAPTER TWO

Dog started barking at the shadows outside the shop, a sure enough sign that Neri's instincts were correct.

A loud bang echoed on the door to the lane. With her carving blade in hand and her pack over her shoulder, Neri crept around the counter and through the darkness toward the stairs. If she could get up there to get Hamlin without being seen, he would be able to no doubt smooth any situation over with his usual genteel charm.

Several dark shadows flitted in organised formation past the windows. With the incessant nighttime heat filtering in, she hadn't bothered to close the shutters so the gaps were still open to the elements.

Hamlin must have woken by now with this noise.

She took a breath and dashed toward the stairs. Halfway up, a fuzzy pair of purple slippers appeared in her line of vision. She looked up to see Hamlin in a neat sleeping suit of fine fabric, trousers and even a long-sleeved waistcoat like one of the lords painted from old tales. Unlike the men in those stories, Hamlin's face set with grim determination. Neri gulped down a squeak as he pushed her roughly around him until she stood on the step above, indicating with his hand that she should go upstairs. When she opened her mouth to respond he pulled her close, his lips pressing against her ear.

"They've come for me. Go upstairs and out of the bedroom window. There's a wall you can drop down onto in the alley."

"Wait, who's come for you?"

A loud hammering hailed down on the shop door followed by the crash of boots on wood. Neri couldn't make out what the knocker shouted but it obviously wasn't a social call.

"Remember that you can trust Niall," Hamlin hissed. "Take what's on the bed too. If you stay here, they will take you and who knows where you'll end up. Don't ever let them find you."

"What about Dog?"

"He has his own way out, don't worry. Remember that Niall will keep you safe. Trust him. Now go!"

Neri tumbled up the steps and into Hamlin's sleeping room with her entire body shaking. She'd only been upstairs a few times to fetch or carry things, but often enough to know that Hamlin was exceptionally messy. Now it seemed he'd turned into a reformed character, the room so neat that his shelves had no clothes on them at all and the piles of books and old papers were nowhere to be seen. She wondered whether he had been planning to run but saw no pack. There were no portraits or personal effects visible either.

A loud bang downstairs suggested the shop door had finally been kicked open. Neri froze to listen but the hum of voices were low rather than raised. She threw open the shutters on the window and stayed as close to it as she could, her mind sticking when she thought of her own meagre pack still downstairs.

No time now. Get out, find somewhere to hide and come back for it once the danger is gone.

Her gaze snagged on Hamlin's bed and a dark, bulky lump marring the uncharacteristically neat blanket. She reached out. A small, leather-bound book the size of an adult hand had been left behind, with a length of leather cord wrapped around the middle and tied in a neat bow. Beneath that lay a scrap of paper, the ragged edges torn by hasty fingers. Neri saw her name scrawled on the top in a thin, spidery hand and grabbed the book.

She flinched as something clonked against the window frame, then a figure appeared balancing on the sill.

"*Vahda.*" The cursing voice was low and hushed. "Come on, you need to come with me."

Niall's head was shrouded in his hood and he didn't sound in the mood for arguing. Neri slid the book into her pack and pulled the drawstring tight, knotting the end. Niall scowled at the delay, but then his gaze flicked to the dagger still in her hand.

"Either come with me or you'll die here," he insisted.

If he thought she was in need of someone protecting her, he was wrong, but voices floated up from downstairs with the echo of meaningful threats and she only had one exit left.

Niall disappeared as she took the last few steps to the window and leaned out. In the glow of lanterns from the street, she could see his outline on the short, sloping roof below. Further down in the alleyway, Dog paced semi-circles, his head pointed up at her.

Neri climbed up to perch on the windowsill, her knees bent against her chest and her hands holding the wooden frame. Panic clenched tight and burning in her gut as Niall moved limber like a cat and leapt across to a stone wall on the other side of the alley. He turned, his legs bent ready to spring and his hands braced against the tiny ledge of stone he balanced on. For that moment, his dark eyes glimmered feral in the firelight from the lane as he looked back at her. Then he dropped down into the alley.

Neri stepped down onto the sloped roof and made her way to the closest point to the wall. She had no hope of matching his gracefulness but she needed to get down somehow and took a deep breath as she secured her pack over both shoulders.

As she leapt, she knew she wouldn't make it to land on her feet. She reached out with her fingertips, the rough surface of stone scoring the skin on her palms. Dropping to the ground, she winced at the jarring in her legs and forced herself upright as Dog appeared beside her.

"Follow me," Niall whispered. "Whatever happens, whatever you hear, stay silent."

Instead of creeping away from the street as she'd expected him to, he inched along the wall toward the shadowed crowd in the lane. Neri kept right behind him, each shuffle of her boots scratching on the dry earth. Dog's hot breath puffed against her bare leg and she inhaled sharply to keep her panic at bay.

Niall glanced behind him with a warning look and motioned with one hand that she should stay put. He didn't look back to check if she was obeying him and rebellion bubbled.

He can't tell me what to do.

As Niall crept closer to the lane, Neri stayed right behind him.

"We know you're a part of the scum that has been opposing the natural law and order of things." An unfamiliar male voice filled the air. "Your so-called resistance has been foiled at every turn and now it's all but extinct."

Neri froze as Niall halted in front of her.

There really is a resistance? And Hamlin is part of it?

She peered over Niall's shoulder to get a better look at the speaker. Silver-haired and tall with a long grey beard, he surveyed the lane with a cold, cruel smile. He stood in front of a row of men, their uniform of grey cloaks giving away exactly who they represented.

"Let me tell you, the resistance is stronger than you know." Hamlin's voice rang out calm and clear. "We will always fight for those you see as undesirable and the folk you've cast out."

Neri bit her lip as the smile faded from the man's face and he stepped forward, hands clasped in front of him.

"Enough. We know who you are and what you represent. Did you think we wouldn't find you? Wouldn't hunt you down to the end? You should have stayed on the other side."

Niall turned and flinched to see Neri so close. He glared

at her and flicked one hand to suggest she should set off in the other direction. When she didn't obey, he dodged around her and grabbed her hand.

"What about the girl?" The man's voice echoed through the otherwise silent night. "We've been watching for days and we know she's been staying with you. We know she's here."

"You tell me," Hamlin replied.

"Stubborn to the last. Very well. We know she has been seen about in a rather distinctive cloak, so we'll find her soon enough."

Neri's skin rippled with chills, her mind flinching to the winter cloak lining the bottom of her pack, its dark reddish brown fabric patterned with feathers of bright orange, gold and grey.

She tried to pull herself free but Niall had a tight grip on her fingers and hauled her behind him as he moved back down the alley. It was either stumble after him or go smack into the hard earth, but being dragged by him meant she missed anything Hamlin might have said. The chilling whisper of blade-metal scraping on a holder of hide caught her attention.

"Any last words?" the man asked.

Niall's step faltered. In the mouth of the alleyway, he came to a ragged halt.

Something swooshed through the air, a quiet swoosh followed by a muffled thud.

Then the realm could have heard a blade of grass drop.

Niall let go of Neri's hand and she used it to wipe the sudden flow of tears away from her cheeks. Hamlin would be dead when she looked back, so she didn't. Couldn't.

Without waiting for Niall, she ran.

She scrambled over the wooden fence that bordered one of the harvest fields still in fallow, her legs aching from her jump. Dog wriggled under the lowest bar of the fence, staying with her.

The memories swelled and threatened to choke her, the image of her mama's body flaring in her mind's eye, the pale, drowned vision of her gramma's coming next. And Hamlin, now she had the imagination of his death vivid before her. She sucked in a sob, her steps tumbling on without any hope of control.

She didn't look back to check if Niall was behind her, focusing only on reaching the cover of the trees ahead. Her feet dipped and snagged on grassy ruts but she refused to stop. Self-preservation surfaced sharp like the slice of a blade.

Hamlin was dead. The Governance wanted her, had enough knowledge of her to recognise her cloak. Her stomach churned, her legs burning with the sudden stint of running.

The edge of the trees rose like a dark wall, but a shadowed figure loomed in front of her and she plunged to a halt.

"Stop there."

She recognised Niall's voice. In the tear-smudged darkness she'd not even noticed him overtake her. His hood, shown only by the soft light from the multi-coloured stars dancing high in the sky, and the terse bite in his tone confirmed it was definitely him.

Neri folded her arms, planted her feet apart and glared, even though he probably couldn't see the full effect in the dark. Dog's bulk pressed against her legs, his hot fur scratching her skin. She took comfort from his loyalty.

"What was all that about?" she hissed, gesturing backwards. "Hamlin- they- he's-"

She couldn't get the words out, a lump forming in her throat. If she spoke them the tears would spring free again.

Niall sighed. "There's nothing we can do for him now. They'll be looking for you next so we should get moving."

Neri refused to budge an inch even though the past snapped up to bite at her. She wouldn't tell Niall why they were after her, not until she was absolutely sure he was worth trusting.

"Why would they be interested in me?" she demanded. "I'm nobody."

Niall shook his head. "I don't know. All I've got is what Hamlin told me, that I was to turn up tonight and guide you to our sanctuary. I didn't know he was going to be- I thought they'd take him away with them. Look, it's not safe out here so we need to get moving now. It's not safe to go back for luxuries either so forget any ideas about getting your stuff."

Neri heard the subtle catch in his tone. The memory of what she'd overheard returned to her then, Hamlin asking if Niall would take care of his effects.

Did that include me? Mama said Hamlin would always look after me if I ever went searching for him, but perhaps he promised her more than that. Perhaps he knew why those men are looking for me, which is more than I do.

Maybe he knew why folk turned up on Mama's doorstep a day after she died to ransack our home.

Neri shook her head and focused on Niall instead of having to review that memory again.

"Everything I own is with me," she said, wiping a hand over her tearful face. "Hamlin said you'd keep me safe, but we hardly know each other. Why should I trust you?"

Niall said nothing in reply, an immovable statue shrouded in shadow. Neri scoped out the nearest edge of woodland. Dog would hopefully follow her if she ran, but Niall was clearly fast on his feet. She couldn't be so sure that Dog would defend her if it came to an actual fight either.

"They mentioned that they've been watching the shop for days," Niall said. "If you stay here or try to run, they will catch you. Either they'll take you with them or they'll decide you're of no use and kill you. I know how to move unnoticed, so follow me and I will take you to safety, but it has to be now."

Neri wiped her face with her hand, any hope of spark or anger draining. She still didn't know why the Governance were after her family, or what they had wanted from her home either. She'd fled to Hamlin straight after that and hidden herself away in the settlement, but now she had nowhere left to run. A woman like her could get work in various settlements; she was strong and in no way work-shy. But the Governance would be hounding her everywhere she went, hordes of grey-cloaks twitching everyone's curtains until they finally found her. Perhaps Niall's sanctuary, wherever it was, would set her up with more supplies than she could get trying to survive alone. She didn't exactly have anything or anyone else to go looking for either. Not anymore.

Neri took a slow, deep breath and waved her hand toward the forest.

"Well then, by all means lead on. But I warn you, one wrong move and you'll regret it."

Without another word or any sign that he'd heeded her warning, Niall set off at a striding pace. Neri followed a few steps behind, her hand straying down to hold onto Dog's collar for support. She clung to him as they walked, taking comfort from his furry bulk pressing against her leg.

The night air was warm against her bare arms and legs, but she shivered from the shock as they blundered through the dark shadows between the trees. Her feet snagged on roots and brambles snared at her skin, but Niall never turned to see if she could keep up with him and his hood would have obscured any corner-eye views. He clearly didn't much care about what state she reached his sanctuary in.

She thought her way through the contents of her pack to keep her mind from spiralling into despair. Three spare tops, her winter trousers and her small packet of miniature portraits she had of her family. Her gramma's songbook.

She made valiant attempts to hold in the sniffs, but the tears soaked her cheeks as she walked.

Poor Hamlin, what did he even do to deserve that?

A twisting corkscrew of grief hit her chest, but she took relief in putting one foot in front of the other and from the leather of Dog's collar biting into her fingers.

They reached another field and Neri stared as Niall placed his hands on the rib-high fencing. He vaulted ninety degrees sideways over it with no sign of obvious effort and she scowled at his back as he continued on without waiting.

Infuriating man.

She followed him over the fence, the acidic ache in her legs erasing any sense of elegance or grace.

Back in the trees, she blundered and stumbled through the darkness. Roots and briars snarled at her bare legs, scratching at skin and scoring cuts. She wrenched her ankle somewhere along the way and lost all track of how long they'd walked for. But none of that seemed to hurt as much as the knowledge that another person she'd cared about had been taken from her.

Whoever that Governance leader is, he's clearly got resources and he killed Hamlin.

She breathed through the angry tension swelling in her chest, pulled her token out from underneath her top and clenched it tight in her fist. It was the only thing she had left of her family now. The unyielding edges of the stone dug against her palm, creating a tinge of pain that focused her mind. She would go to Niall's sanctuary to start with. She could offer to earn her keep, but if they weren't willing to let her stay then she could only hope they'd at least let her rest and refuel there.

When Niall stopped a long time later in a non-descript cluster of trees, Neri was so surprised that she almost cannoned into his back. Dog's tongue lapped against her bare legs and the attention stung, which meant her cuts were still raw.

Niall shuffled his shoulders and Neri realised he'd been carrying a large pack the whole time. He pulled out two mounds of soft blanket and a large wooden box. His eyes widened in the moonlight when he finally looked her way.

"You're all cut up." He stared at her legs.

She glared back at him. He'd seen her wearing shorts, yet he still set a blistering pace through dense woodland and now he was surprised. Her stomach growled and her emotions swirled around her weary, wrecked mind. She simply stood there staring at him, one hand still on Dog's collar.

Niall's dark eyes burned into hers, ringed with sunken hollows of shadow. In that first glance, he looked dead. She glanced down at Dog instead to avoid that gaze. Sensing her attention, Dog wagged his fluffy tail and she frowned back at him. She hadn't even thought of how she would feed him. She turned to voice this to Niall but he was busy opening a wooden box, taking out bread and cheese.

"It's nothing fancy but it's easy to carry and keeps well without spoiling in the heat. When we reach the sanctuary, you'll find much better food."

He offered her a large chunk of bread, over half of what was there, and a wedge of cheese. She immediately broke the bread in two, taking the smaller half for herself and holding out the bigger half for Dog to snap up.

As she ate her food, she vowed that she would find some wax from somewhere, make enough candles to sell and then buy a backpack to fill with food for Dog. But before any of that was possible, she needed answers.

"Before we go on any further, you need to tell me why they were after Hamlin. He said they'd come for him. Anyone with sense will recognise the grey-cloaks and what that means, but why Hamlin?"

Niall's brow lifted at the demand. He chewed his lip for a long moment before sighing.

"He knew it would happen eventually."

Neri frowned. "But why? Was he really part of some resistance? Does such a group even exist?"

"Why else would he say it?" Niall scoffed. "I can't explain it to you, but let's just say there are folk out there who want to ruin lives by dividing folk and the land, taking away everything they have. They take and give nothing back. So, it would be surprising if there wasn't anyone out there willing to fight."

That I can believe. But it still doesn't explain anything about who any of these folk actually are.

When she looked up, Niall's eyes were fixed on her chest. She glared at him.

"What?"

He pointed, as if that somehow made his behaviour any better.

"That charm is an unusual token to have this far east," he said. "Is it a family thing? Heirloom from somewhere other maybe?"

Neri looked down and saw her token. She grabbed it and dropped it under the neckline of her top but the damage had been done.

"It was my mama's, a bit of rock she had. Are we

27

moving on then?"

Niall bit his lips together and frowned at her. After a few moments, he nodded. Neri wondered if he'd intended for them to rest a while, but she couldn't exactly take back her prickly attitude now.

Niall repacked his pack and set off again. Neri couldn't tell if he was going steadier now that he'd seen her injuries or if she was imagining it. Either way, the slower pace was welcome. Her muscles ached. Her bones felt creaky and her head thumped. Steep hills urged shooting pain through her weary limbs. She kept her focus on her steps until Niall stopped again, this time at the edge of the forest. The odd pinpoint of light in the dark came from a settlement below them, but she had no way of knowing which one or how far they'd travelled.

"We'll rest here a while," Niall said. "Take this blanket and sleep. I'll wake you when it's time to move on."

The flat tone of his voice held no hint of emotion. A tremble of rebellion rose up at being ordered about, but Neri's belligerence failed her. She took the blanket that Niall held out to her instead and spread it on the ground. As Dog lay down next to her, she pressed herself close to his reassuring bulk and shut her eyes.

Niall settled somewhere nearby and she wondered if he intended to sleep. Whether he did or not didn't matter; she would stay awake until daylight. As she lay there with the sounds of rustling animals and the odd hoot of an owl, she tried to put the thought of Hamlin from her mind. Self-preservation cautioned that thinking of him now would only slow her down, but she couldn't stop herself from reliving the horror over and over.

Thoughts of Hamlin stampeded around her head, his kindness to her unwavering right until the end. She tried to ignore the gutting knowledge that none of it mattered anyway now. She had no family and no home left.

I can only hope I'll be half as lucky with this sanctuary as I was at the shop.

CHAPTER THREE

The suns were beginning to sink by the time they left the forest the next afternoon. A whole day of walking with very little food, and Neri had to acknowledge that Niall had given her way more than her share. She wanted to ask whether they should be finding or bartering for a horse, or at least a ride on a passing cart or carriage, but she kept her mouth shut. Even if Niall agreed, she'd have to admit that she had no coin or items to trade for a ride, let alone a horse.

She had no energy to demand answers of him either, although when a large flock of crawbirds flew overhead and they both looked up, he didn't move to tap his chest twice as protection. By the time he led her through a derelict settlement with no sign of folk in sight, Neri felt like fainting right there on the hot earth.

Niall came to a stop some moments later outside a small wooden gate and Neri lifted her head, hardly daring to believe they had made it. She stood behind him and stared up at a detached dwelling made of stone set at the end of a row.

White paint peeled off the crooked window shutters and the weathered stone slabs looked like they were at the point of crumbling. Only the garden appeared as a thing of beauty, an array of wildflowers throwing up bright colours among the yellowing grass that wilted in the oppressive heat.

Despite the dilapidated outside, Neri dared to hope for a soft set of blankets on a floor somewhere and maybe a full meal. Given the state of the dwelling, a place to bathe was probably pushing it. Even the gate hung off of its top hinge and creaked in protest when Niall pushed it open. He glanced around him as if checking for enemies and strode to the front door.

Neri followed. Her skin had caught the suns, prickling and tight, and her remaining shreds of resolve filled her with apathy. Only the thought that Dog could get water and possibly food inside stopped her from collapsing right there on the garden path.

Niall opened the door and stood aside to let her pass. Pushing down the wariness in jangling in her mind, Neri took a deep breath and walked into the dim coolness of a hallway, her fingers drifting over the dagger hanging ready by her hip. She blinked away the dazzles still twinkling in her eyes from the harsh sunslight outside and her mouth dropped open.

Murals adorned the warping wooden floor, lined with mixtures of vivid paint and chalk. To her left a small herd of unicorns galloped across the wall, and a vast watercolour tree climbed up to her right. Rainbows, flowers and mythical beasts held court all over the hall. In comparison, the stairs running up the left wall were bare, unmarked wood, but the banister was glowing as if someone routinely cleaned it.

Neri tensed at the sound of the front door closing behind them, then wooden bolts sliding shut. She clenched her fingers tighter around Dog's collar, her insides twisting into anxious knots. Niall opened a door to the right and indicated with his hand that she should go through. She eyed him for a moment with her mind firm on the dagger beneath her fingertips, then walked into a large room.

Sunslight danced through a bay window that dominated the wall to the right. An abundance of colour burst from paintings on the walls, and freshness wafted from the forest of potted plants that stood everywhere. Neri noticed the mismatch of furniture too, one battered purple sofa sitting in the middle of the room, accompanied by one paisley armchair and one brown leather one.

A woman got up from the sofa and approached with a serene smile. Neri took in the wild thatch of red hair and the ruddy complexion. Friendliness didn't often come easily and kindness wasn't always free, but this woman was smiling kindly enough. For now.

"Ma, this is Neri," Niall announced. "Hamlin sent her."

Neri turned to look at him in time to see the back of his hood disappear around the doorframe. Aware she was being scrutinised in depth, she turned her attentions downward to where Dog stood panting heavily under his thick coat. So far, he'd only managed to gain a drink from the river they'd passed earlier.

"Could we hold the inspection for a moment?" she

asked. "Dog hasn't had a drink for a fair while and it's baking buns out there."

She held onto his collar and expected some kind of reprieve for her boldness. The woman broke into a gentle smile and held her arms out wide. When she clucked her tongue, Dog moved. Neri released her grip on his collar out of shock as he left her side, aggrieved that his allegiance could shift so readily to this stranger. The woman ruffled Dog's fur and looked up.

"Dog and I go a long way into the past," she said with a chuckle. "Hamlin used to bring him here when he went away on his journeys. He's welcome here and so are you. We have a spare bedroom you can use and of course you're welcome to eat with us at mealtimes."

Neri's bottom lip dropped before she could rein in her surprise. She'd expected some kind of resistance after Niall had brought her in unannounced, but nothing appeared to ruffle the woman's calm.

"I'm Ma Kath, Ma because I look after everyone here at the sanctuary, not because I ever had children. You're welcome to stay as long as you need to. All I ask is that you don't tell anyone that this place exists. If Hamlin trusted you enough to send you here, I believe we can trust you too."

Bewildered, Neri nodded.

Who would I tell? The sharp sadness twisted in her chest again.

Ma disappeared into the hall without another word, leaving Neri alone. Dog padded back to Neri's side, staring up at her as if to beg her forgiveness for his disloyalty. She stroked his large head and wondered how long she could stay before her welcome was outlived. The suggestion of a bedroom, possibly with an actual bed and mattress, became irrepressibly enticing.

Then again, if I do have to move on, perhaps this will be the safest place for Dog to stay, even if it's without me.

Ma returned with a large wooden bowl full of water and to her credit she laid it close to Neri's feet. Dog fell on it and lapped like a condemned beast. Neri almost smiled when the cold, wet flow of his exuberance slopped over her boots, but she couldn't let her guard down.

"Now my dear, I'm not going to pry." Ma fixed her with a determined look. "But if you need to talk then I won't judge. First, let me show you your room."

Neri parted her lips, halfway to arguing and halfway to issuing gratitude. Words failed her when Ma took one of her sweaty, clammy hands and held it tight.

"You look so much like your mama."

Neri inhaled and gulped at the same time.

"I-" She spluttered.

When she didn't reply, Ma lifted her free hand and waved a faded portrait under Neri's nose. The small image on crumpled paper must have been sitting in Ma's pocket already, almost as if they'd been expecting her to arrive.

Neri stared down at it, devouring the sight of the familiar faces etched in coloured lead.

"That's Mama, and Gramma's there too. And that's you. Is that Hamlin? It is."

Ma Kath pocketed the portrait again before Neri could fully devour it.

"I hope that settles your mind about us at least a small amount," she said. "If Hamlin is gone then you owe it to him to continue his work. If we give you enough wax and a space to work, will you?"

The deep green eyes, narrow like a cat's, stared without blinking. Neri's bluster and doubt died on her tongue, her head bobbing in a nod of its own accord.

Ma smiled with tranquil brilliance once more and let Neri's hands drop. Exhausted, Neri followed her into the dim hallway and up the bare wooden staircase. She hesitated on the first floor to study the various doors all closed to her and almost missed Ma disappearing behind a towering storage wardrobe made of dark reddish wood.

This opulence was a far cry from the settlement at the base of the thriving citadel she'd known for most of her life, and the single level dwelling her family had lived in. Even Hamlin's shop ranging over the two levels had none of this faded grandeur.

She took a few steps forward and peered around the corner. Ma stood in an open doorway, hidden between the wall and the wardrobe's side. A narrow staircase disappeared up to the left and Ma led the way up. With one hand on her dagger, Neri glanced over her shoulder to check nobody was sneaking up behind her and took the stairs as fast as her weary legs would carry her, her free hand trailing over the lumps and bumps of the bare stone wall.

How much effort must it have taken to build the dwelling this high? It's almost palatial.

She emerged into a large, airy room with a door in the

opposite wall. It led to a short ledge cut into the slope of the wooden-tiled roof, big enough for two folk to stand on and walled by more stone. Two large plants stood against the walls in earthen-worn pots, their wide green fronds wilting in the heat.

"I'm staying in here?" she asked.

The narrow bedframe in the corner had a plump-looking mattress and even matching covers in soft golden brown. The last time she'd seen matching covers made with such care was at home on her gramma's bed, and those were old and continuously re-stitched.

Ma Kath nodded, her green eyes dancing an amused tango with her smile. Neri rotated on the spot, her weariness fighting and winning against any reservations she still had.

"Eva says the dinner is ready."

Niall had the silent footsteps of an alley cat and his voice made Neri flinch. She cast her eyes over her shoulder to him, noting that his hood was down and his copper hair was now swept back from his face. He watched her in return, the dark eyes alight with intense curiosity.

Neri managed to quell the alien urge to run toward him and throw her arms around his neck. She wanted to thank him for bringing her to somewhere she could rest in comfort and immediate safety, but she resisted. He'd done his duty to Hamlin, nothing more. He disappeared back down the stairs and Ma Kath headed after him, looking back as she waited for Neri to follow.

Neri didn't want to leave the room but couldn't risk being disagreeable, not until she knew the true trade for such kindness. So she followed Ma without complaint back down the stairs and through a glass door at the end of the entrance hall into a large kitchen.

The wooden floorboards were cracked but the counter surfaces shone with loving care. A young woman stood ladling soup into large bowls. With her wavy red hair and elegant face that held a faraway expression, Neri could easy believe this was Ma Kath's daughter. The same couldn't be said for the female ball of energy with the cascading yellow hair that sat on top of the counter, crammed into a small corner between the edge of a cupboard and the wall. She wrote furiously on a piece of paper while drumming her feet together, completely oblivious as other folk cascaded into seats around the table.

By an act of chance, Neri sat next Niall when chivvied to join the others. She took the bowl of soup Ma Kath held out and then a chunk of bread from the proffered platter. The others held meaningless conversations, mostly at Ma's insistence, but Neri didn't join in. She kept her eyes on her bowl and tried to be as inconspicuous as possible while all throughout the meal Niall's leg jittered and bounced beside hers. He seemed uneasy sitting still, and a wave of kinship swamped her full of understanding toward him.

The moment the bowls were empty, Ma's attention turned Neri's way.

"Everyone this is our newest resident," she announced. "I'm sorry, I'm so bad with names."

Neri mumbled her name, her cheeks flushing as she avoided several scrutinising pairs of eyes. Ma nodded and went around then to introduce everyone at the table. Eva, the young redhead who Ma insisted was no relation, gave her a curt nod. A paint-splattered young man called Matty smiled at her and of course she knew Niall already.

"We also have a few others who are out a-wandering at the moment," Ma added. "No doubt you'll meet them in time."

Neri nodded but uneasiness settled like a weight inside her. The brief mention of a resistance had her expecting something out of a fable, lines of battle-ready warriors queuing up to take on the enemy. This was little more than a dysfunctional family with the brief mention of 'a few others out wandering'.

This is it? She tried to withhold the accusing frown quivering on her brow. *They're more likely to be growing a bit of herbal and talking about spirit-lines than fighting an entire regime like the Governance.*

Everyone stood up to go about their own business, but Neri didn't have the heart to mention she wouldn't stay more than a day or two without some kind of reassurance. Only then did she realise nobody had mentioned the blonde girl still sitting on the worktop still scribbling away on her scrap of paper.

The suns started to sink outside, the heat lingering around them. Neri's mind wandered to the bed upstairs that was miraculously supposed to be hers for the time being. She got up, hoping nobody would notice her sneaking upstairs, and found Dog looking at her with expectant silence. She cursed under her breath and blushed when Ma turned to look at her. She hadn't thought about how she'd feed Dog either. She glanced at Ma, then at Dog, wondering how to broach the subject.

Ma smiled and took a comical sidestep toward a cupboard in the corner. Dog's nose loomed forward, his eyes widening to the size of platters as he watched.

"I always keep food here for dear old Dog." Ma chuckled. "Not easy to get the special pellets the local brewer used to make anymore but luckily they last forever. Then again, he'll eat anything. Including *my favourite mat.*"

Dog gave Ma a wide-eyed smile and slunk over to the bowl of food as she lovingly chastised him.

Neri hovered by the counter until he'd gorged himself suitably, aware of Ma now cleaning like a demon at the neat stone sink. She knew she should offer to help, but she couldn't see how anything she could offer to do would be a help rather than a hindrance. The moment Dog's bowl was empty and half the kitchen floor had been slopped with water from his bowl, Ma planted a determined hand on Neri's shoulder.

"Come on then, follow me," Ma insisted, sweeping her through the hall to the living room. "We call this the den. We're an odd bunch to be fair, but you'll soon get used to us."

Neri resisted the temptation to say she wouldn't be there long enough to get used to them. Everyone was being so kind to her, suspiciously so, and that made her wary.

But it seemed evenings were a social time for the household and she didn't dare say anything rude while the promise of the bedroom was still upstairs.

Eva slipped onto the window seat in the large bay with

a book in hand. Matty started waving a paintbrush across a blank space of stone on the wall. Ma sat on the sofa and Neri spied a sprig of blonde hair sticking out from underneath, which suggested the pixie from atop the kitchen counter had since moved to lie there.

She had three choices. She could stand there like an idiot, sit next to Ma on the sofa or find some excuse to disappear upstairs. Even Niall appeared at home, sunk low on one of the chairs with his head thrown back against the fabric. He raked strands of hair back from his forehead with a lazy hand and closed his eyes, letting out a tumbling sigh.

When Ma patted the sofa cushion beside her, Neri's decision seemed to be made. She occupied the tiniest section of sofa she could manage and glanced again at Niall. He seemed to be asleep already, but his head was trained in her direction and she caught his eyelids flutter open a crack then closed again.

"Tell us a little bit about you, Neri," Ma suggested.

Neri hesitated while Ma picked up a ball of wool and some wooden needles. With the repetitive clacking filling the room, at least she wouldn't be talking into a complete wall of silence.

"Hamlin took me in when my mama died," she began. "That was almost a winterspan ago. Until last night, until- Sorry, I don't seem to bring folk much luck I'm afraid."

"Oh, tosh." Ma's tutting danced into the crescendo of clacking noises. "Nothing about what happened to Hamlin was your doing. The Governance is behind this and they alone have his blood on their hands. It won't be forgotten either, I assure you."

Given her furious scowl and the sudden increase in determined needle clacking, Ma had a serious hatred of the Governance. Heartened by the vehemence, Neri managed to unwind her tense shoulders a little more.

"I didn't hear what they said to him or anything," she insisted. "I'm definitely not a fan of theirs for my own reasons, but I have no idea who they are."

Ma seemed to understand, her green eyes flashing. "You're in the right place then. The Governance are-"

"Ma." Niall shook his head with a warning look. "No need to bore her with all our backstories."

Ma rolled her eyes. "She deserves to know. Worst case, she thinks I'm a nut like everyone else around here."

"Oh sure," Niall grumbled. "Nut is the first thing we want new folk to think."

Neri might have laughed at that under normal circumstances, but she turned to Ma instead.

Whatever nonsense she comes out with, the Governance killed Hamlin and they're after me too, but I have no idea why.

"You've heard of the split between the east and west?" Ma asked.

Neri blinked. "The old fable about the cursed forest and how it keeps the east and west from fighting?"

Ma's needles flew faster and faster, her eyes narrowing.

"That's the one. The Governance are ripping up our land and they're afraid someone will find a way through the woods. If the west can make it through, they'd have a fighting chance of taking them down. They always had a mighty fighting force."

"So you're saying the Governance are against the union of the east and west, but there are folk out there looking for a way to unite the two? What did any of this have to do with Hamlin?"

And what do they want with me?

Ma sighed. "Let's just call ourselves a group of folk who don't want the Governance to succeed. They took over by force and they're running folk into the ground, but we're convinced-"

"That's enough." Niall's voice rolled off the walls, deep with warning.

Ma gave him a 'really?' sort of look, but said no more as he slumped back in his chair. Amazed that Ma was obeying him, Neri frowned in Niall's direction. Instead of being ruffled by her disapproval, he tipped his head back against the chair and closed his eyes again.

"You must be tired." Ma gave her a knowing smile, as though Niall's behaviour was totally normal to her. "Perhaps you'd fancy an early night instead, get yourself settled, hmm? Plenty of time to get to know everyone when you're feeling fresh tomorrow."

Neri shot to her feet. "That's probably best."

Without looking at anyone, she mumbled an awkward "night" and hurried out of the room. At the top of the stairs she glanced back, but nobody was following or watching her. She rounded the wardrobe, trying to ignore the thrill of childish secretiveness at the door hidden next to it. Darkness had finished falling outside but a small glow from above lit her way up the stairs, and she found a solitary candle flickering in an empty corner of the room.

Did Hamlin mention me somehow to these folk before he died? She wondered. *Maybe Niall did, although he wouldn't have been able to get here and back to the shop yesterday, not without a horse, and why would he leave a horse behind if we were travelling back here?*

Even more concerning, she didn't know how they could be so trusting of her candle-making skills without any proof, yet they seemed to be. It also didn't explain why the Governance were after her, but she could easily believe that her mama used to be involved in resistance sort of stuff.

These folk clearly want to bring down the Governance though and I've got nowhere else to go, nobody I want to run to.

She couldn't risk agreeing to help or stay long-term, but having something to work with and eventually sell on wherever her next journey took her was a reassuring thought.

Neri eased herself onto the soft bed fully clothed as Dog collapsed in a panting heap by the ledge door. From beneath her shorts, she pulled out the book and paper that Hamlin had left with her name on. She would wait to read it until the morning, when emotion would be further away from her than it felt now, but it was all she had left of Hamlin and she would keep it safe.

She pulled up a corner of the thick mattress and slid the parcel beneath it. Then she pulled a hair free of her head and curled it on top of the parcel, lowering the mattress down. If anyone went rummaging for secrets and tried to cover up their sneakiness, she would know.

Still not feeling calm about sleeping in a strange place, she eyed the room again. Her gaze settled on the solitary wooden chair in the far corner. After a moment's pause for what her hosts might think, she got up and took the chair down the stairs to the door that shut her room off from the communal hall, wedging it underneath the handle.

Settled on the bed once more with her eyes closed, she tried to ignore her imagination leaping at every fleeting creak and sigh from the vast dwelling.

So this is the great resistance. She rolled over onto her side with a disagreeable huff. *Either way, I'm safer here than I am out there.* She let the thought lull her toward slumber. *For now.*

CHAPTER FOUR

Heat seared Neri's fingers and her mind went from sleepy to self-aware in seconds. She wasn't in the shop and definitely wasn't sleeping outside. The memory of Hamlin and her long walk to the sanctuary with Niall jolted her upright and she stared at the sanctuary room with her pulse racing.

She glanced down to see her hand still hanging over the side of the bed, with Dog panting beside her. Given the bright light and stuffy heat, Neri guessed she'd slept late. Casting another look around the room, she noticed a pile of candle stubs in the far corner. If someone gave her some big stones and a slab of concrete, she could melt the stubs down. She would also need some firewood and a boiling pot, but the door that opened onto the roof ledge would provide enough air.

Her stomach growled, reminding her she'd have to face the house's other occupants to do any of those things. It was either suffer that or starve, but then they had been kind to her so far.

"You need to go outside?" she asked Dog.

He huffed to his feet, his tongue lolling out of the side of his mouth as he followed her down the stairs. She removed the chair from the door at the bottom and crept through the dwelling. As she approached the entrance hall, the memory of bolts sliding on the front door echoed in her mind.

Dog hadn't shown any signs of being desperate to go for a proper walk so far, and he was lazy at the best of times, but Neri decided she would take him outside for the necessary.

If they try to stop me from leaving then I know they can't be trusted. Then I need to find out why the Governance are interested in me.

The hallway was deserted and she almost reached the front door when Ma Kath appeared in front of her.

"I've found what you'll need for candle-making," she said with a soft smile. "I'll pop it up in your room. There's a stone slab and a pot for melting, as well as a few old moulds you can use."

Neri nodded and sidestepped around Ma. She lifted the catch on the front door but it stayed locked. The bolts at the top and bottom weren't drawn across, so the only thing keeping it shut had to be the old keyhole. Turning around, she caught the slight hint of amusement drifting across Ma's otherwise impassive expression.

"I'm going to take Dog out," she announced.

That should have been reason enough for Ma to set about unlocking the door for her but the woman didn't move. After a standoff of silent staring, Ma indicated back toward the kitchen.

"We have a garden he can lounge around in. He never was one for chasing creatures or exerting himself too much. We do need to be cautious about being seen outside, what with the Governance everywhere these days."

Against her better judgment, Neri resisted the temptation to push the issue. Without openly holding her hostage, Ma's insistent manner dictated that she was supposed to stay inside.

If I insist, they might show their true colours and we'll all know I'm a prisoner here. Better to be cautious and play along for now.

With a slow nod, she took measured steps away from the door. Ma led the way through the kitchen and pointed to an open door at the back that let in shining rays of heat. Keeping one eye on Ma as she passed, Neri stepped outside.

The dazzling blaze of sunslight beat down on an unkempt patch of grass that ran along the length of a garden, walled in by high wooden fencing. A small pond had been dug into the earth, bordered with stones and filled with the trickling sound of a fountain. She'd seen a couple of gardens before outside the more affluent dwellings in her childhood settlement, but she couldn't imagine Ma or any of the others ever living that kind of life.

Small trees and large shrubs grew around the edges of the grass, the scent of fresh and earth filling the air. The drowsy fragrance coming from a lilac tree were mixed in and delicate sprigs of jasmine climbed one of the fence panels. All the while the trickling of the fountain enhanced Neri's overwhelming desire to lie in the grass and forget whatever waited outside.

Dog seemed happy enough, disappearing behind a bush full of enormous round blooms of purple and blue for a minute before finding a shady patch of grass to lie on. By that point Neri's only thought was to get him a large bowl of water and find a way of bringing her candle equipment down so she could work outdoors.

The oppressive heat beaded sweat across her forehead but a sudden breeze stroked the perspiration away. Looking up she located gaps in the fencing only large enough to fit a thin book through, and then square holes in the wooden slats that ran overhead. The garden wouldn't provide any escape if the Governance came calling, especially for Dog's hefty bulk.

A scraping noise brought her round to face the kitchen door. Niall stood leaning casually against the wall of the house, his gaze fixed on her. She wondered if he'd been told to guard her in case she tried to escape, but before she could find anything to say to him he stumbled forward.

The blonde pixie girl from the evening before shot past him, her flyaway hair fluffing around her shoulders.

"Hi." She beamed with innate sunslight in her voice. "I'm Emelyn, folk often forget me when I'm on top of the walls or squeezed into a small space somewhere, so we haven't been introduced properly. I'm a scribe or trying to be. Sit please and I'll get you some breakfast."

Overwhelmed by the burst of unshakeable energy, Neri did as she was told, thudding down onto the grass. As Emelyn dashed off toward the kitchen again, Neri saw that Niall had disappeared back inside.

When Emelyn reappeared a minute later, she had a plate full of mixed egg and fresh honey-bread in one hand and two large bowls of food and water for Dog balanced in the other. Neri took the teetering plate and sank onto the grass with it on her lap, flinching when Emelyn sat next to her.

After the first few mouthfuls, Neri's defensive confidence had settled enough to be almost ready for the oh-so-innocent questions.

"Do you come from around here?" Emelyn asked.

Neri shook her head, using the convenient act of keeping her mouth full to avoid answering. Unperturbed, Emelyn soldiered on. None of Neri's non-committal answers dimmed her sunny smile or dissuaded her from asking.

"Well, I hope you will stay a while," Emelyn insisted eventually. "We could use a candle maker. We have to go into the next settlement like everyone else at the moment, or make our own but there never seems to be time, and the Governance are always lurking around lately. Hamlin used to send us some though whenever Niall went to visit. He was always so sweet."

Neri's chest swooped at the thought of Hamlin, her previous brief break from her emotions fuelled by food now over.

"I didn't know him long. Only for a winterspan, and only because my mama wanted me to go somewhere safe when she died."

Emelyn sighed. "It's so sad. But Niall said Hamlin taught you to make candles?"

Neri nodded. Her attention had drifted and now she

noticed Emelyn's clean, bare feet. She wondered how it would feel to remove her boots and socks. The few days of heat and sweat since leaving the candle shop would no doubt stink out the garden if she took them off so she decided against it. She would ask for water and a quiet place to wash first. Unless Ma had a small enough bucket; then she could take the water up to her room and wash at leisure.

"I was hoping I might be able to get clean?" she asked.

Emelyn bounced back up to her feet again.

"Of course! I'll show you. I can give you some clothing as well because I'm not that much bigger than you."

Neri stood up and quelled the temptation to tear her hand away when Emelyn grabbed hold of it.

With a flicker of amusement at Emelyn's boundless enthusiasm, she let the girl drag her into the dwelling and up the creaking stairs to a room set specifically for bathing. The stone walls held out the heat well enough and even the tiniest breeze came through the un-shuttered window gap. A large wooden tub for bathing in was already full of water.

"It's clean, don't worry," Emelyn babbled happily. "It's Niall's job to empty it and Eva's job to fill it each morning, but Matty rises late and Ma only bathes in the evening, and I did last night, so nobody will have used it yet."

Neri turned in the bathroom doorway and clasped her hands in front of her, waiting. Emelyn stared at her for a moment before slapping her palm to her forehead and leaving in a flurry of apologies. Neri shook her head, but something about Emelyn's excitable manner made her smile. She shut the bathroom door behind her and swirled her fingertips through the cool water.

There were no drying cloths available save for a small, blue one, but she resisted using that. The air would dry her out fast enough without her needing to use their items.

A sudden, short burst of hammering hailed on the bathroom door. Neri jumped and her knee ricocheted against the side of the tub. She swore under her breath.

"I've brought you some fresh clothes and a towel! Can I bring them in?"

Emelyn's voice bounced around outside the door and Neri grumbled under her breath. She opened the door and peered through the gap, still half expecting some kind of ambush.

Emelyn stood alone, beaming back at her. She held out a messy bundle of clothing and a large brown drying cloth which Neri leaned forward to grab.

"Oh, that's a lovely necklace." Emelyn pointed at Neri's neck. "Is it something you found or a gift from someone special?"

Caught by surprise, Neri blurted out the truth.

"It was my mama's. She gave it to me before she died, but said it was always meant to be mine."

Emelyn nodded, hovering as if she expected something more. Neri took the clothing from her and said thanks before closing the door again.

It is quite an unusual type of stone, I guess. Although Niall noticed it on the way here as well. Surprising considering it was in the dark, and he doesn't seem the type for trinkets.

She soaked her hair first then dabbed herself dry with the towel, frowning at the pink patches of sunburn on her upper arms. As she changed into her borrowed clothes, she had the oddest temptation to hum a tune. Emelyn's blue shirt with short sleeves was so clean it felt like animal fluff, and Neri took the time to replace her grimy shorts with Emelyn's neater black ones. With a few remaining clean clothes wrapped over one arm and her dirty ones over the other, she opened the door.

She jumped in alarm, but if Emelyn noticed the reaction while standing right outside the door, she didn't hesitate long enough to comment on it.

"I know you'll want to get started on the candles, but I want you to meet Finn first. He's been out travelling but he's back home now."

Neri nodded.

"I guess I should at least try to make a good impression while I'm here," she said, aiming for humour.

Emelyn blinked at her, then beamed again.

"Great! Oh, take those upstairs first."

Neri did as she was told, taking her mix of clean and dirty clothing to her room. Madness to think of it as hers, but for now it was.

She hurried back down and followed Emelyn through the dwelling. The kitchen showed signs of lunch being prepared, but Ma Kath merely turned and offered a serene smile. At her side, Eva didn't turn around at all.

Emelyn bounced out into the garden and Neri took a deep breath before following. It had taken her several handspans of days to get comfortable at Hamlin's and now she had to start all over again. Her usual sense of self-preservation surged once more at the thought of meeting yet another stranger. Despite how nice everyone seemed so far, she couldn't find any reason for their kindness. Until she did, she would stay on her guard.

The suns splayed fierce tendrils across the garden, wicking away at the freshness on her skin. A man she didn't recognise lay back on his elbows around the small pond, bare-chested and lithe with a hint of tanned muscle. Emelyn kneeled next to him already, her fingers marvelling at the length of his sandy hair.

Neri tensed as an awkward flush crept over her cheeks. Niall lounged beside the unknown man with all the confident languor of a jungle cat, his upper body also bare.

Typical.

The first time she had seen him without the uniform cloak, and she had to see him half naked. She resolved to ignore Niall as best as she could and followed Emelyn's beckoning finger summoning her to join the group.

She stood, not comfortable enough to sit amongst strangers, and met Finn's critical gaze with a similar one of her own. He looked older than the rest of them, maybe about thirty winters young, and he smiled at her with lazy confidence.

"Neri, this is Finn." Emelyn eyed them with buoyant hope. "Finn, Neri came from Hamlin's."

Finn nodded and held out a hand without making any effort to sit up. Neri guessed he meant for her to shake it, but that would involve her leaning right over him. She also got the distinct impression that he might not let go straight away from the way he was looking her up and down.

She lifted her arm in greeting instead. "Hi."

Finn's hand dropped into his lap. His gaze flicked to Niall, but Neri could only focus on one of them at a time right now.

"So, you were there when Hamlin died?" Finn asked.

Out of the corner of her eye Neri could see Niall freeze, but it was Emelyn's sharp intake of breath that she noticed most.

"Yeah." She had to nod. "I'll miss him. He was kind to me right up to the end."

Finn shrugged. "But you didn't have anything to do with it? You're not one of them?"

Niall sat up, one hand reaching out as if he could snatch Finn's words out of the air.

"Finn!" Emelyn sounded horrified. "Of course she isn't."

Neri folded her arms. She guessed she and Finn would never be great friends, but she also recognised the lingering smile on his face.

He enjoys creating discomfort and drama, probably thrives on it. Well, I'm not indulging him.

She held his unyielding gaze.

"One of who?"

His eyes narrowed, recognising someone who wouldn't back down straight away.

"The Governance, those that ravage our land."

Neri shook her head. "No, I've never had anything to do with them. I didn't have anything to do with what happened to Hamlin either. I wouldn't repay his kindness with betrayal. But he's the reason I ended up here, so I should start the candles now. Excuse me."

She shot Emelyn an apologetic grimace and turned away before her anger could show on her face. She didn't dare look at Niall.

Without waiting for Emelyn to protest, she powered into the house, through the hall and up to the attic room. She almost fell over Dog who sat waiting for her on the landing. A quick glance over her shoulder and she saw Emelyn scampering behind her. She held in a groan and continued up to her room.

She sat down by the long slab of concrete Ma had mentioned leaving for her, along with a large stone boiling pot and a hewn stand to hold it over the fire. Stones were stacked in a pile on one end next to a bundle of kindling. She could use those to create and then contain the fire to melt the wax. A pair of long tweezers made from blade-metal lay on the stone to pull out any remaining strands of wick, next to some lengths of string for making new ones.

Blade-metal isn't cheap for coin or easy to trade for neither. Neri frowned. *So they either have access to old wealth, or they've stolen it from somewhere. Or it belonged to whoever lived at this dwelling before these folk did.*

Neri took solace in the surge of purpose that coursed through her. The roof-ledge door was flung open wide and soon a tiny fire blazed. Hamlin had taught her well how to feed a fire enough to keep it blazing but not out of control, and she let that familiar practice soothe her. She focused solely on her task, only vaguely aware of Emelyn perched on the chair near the top of the stairs to watch.

When the candle moulds were filled and settled in a cool, shaded corner, Neri poured a jug of water over the fire and moved the boiling pot away from the smoke. She intended to keep an eye on the remains until it was cool enough to handle but malleable enough to mould into shapes. Emelyn threw her a small cloth and she took great relief in wiping her sweating brow.

"You're lucky you have a gift," Emelyn said.

Neri raised an eyebrow and dropped her aching body onto the bed. Staring up at the ceiling, she laughed.

"I doubt it. You said you are a scribe? Is that not a gift to be considered lucky to have?"

She turned her head, catching Emelyn's enthusiastic smile.

"I'm very lucky too. We all are touched with good fortune here. Perhaps it was fortune that brought you to us."

Neri sighed and shook her head. She got up again, restless despite the aching, and prodded the excess wax with her tweezers.

"Niall brought me to you," she insisted. "Hamlin put him up to it I think, but I have no idea why he did. I don't think it has anything to do with fortune."

"But surely you know that gifts are... well, a gift?" Emelyn asked. "The gifts we get from the land at birth are a blessing."

She sounded so surprised, with a slight rivulet of disappointment in her tone. Neri took pity on her, trying not to let her amusement show.

"Of course they are, and many folk are truly gifted. I don't have much in mine, the ability to warm slightly which comes in handy."

She stopped short of asking what everyone else's gifts in the dwelling were. Land-gifts were becoming less and less common if the rumours folk told were true. Some tales told of folk who could wield water and summon earth-spirits or commune with animals as easily as breathing. Most folk ended up with some small gift still, but Neri had never set much faith in hers. Better to rely on wits than on gifts. But then Niall clearly had some kind of affinity with movement, his ability to walk without tiring and leap over fences without a struggle likely coming from the air element.

"My gramma was a wonder with herbs though," she added. "She could weave any information into tales and folk used to come from all over for one of her healing brews."

It felt strange to be talking so much after almost a year of keeping to herself. Emelyn was smiling at her still, despite her dismissive words.

"There is hope for you yet," Emelyn decided. "We leave our footprints on the land, but knowledge of its wonders and mysteries are all we take with us when we go. I suppose that's true of all realms."

Neri smiled to herself and said nothing. She could easily handle Emelyn's ethereal mentality, convinced the girl just wanted to be friendly. Everyone knew that there was the east and the west, separated by the supposedly cursed forest. Legend told of the forest keeping folk from crossing through by land-magic, but she reckoned there were more likely beasties that would happily eat folk who traipsed into their territory before they even made it halfway across.

She prodded the cooling wax once more and then held her hand close to the surface.

"Would you like a small sculpture of something?" she offered. "I'm better at carving than I am at moulding, but I can try."

She pointed to the leftover wax. In one fluid movement Emelyn slid off of the chair and came to peer into the pot.

"Could you make a bird, like a simple token? I'd like to carry one around with me, to remind me we can all have wings in our souls should we need to soar."

Neri smiled. Emelyn spoke like she still addicted to the wonders of the world and her own dreams, and up in an attic room without any others around, her enthusiasm became infectious.

Neri took a slow, deep breath and pushed one finger into the gloopy wax, slightly hotter than she'd like to handle but she could bear it. She scooped a handful out of the pot and sank to her knees on the concrete, setting the wax down and smiling up at Emelyn's wide-eyed curiosity.

"I'll need to be on my own for this bit. Call it elemental giftery."

Emelyn caught the joke and grinned, bouncing up and down on the balls of her feet.

"Of course, I can't wait to see it! I'll leave you some food at lunch time behind the door."

She ran off down the stairs, her feet thumping softly in a higgledy-piggledy drum roll on the steps. Finally, blessed silence settled. Neri funnelled the wax into rough feet and thin, spindly legs with her fingers first. Then she used the tip of her carving blade to score a gap between the legs and set the bulk of the body. She frowned and leapt up, setting another fire and throwing more used candle stubs into the pot. Then she set about fashioning large wings, reaching out.

When the rough shape of a bird was formed and set properly, she would carve the detailing, but before that she needed more wax to create the head and a long, thin tail. A regal, elongated neck grew, and the teardrop dome of the bird's head formed. She tapered the end of the wax into a beak, travelling back up the head and forming a ridge she would later carve into a thin plume to match the tail.

As she worked, she remembered the book her mama used to read to her, back when she was a dreamy young girl in a barely known settlement far to the east of the eastlands. The memory reminded her of one poem in particular, and her mama's words echoed in her mind.

"These poems were written by your gramma. She's a scribe, a very talented one. One day you'll have your own gift of creation, I truly believe that. Now which poem shall we read?"

Always Neri would clap her hands in excitement. Always she would ask for the *Lamentation*. Her mama would smile knowingly and turn to the page that showed a large bird, its feathers blazing red and gold.

Neri hadn't thought about that memory in a while. She let it fill her thoughts, refusing to think about her gramma's poetry book that had been in her pack at the candle shop.

It was now likely in the clutches of the Governance or shredded in a lane somewhere. Her gramma had never bothered to publish her scribings, insisting they were known only by the three of them and it would stay that way, their family secret.

Neri took the last of the spare wax and realised the bird's tail was already hardening too much to sculpt new wax onto it.

We'll go no more a-wandering to distant borrowed lands

The *Lamentation* poem danced through her mind as her fingers began to skitter with rapid feverishness over the wax.

Where rain falls soft and fairies sleep with meadowsweet in hand

The fire was still simmering on old kindling, so Neri reached over and heated the tweezers.

Don't stop to talk to strangers, no sweet words in your ear

Using the hot blade-metal to melt the rear of the bird, Neri pressed the spare wax onto the sculpture.

For the veil now is lifted and the firebird is here

With long sweeping strokes of her curled fingers, a thin tail grew and ended in a bulb of what would eventually resemble flame.

Neri slumped, her wax-stained hands thudding back against the concrete to support her. She reviewed her creation with a critical frown as a soft, irregular thumping on the stairs heralded Emelyn's arrival. A moment later, curious green eyes peered over the top step along with a hand holding a sandwich on a plate.

"It's not complete yet, I still need to carve it," Neri warned. "It's a crawbird though, or it will be."

She waited for the inevitable wrinkling of Emelyn's pert nose, the questions about why she'd chosen a crawbird when they were an omen of death.

But Emelyn's eyes shone.

She put the plate on the floor and crept forward until her nose almost touched the wax figurine.

"It's beautiful. Why choose a crawbird?"

Neri shrugged. "My family was never that big on superstition. They taught me that even crawbirds are creatures, as good and bad as any of us."

"We'll go no more a-wandering to distant borrowed lands," Emelyn whispered. *"Where rain falls soft and fairies sleep with meadowsweet in hand."*

Neri, having turned to check on Dog, whirled around.

"Where did you hear that?"

CHAPTER FIVE

Emelyn's eyes widened. She opened her mouth, hesitated, then shut it again. Neri stared back at her, astounded.

Nobody should know that poem other than me, nobody living anyway.

True, she had left it in her pack at the candle shop. Maybe Hamlin had found a spare moment to sneak in and take it. She tried to think of when she'd last checked on the book but couldn't remember. Had he given it to Niall to take with them? Or perhaps gramma had lied about it being only for the three of them. Maybe Ma Kath had heard it if they all knew each other. None of those thoughts stopped her heart pounding.

"Everyone knows it," Emelyn mumbled. "It's an ancient lullaby, practically common sense where I come from."

Neri narrowed her eyes, suspicious. That seemed enough to send Emelyn skittering out of the room and down the stairs in a tumbling thumping of feet. With chills rippling over her skin, Neri wondered what she'd somehow stumbled into. The possibility of her Gramma passing someone else's poetry off as her own entered her mind and just as quickly sailed out of it.

She wouldn't have stolen someone else's work. I saw her create and she had no need to. If Mama was friends with these folk, it would make sense they might know Gramma's poems. Or it's a chance occurrence that someone else wrote something similar.

Feeling bad for unsettling Emelyn when the answer was probably quite simple, Neri crossed the room and picked up the plate. Despite her uneasiness, she devoured the two slices of honey bread teetering with whipped egg and gave the crusts to Dog.

"What is this all about, huh?" she asked him.

He answered by getting up, turning a circle and flopping in a panting heap on the floorboards by the bed.

Hamlin's parcel. Maybe that will tell me something.

When she raised the mattress, the book and paper were where she'd left them with the one hair still curled on top. She opened up the folded piece of paper first, noting the hastily torn and uneven edges.

My dearest Neri,

I apologise for the journey I am about to send you on, but please trust me when I say Niall will see you safe and well. Trust the sanctuary and keep Dog with you. He will show you the way when it seems hidden from you as he is an excellent judge of character. If you believe in nothing else, follow his lead. I am glad to have known you even at the end of my time. The item I have left you is of particular value. Please keep it safe. There may come a time where

you meet the Lady who can make use of it.
  Carry on carving, you have a true gift.

Yours until the end,

Hamlin.

His eloquent voice seemed to roam in the room with her, leaping from the page to fill the air with his spirit and a faint sound of ticking. Memories of blades slicing filled her mind but she shook her head to clear them.

Almost afraid to find out what secrets were held amongst the pages of the book, Neri dug her fingers into the edges of the book and flipped open the hide-bound cover.

The middles of the blank pages had been cut out. In the hollow of the book lay the slim gold pocket watch that she had never seen Hamlin without.

No further note or clue in the cut pages of the book or inside either of the covers indicated who she should give the watch to, other than a 'Lady'. For the time being, she slipped it into the pocket of her borrowed denim shorts, but not until she'd held the watch to her ear for a long time to hear the steady, faint tick.

The afternoon sunlight still shone full and beaming outside the balcony door, so she decided to begin carving the crawbird. She knelt down, the pang of bruising aching on her knees, and took her carving blade in hand. Whittling the feet first, she worked on the claws and then moved up the legs. The *Lamentation*, her gramma's poem that

Emelyn mysteriously knew the words to, danced once again in her mind.

Her gramma's poems weren't known, but then they'd not had many true friends in their settlement. Soon after the initial throes of innocence settled, Neri preferred digging out her mama's old slips of lead and sketching on any surface she could find.

When she died I moved from sketching to carving.

The thoughts circled until she'd carved an entire underbelly of bird plumage. Sweat beaded on her brow as she worked and dripped onto her bare shoulders, trickling down her back. Her top stuck to her skin and she had to fork savage handfuls of hair back at regular intervals.

She crept down to the second floor only once throughout the afternoon to relieve herself. Dog disappeared at one point for about ten minutes then reappeared to sit with her. She assumed he'd begged food from Ma Kath and they let him out into the garden. Emelyn didn't come back at all.

Unable to settle, Neri bit her lip and cut the first line of the bird's eye. The sounds of folk going to bed or to spend the rest of the evening in their rooms echoed below, but it was only after night had long since fallen that she considered herself done.

The crawbird stood with its fully carved wings spread wide and the noble neck holding the regal head high. Neri clambered to her feet and stood to assess her efforts from a distance. She'd done a little too well with the eyes which followed her about the room as she moved.

Her stomach grumbled until she conceded and crept

down the steps to see if anyone had left any food at the attic door for her. She found a wooden plate of bread along with a bowl of cold vegetable soup and a lump of hard cheese, which she took up and stood on the balcony to eat. The balmy evening air cooled her skin as she looked out over a candlelit town in the distance.

A soft caw followed a flutter of wings as a lone crawbird landed on the balcony beside her plate.

"Suppose I'm not getting my crusts," she murmured, knocking them off the plate toward the bird.

Intelligent inky eyes blinked as the sharp beak opened, dropping a small pebble beside the plate.

Neri smiled, waiting until the bird had taken the crusts and hopped back out of reach.

"Thank you. I don't usually get gifts before food."

She picked up the pebble between forefinger and thumb, amused. The crawbirds she had fed in younger years often came back again and again, sometimes with their babies. After a while, they brought her small tokens in exchange for the food, a sturdy piece of string, a sharp rock, sometimes even coins.

The pebble glinted in the dim firelight, pearlescent white and utterly smooth. Neri pocketed it as the crawbird took flight into the dark night.

Now I have to work up the energy to take the plate back down to the kitchen.

She turned to go back in and jumped. The plate slid from her fingers, bounced off the balcony wall and tumbled down toward the tiled path below. A second later, a clattering noise echoed through the quiet air.

Niall stood leaning in the doorway, the sleeves of his shirt rolled up and one eyebrow lifted in amusement at her skittishness.

Neri glowered back at him. She'd been immersed in her thoughts but not so deeply that he should be able to sneak up the stairs without her hearing.

"A pet of yours?" he asked.

"What- oh, the bird? No, just a passing friend."

She edged into the room and flattened her back to the wall in pre-emptive defence.

"You have curious friends, like that carving." He nodded at the wax crawbird. "It's almost real. I feel like it's watching me."

Neri shrugged. "I'm not sure what else I'm meant to do to be honest. You brought me here but nobody's actually said much since, and I'm not going to assume I can stay here forever, even if you are meant to be part of some great anti-Governance movement."

A legitimate suggestion, but then Finn's question wandered through her mind. They could easily claim that she'd gained Hamlin's trust and ratted on him to their enemy. He would, as a gentleman, try to find a way of keeping the poor, defenceless young woman safe after he was gone by palming her off on his friends. Niall would have taken her to the sanctuary at Hamlin's request, as he had done, then she could infiltrate them. They might be assuming that she was a spy.

"Well apologies for the inconvenience," Niall muttered. "But we don't trust outsiders easily."

Wanting to avoid a stand-off, Neri crossed the room and

checked the candles. Unable to do anything until they set, she grabbed the slender carving blade and started scoring lines into one of the ready-made candles.

"So, what brings you up here? Or did you just want to check on my efforts?"

She nodded to the line of candles already in a row along the wall and Niall smirked at her prickliness. Too busy eying him warily, her blade slipped on a bit of wax and scored a shallow cut along the pad of her left thumb. Uttering a quiet curse, she sucked the tip into her mouth.

"Would you consider Emelyn a friend?" Niall asked.

Surprised, Neri looked up, her thumb still pressed to her lips. With the coppery tang of blood on her tongue and the zinging ache of cut skin not yet dulled, she frowned, unwilling to risk being guilt-tripped into whatever was inevitably going to come next.

"I don't know her," she said carefully. "But she's been kind to me so far, and friendly, so I suppose you might call her that."

Niall nodded and sighed, his long fingers raking his copper hair back. From this one movement, Neri noticed the dark rings around his eyes and his gaunt, pale tiredness.

"To tell you what I think I need to-" he hesitated. "I have to explain a whole bunch of other stuff you're probably not going to believe. About exactly how far land-gifts go."

He stalled, silent for a moment. Aware he wanted her full attention, Neri stood up and moved to sit on the bed. After a pause, Niall clasped his hands behind his back.

"Do you believe what the legends say about the forest

between the east and west?" he asked. "That it's impossible to pass through because of long ago sorcery?"

Neri groaned and put her forehead in her hands.

"Not you as well, I thought Emelyn was the fanciful one."

Niall flicked a look of irritation at her. "Humour me then. Are you one of those who assumes trained hunters go in and never come out because they're eaten by wild-wolves or similar?"

She shrugged. "I guess I must do. We are born with land-gifts, but I haven't seen any proof of actual sorcery. We've all heard the tales, but until I see it I'm a non-believer. Being able to warm water a little or move items with will a short way are not the same as an entire swathe of woodland that eats folk."

Niall released one of his hands from behind his back and rubbed the rough stubble on his chin. Uncomfortable under the intensity of his stare, Neri pulled her legs up onto the bed and picked at the congealed wax on her fingers instead.

"So, you reckon it's merely normal, natural dangers?" he pressed.

Neri rolled her eyes and decided she had to move him on toward the real reason for such a random conversation.

"What other explanation is there? Are you seriously telling me you believe that three ancient brothers cast powerful sorcery to put a cursed forest down the centre of the land to stop ancient lineages from warring with each other? Why even bring it up, unless you're offering to go into the woods and prove me wrong?"

Niall shrugged, a patronising smile growing across his face.

"Maybe I will. What do you believe in then?"

Irritated, the words sprung out of her mouth before she could check them.

"I believe in life. I believe in being kind to those who need it, and destroying anyone that isn't. You don't need magic or fortune for that. If it is out there, I've never seen it, and it'll probably bring more trouble than benefit with folk like the Governance lurking."

Niall folded his arms, regarding her with narrowed eyes.

"Finn still seems to think you could be one of the Governance," he announced. "I haven't told them what we overheard yet, about them knowing which cloak to find you in, but it's a curious thing for them to know about."

Neri could understand that, mainly because her rational mind was always suspicious of unknown folk. Her emotional side took offence immediately.

"My gramma made it for me and it has some distinctive fabric and patterning, but I am *not* one of them, believe me. What Ma said about them is true enough and I have my own reasons for hating them."

Thoughts of the men in hooded dark grey cloaks moving through the shadows to ransack her family's dwelling after her mama and gramma died filled her head, but Niall didn't need to know about that.

He raked his hand through his hair. As she did so, her own hair fell across her eyes and she found herself mirroring Niall's actions, pushing the strands away from her face with both hands.

"They're getting desperate now, what happened to Hamlin proved that." He hooked his thumbs in the pockets of his trousers. "I thought it fair to update you, but not everyone is convinced about what brought you here so if the mood is off, that's why."

"*You* brought me here, and I wouldn't have anything to do with the Governance if you traded me all the riches in the realm. But you lot go ahead and believe whatever you like."

Niall's mouth twitched and Neri saw his shoulders lower slightly.

"Everyone's agreed that they're happy for you to stay here," he said. "But it's your choice. You can choose to leave and nobody will hold it against you. It's dangerous out there though, and you need to be aware of that. You barely made it out of the shop alive."

Neri ignored that not-so-subtle suggestion of her helplessness. She sank back onto the bed and stared him out.

"I'll consider it," she said. "I don't know why they were looking for me at the shop, assuming my gramma didn't make a similar cloak and forget to mention it."

She couldn't imagine that being the case. Her gramma had been kind but frugal with fancies. A cloak that finely lined and woven would have fetched a handsome trade in even the more salubrious of markets. Niall didn't look convinced by the suggestion, his head tilting sideways as those dark eyes roved over her face, seeking answers.

Or looking for weaknesses.

She sat up and gave him a dismissive look.

"If they want me for something, I won't be going easy. I don't fancy being used as bait here either whenever I inevitably become useful. I'll consider the offer to stay for a short while and make as many candles as I can. After that, I'll see."

Niall tugged the rolled cuffs of his shirt, staring down at his boots.

"Why are you so against them then?" he asked. "If you want us to trust you, you need to give us something back."

"What, collateral?"

"No." He was trying not to smile. "I mean you need to trust us in return, let us in a bit."

Neri scraped at wax on her little finger.

I doubt the truth can go against me as long as I stay vague. No names, no specifics.

"Okay," she sighed. "About two winterspans ago, my mama got sick. Then Gramma disappeared and turned up dead. The local watch said she must have been going addle-brained, but she was sharper at sixty winters than most folk are in their whole life. When Mama died ten months ago, a bunch of grey-cloaks arrived at our dwelling the day after to ransack it. I was out but came back in time to see them."

Niall froze. "Did they catch you? See you?"

"No, I hid in the opposite alleyway until they were gone. Mama told me if I was ever in trouble or lost, I was to go to Hamlin and give him a letter she'd written. She hid it rolled up inside the hollowed leg of her bed, so that's what I did. I stayed with Hamlin until you showed up and suddenly everything's fired up in my face again."

Neri focused on her fingers, unwilling to see any pity in Niall's eyes. She hadn't even admitted this much to Hamlin, although he must have guessed the bulk of it when she turned up on his doorstep with her mama's letter in hand.

"I hung around long enough to coin them," she continued. "My family I mean. But there were men waiting there too. I grabbed a pack with the few things I couldn't part with and fled. All of that is gone now. I didn't even remember to get my pack when I left Hamlin's."

A quick glance up and Niall's eyes were wide and dark with pity. Neri shrugged with a self-deprecating chuckle.

"So yeah, my mama died sick. My gramma's death is still unsolved, at least in my eyes. Then they killed Hamlin after he was so kind to me. If their passing is all courtesy of the Governance then they're my enemy too."

At least if they trusted her, she could eventually go outside without locked doors stopping her. If they crossed her later on, she would be able to run.

"It'd be too dangerous for you to leave," Niall insisted, his tone turning sullen. "If they sent one of their main men to collect you back at the shop, you must be important to them for some reason."

His gaze left her eyes and slid downward. Neri froze, but it was the quickest of flicks toward her chest. She remembered his behaviour when looking at her token in the forest and Emelyn's interest in it also. She shrugged, uneasy.

"I don't know why. Mama never mentioned having

anything to do with any Governance and neither did my gramma before she died. They probably have completely the wrong person. I'll be of no use to you then."

Niall grinned. His lips curved up and his cheekbones bunched, forming dimples at the edges of his smile. Even his dark brown eyes sparked with a sudden sense of wicked mirth.

"I don't know about that. Candles are more than enough for us right now. If you decided to stay properly, we wouldn't ask any more of you than that."

Neri had to accept that. If she helped them with candles, they might even give her the chance to come and go as she pleased one day. She could earn their trust as she had earned Hamlin's.

"Maybe I would be safe here, but I'd want the knowledge that this place wouldn't be a cell. If I come back, I want it to be my choice to make."

Niall straightened up suddenly, making her jump. He frowned at her skittishness but walked a few paces toward her.

"It will be, but we need to know we can trust you first. Trust takes time," he hesitated. "I suppose that goes both ways."

He shrugged and turned toward the doorway, but Neri couldn't stop herself from calling out after him.

"I have to ask, why me? Did Hamlin really want to keep me safe in the end, or is there some real reason you're all being so polite? If I refused to follow you here, or said I had no idea how the candle-making worked, what then?"

She had to know. The idea that Hamlin was involved in

using her life and the Governance's interest in her hurt more than she wanted to admit.

Niall turned with one hand on the doorframe and his mouth curved up, a gentle smirk that insinuated he would not give her any more sensible answers for the present.

"Hamlin wanted to keep you safe in his last days, no ulterior motive. He was always a complete gentleman. But for my part, if you refused, I'd have thrown you over my shoulder and carried you. Or dragged you behind me screaming. Either way, I promised Hamlin I'd get you here and here you are, no harm done."

Neri hesitated, assessing whether the glint in his eyes sparked from humour or truth. Then she rolled her eyes at him. She might as well try to ask one final question.

"Is this some kind of sorcery cult then? Are you eventually going to tell me that you lot howl at the suns and that this place is built on some ancient spirit lines, or try to convince me that tricks of the light are down to some deep spiritual magic instead of someone throwing spark-stones? That's all I've heard folk mention since I've been here."

Niall's smile grew wider. "I don't think we could be called a cult, and I don't know about any relevant spirit lines nearby. Although Finn does howl at the suns sometimes, but then he loves to dramatise things."

Neri had to smile at that. Niall remained there for a moment, watching her until the atmosphere turned awkward.

"I should get on with this." She grabbed her candle and blade in hand.

Niall glanced at the darkness outside the balcony doors.

"You should get some sleep," he retorted. "It's got to be near stars-wane at least."

Neri shrugged. "I don't tend to sleep much."

"Nightmares?"

"Something like that. Still, I am grateful to you for bringing me here."

He chuckled. "But not enough to want to stay, I'm honoured. Never mind, rest while you can."

He left her in peace with a smile lingering in his wake and Neri glanced at the blankets on her bed, trying to soothe herself by working out how thin they'd have to be to reach the ground.

With her stomach growling, Neri went down for a wash and to sneak some food. She found the bathroom empty and spent time picking and rinsing the wax from her hands. She even used a minimal amount of the apple soap on the side to cleanse her hair.

Without realising it, she started to hum. The old lullaby without words that her mama used to sing soothed her further. The status quo could always shift in her favour. She didn't exactly have anywhere to get to in a hurry either.

With her hair unknotted and her skin clean, she felt able to pull on the second set of fresh clothes Emelyn had left her, another pair of shorts and a dark green shirt without sleeves.

Neri left the bathroom absorbed in her thoughts and ran straight into Finn's chest. She moved to dodge around him with a mumbled apology but he blocked her path.

"I hear you might want to join our great cause," he said with a grin.

Neri frowned and took a step back.

"Talking in corners already? I told Niall I'd consider it short-term. Besides, by all accounts you don't trust me being here, so quit leering."

She expected a roll of his eyes or some sarky comeback. His expression slipped, a darker seriousness shining as his eyes narrowed and his mouth thinned.

"Don't make the mistake of thinking I won't do anything to protect those I care about," he murmured, his voice low and hushed but sharp as blades.

Before Neri could veer back, his smile reappeared, as though she'd imagined that slip of his expression.

"Having you here will at least be interesting," he said, stepping close.

He stood a head and shoulders taller than her in the narrow hall. Neri flinched as he found no difficulty in grabbing her hips and bodily lifting her to set her aside so he could pass, as if she'd been the one blocking his way.

Frozen in outrage, she couldn't dredge up a single word of protest. Finn added insult to the assault by turning back and winking at her.

Bristling with uneasiness, Neri fled back up to her room without going down for food. Despite the balcony doors being open and the faintest hint of a breeze brushing against her skin, the heat of mortification radiated through her. For him to even get close enough to catch hold of her without receiving a suitable injury in response proved she was getting careless.

Next time, I'll make sure he doesn't get away from that unscathed. Neri threw herself onto her bed. *Seems like staying here will be interesting indeed.*

CHAPTER SIX

Neri wandered through the silent dwelling early the next morning, leaving Dog asleep by the bed. She peeked into the den on her way through to find it empty, then carried on through to the kitchen. There was nobody in there but on the counter was a large bowl of green berries and a pile of breadcakes. Someone, Ma Kath most likely, had scrawled a small note that read 'Help yourself'. Neri smiled, wondering if the note was for her benefit. After two sweetened breadcakes and a handful of berries, she wandered out into the garden.

Worry about the situation had kept her from sleeping most of the night but she'd waited for the sunlight to rise before sneaking down to sit in the garden.

She settled herself next to the pond and glanced over the stones. Two golden fish swam around each other and the fluid swish of their movements steadied her senses. Calm enveloped her and a vision of snowy forests with bright flowers peeking through filled her head. She closed her eyes as her skin chilled beneath the lull of the morning heat. In her mind's eye the snow melted, draining into a nearby river that had been frozen moments ago. For the first time in a long time, Neri delighted in her imagination.

Knowing it couldn't last, she opened her eyes and looked down. The golden fish merged into one, taking a familiar shape. Flames flickered in the water's surface and Neri stared in amazement as the vision of the crawbird she'd carved flickered as if made real. The dark teardrop eyes fixed on her, its body and jagged wings wreathed in untameable fire.

The bird winked once.

Entranced, Neri reached out and her gaze snagged on her fingers. In that instant, the vision vanished. In front of her lay the same murky pond as before with the two golden fish still drifting around each other.

Blinking her eyes tight shut and opening them again, Neri shook her head.

I'm seeing things. Too much talk of sorcery and myth lately.

She clambered to her feet and turned to go back inside, only to find Niall leaning against the kitchen doorframe, his gaze fixed on her. Rattled that he'd managed to sneak up on her again, Neri wrapped her arms around her chest.

"Do you enjoy spying on me?" she asked.

Niall grinned and pushed away from the wall.

"I want to show you that you can trust us. We're going to take Dog for a walk."

Neri eyed him with disbelief. "What, after all the warnings about staying safe inside?"

Niall nodded. "I have to scout the area. It's something we do regularly, but we thought you might want to come with us. Ma said you were talking about going for a walk before. Now's your chance."

They're testing me.

If she tried to run, they'd assume she was off to the Governance with their location. But if she returned with Niall under her own steam, they might not watch her so carefully the next time she left the house.

I don't have any supplies yet either so I wouldn't get far even if I did run.

Neri nodded. If the excursion achieved anything, at least Dog could have a bit of a stretch.

"I'll go fetch him," she said.

Niall stepped aside as she approached, giving her scant room to squeeze past into the kitchen. She frowned as she flattened herself as best she could, but shivered as the hem of his shirt brushed her passing wrist.

"Watch out for Emelyn too," he called out. "She's determined on chaperoning us. Her words, not mine."

Neri didn't turn back as she reached the hall, the smile in his voice too obvious to be anything other than a taunt.

She almost stumbled into Emelyn waiting for her by the stairs to her room, Dog already awake and wagging his tail, apparently ready to go.

"Don't let Niall scare you off," Emelyn didn't bother with any greeting. "Are we going out?"

Neri nodded. "Dog needs a stretch, and I- is that my cloak?"

She stared at the obvious mound of fabric in Emelyn's hands. Emelyn held it out hurriedly.

"I didn't steal it or anything. I wanted to ask where you

got it from. I want one but in green."

Neri blinked, amazed that not only had Emelyn gone through her pack in order to find the cloak, but also had no qualms about admitting it.

Is that how she knew Gramma's poem? She somehow managed to search my pack?

She tried to think of any time before the incident when Emelyn could have gone through her pack, while Emelyn stared at her with expectant wide eyes.

Either that, or someone else went through everything and told her.

She bit her lip, her mind on the book Hamlin had given her. No time to check that now, but she would need to find some way of keeping her stuff more secure.

"It's not a common item," she admitted. "It was made for me."

"Can I borrow it? Not for ages, just while we're out for the walk."

Neri hesitated. "Is it safe?"

Thoughts of the Governance mentioning a distinctive cloak filled her head. Emelyn shrugged.

"We're a long way from other settlements, so it should be. I know it's warm out but it's been a while since I've seen anything as fine as this. Please? I'll be so careful."

Neri held back a chuckle brewing in her throat at the childlike pleading.

"I suppose so?"

She flinched as Emelyn did a violently excitable jump and swirled the cloak around her shoulders, the edges of it brushing the doorframe. Neri tried not to cringe thinking about splinters as Emelyn bounded past her with Dog plodding at a much more dignified pace.

Niall stood at the bottom of the stairs, his foot tapping an impatient rhythm. He stopped as Emelyn cascaded past him, his gaze lifting to Neri.

She pulled a face at him as she passed to follow to the door, which did nothing to dim his grin.

From sullen to sunslight in the space of a day, just my luck.

The moment she stepped outside, the severity of the muggy heat hit her. Blinking in the dazzle of daylight, she stopped at the garden gate and turned back to find Niall a few paces behind her. She stood aside to let him take the lead with Emelyn and followed them to the edge of the forest at the end of the lane.

Her mind twisted around until they reached the cool shade beneath the trees, but worries about the sanctuary, the candle shop and all of the recent events seemed to ebb to a distant echo. The occasional scuffle of an animal in the undergrowth they trampled through or the trill of a bird high above circled a consistent, peaceful silence.

"So, what's the eventual plan?" She called ahead. "Are you expecting me to stay long-term, or should I be stockpiling?"

Niall turned his head back enough for her to see the frown on his face and slowed so that they were walking side by side.

"That's up to you. We'd prefer to have a candlemaker with us, but we can source them elsewhere. Whether you'll fit in as one of us enough to stay is another thing entirely."

Emelyn slowed her pace to walk alongside them with a loud giggle.

"Nobody 'fits in' with us. We're all odd in our own ways."

"I already know that you lot are into all the sorcery stuff." Neri waved the idea away as irrelevant. "I'm not bothered with any of that, even if you lot do dance around naked and chant at the suns or whatever."

Niall snorted. "I doubt any of us could be accused of chanting at the suns or dancing around naked, not in public anyway."

"I'm going to scout ahead," Emelyn announced.

Before Neri could ask if it was safe for her to just run off, she ran off.

"Is she…" she wasn't sure how to ask.

Niall halted without warning and turned to face her. Fears bubbled up instantly, wild thoughts about him bringing her there to dispose of her flooding in. Nothing noteworthy looked visible around them and she lowered her hand to Dog's collar.

Niall grinned. "Don't worry about her. She's capable of looking after herself. Now, I brought you here because I wanted to prove something to you."

He held out a long brown rag. Neri took it with hesitant fingers as he stepped forward.

"Blindfold me," he demanded. When she opened her mouth to argue, he chuckled. "I'm giving you a chance to render me vulnerable and you're hesitating? I can easily outrun you."

She felt the challenge being extended and her lips

curved up. She took each end of the rag in her hands and stepped close. Niall turned around and she reached up to settle the fabric over his eyes, tying it tight with a double knot. After making sure it was secure she stood back, wondering why her fingers were zinging with energy when she didn't plan to run yet.

"Now, I'm going to count ten handspans." Niall clasped his hands behind his back. "If you want to run, or to hide, now is your chance."

Neri smiled mischief of her own. This wasn't the kind of 'scouting the area' routine she'd envisioned when they left the sanctuary.

He'd said she couldn't outrun him and he was right. She could try and hide but he had the advantage of knowing the area. Then she spied a crooked tree. It stood bent over with bark gnarled enough to climb, but still tall enough to provide adequate height and foliage for hiding.

"Okay, when you're ready then," she said.

He started counting out loud. When he called ten, she had already reached the lower branches. She managed to find a good vantage point in a dipped branch that gave her a comfortable place to sit. From there she could make out a deserted lane running right past where they were.

When Niall reached twenty, she quietly worked a couple of dry branches back and forth until they broke free. She threw one high into the trees in front of him. It made a loud noise as it hit a tree nearby. The second stick arced into the branches a little further on, rustling the leaves loud enough to reach Niall's ears.

She grinned when he reached twenty seven and lifted

the blindfold. He wasn't playing fair, but then she played a game of her own. He glanced around and she caught the bitter disappointment on his face. He actually thought she'd tried to run.

And he's actually upset about it.

He continued to spin, looking at the ground for possible tracks. Dog spoilt the ruse by pacing back and forth near her tree, but he made enough ground on each pass that it looked like he was waiting for Niall instead. Neri smothered a laugh as Niall approached Dog and bent low.

"Where'd she go then?"

She decided the time had come. She had two sticks left in her grasp. With one hand high above her head, she used all her strength and effort to throw the first stick as far as she could.

The effort was worth it. Niall whirled around at the noise as the stick hit a tree trunk nearby, his face a picture of hope mingled with bewilderment. When he next passed beneath her, Neri opened her hand and let the last stick drop behind him. Once again, he span round, cat-like reflexes useless against her playful cunning.

She swung her feet back and forth until the branch started to rustle its leaves. This time, Niall looked up and she couldn't help it. She waved.

He frowned as she shimmied along the tree branch to prolong her victory, pretending to be escaping out of reach. Dog barked, his tail wagging as he danced back and forth beneath her.

"Funny, everyone expects folk to try and run." She smirked down. "You would have done the running away for me."

She scooted back along the branch to the trunk and slid down until her feet touched the ground. The short while of having the upper hand made her feel powerful and she grinned at Niall. He now wore the rag around his neck where he'd pulled it down, but she couldn't read his expression.

"I guess this was meant to be like an initiation trial," she conceded. "I can't promise that I won't go my own way, but I'll take some time making my decision. You'll have to be content with that."

Niall raised his eyebrows and held her gaze but didn't reply. Unnerved by the unbroken eye contact, she folded her arms.

"Was that it, or is there actual scouting you have to do?"

Niall shook his head and walked past her without a word. She followed him back in the direction of the dwelling, wondering if she'd actually managed to ruffle him for once.

So this whole outing was a test. Unless Emelyn did the actual scouting.

A cacophony of cawing filled the silent air, panic in every urgent note. Neri twisted around, scanning the trees. No sign of Emelyn or her cloak. She opened her mouth to call to Niall, but he was standing still too, his head cocked and his stance rigid as a voice pierced the air.

"What are you doing?! Let go of me!"

Emelyn.

Panic flared in Neri's chest as she twisted right toward the sound.

"Stop it!"

Neri started running. Before she could make it more than three paces, something warm and unyielding caught around her wrist. She hissed as the weight hauled her toward the ground, her free hand coming out to break her fall.

She pulled her arm free of Niall's hand as he crouched beside her, but when she tried to get to her feet again, his arm landed on her back to hold her down. She glared utter fury at him but he pressed a finger to his lips before pointing it in Emelyn's direction.

"Shh," he whispered. "Nothing we can do. If we try to rescue her now, they'll take the lot of us. We need to get the news back to the sanctuary."

Neri's anger simmered as a jolt of fear crunched her stomach into a tiny ball. He had a good point and memories of Hamlin's final moments and the sheer number of grey-cloaks crowded around swelled. She balanced beside Niall in a ready crouch, her fingertips pressed against the ground. Dog seemed to sense their urgency and dropped to lie on his belly beside Neri's feet with his ears cocked and eyes alert.

Neri tried to keep her mind sharp despite her chest pounding and her limbs jangling with nerves.

Through the grass she could see the worn-down dirt track bordering the forest, a large crated cart standing on one side with several grey-cloaks slamming shut the gate. Neri squinted but she couldn't see Emelyn inside. A heavy rumbling started up as the cart set off, clattering faster and louder as it turned a corner.

A quick glance at Niall showed him looking uneasy, his lips pinned together and his dark eyes flicking back and forth with watchful caution. He'd washed his hair since they'd reached the sanctuary, and the auburn strands were lighter and more autumnal than she'd first realised. He'd removed the hair around his mouth as well, something she'd not noticed earlier, making him look more own her age.

I wonder how old he actually is.

She shook the thought away, reality crashing in once more as Niall stood without warning. When he held a hand out to help her up, she grabbed it, determined to run like mad back to the sanctuary.

"Well, if that doesn't prove you can trust us, I don't know what will," Niall muttered.

Neri glared back at him. "Never mind that. We need to let everyone know."

He nodded and set off at a powerful pace, Neri almost running to keep up with him. As the dwelling came into view, a few faces disappeared behind the drawn lines of the drapes covering the window.

Neri followed Niall up the path and slipped into the sanctuary of the entrance hall. As she waited while he shut and locked the front door, her eyes drifted over the chalk sketches on the floor. Crouching low, she passed her hand over a depiction of a fire-eyed white unicorn fighting a dragon. Without disturbing the picture, her fingers hovered over the unicorn's proud head.

If the Governance were the sanctuary's enemy, then maybe she was standing on the right side already. Of course all the cryptic suggestions of spirits and magic were complete nonsense, but she knew that beyond the airy fairy aesthetics, there was a family dynamic in the dwelling that was worth saving.

Niall moved out of her way and disappeared into the den, leaving the door open for her to follow.

"Emelyn's been taken," he announced.

Ma shot up, her mouth dropping open. Eva and Matty sat in the far corner, their heads popping up in horror. Finn was nowhere to be seen but Neri couldn't even bring herself to be relieved.

"Where?"

"The wale woods. A cart and several grey-cloaks."

Ma sighed. "That is unexpected. Poor Emelyn. We'll need to have a think about this."

Neri folded her arms and clenched her fists, astonished.

"Aren't you going to go out after her?"

"Not yet," Ma said. "We need time to think, to plan. Don't worry yourself about this. It's not your doing."

Neri closed her eyes in torment, the truth burbling out before she could stop it.

"They took her because they thought she was me! All that stuff they said at Hamlin's- when he... when they... she was wearing my cloak!"

Several astonished pairs of eyes fixed on her, silence dropping like a storm cloud after her outburst.

"Well now, what's with all the shouting?"

Neri twisted around to see a short, slender woman beaming at her. A purple-haired, brown-skinned woman, wearing a swathe of pale yellow fabric wrapped around her body. She was tiny, age only showing through spidery lines around her eyes and the immense aura of wisdom that radiated from her.

"Emelyn's been taken," Ma Kath explained, getting to her feet.

The unknown woman's expression dimmed, but although she had an air of sadness about her, she didn't seem surprised.

"We must convene on what it to be done," she insisted. "Sorry to hustle you out my dear, I'm sure we'll have ample time to converse later."

Neri stood for several moments before realising that the woman was speaking to her.

"Neri, this is Moonshine," Niall said, his tone weary with resignation. "We need to discuss this as a group."

Neri glanced at him, her heart sinking even as she nodded. She understood them not wanting her as part of their discussion. Her game with Niall earlier might be a small mark in her favour, but she wasn't one of them.

She slipped past the woman and took herself out to the garden, forcing aside the sense of being in the way. She settled beneath the *liliam* tree and turned her face up to catch the scent from the tiny purple leaves.

If I hadn't let Emelyn wear my cloak, they wouldn't have taken her.

She couldn't guarantee that. They might have questioned her and let her go, or they could have taken her anyway, but the cloak certainly hadn't helped.

She pulled off her boots with the pit in her gut deepening to a chasm at the thought of losing the cloak. It was only fabric, nowhere near as valuable as a person, let alone one as cheerful as Emelyn. But she missed her family deeper than she could even admit to herself. Running to Hamlin's from all that had gone before helped her block the pain, the need to survive encompassing all else. But now she had nowhere left to run to.

"I brought you some water."

Niall's voice broke through her introspective meditation. He approached with a wooden cup held out and a bowl for Dog too.

Neri took the cup from him and drained half of the clear water inside as Dog did the same with his bowl. Niall stood with his hands in his pockets and moments of silence passed, but he showed no signs of going away.

"Are you going to help her at least?" she asked.

"Of course. But we can't go charging in. We need to be smart."

"I want to help."

He frowned. "I just thought it fair to update you. Not everyone is convinced about what brought you here so if the mood is off, that's why."

"You brought me here, but you lot go ahead and believe whatever you like," she retorted. "But who's going after Emelyn?"

"What do you mean?"

"Who's going to find her, rescue her?"

Niall sighed and rubbed a hand over his face. "You don't need to worry about that."

Neri shook her head, refusing to succumb to such a lazy brush-off. She ignored the tired circles around Niall's eyes and the weary slump of his shoulders, determined to get answers.

"Do you at least know where she's been taken? You said taken, not that she's been- she's not ended up like Hamlin, so there must be a chance of going after her. You're not just going to abandon her, are you?"

Niall raised his eyebrows. "We're not going to abandon her, but she's not your concern. It's also not exactly a case of strolling into their lair and saying, 'oh please give us our friend back' like we're asking if she can come out to play."

Neri snorted a laugh at his sarcasm. Whether it was foolish bravery in the safety of the sanctuary or fierce vengeance at the thought of losing a fourth person who'd shown her kindness, she couldn't bear the thought of doing nothing and letting Emelyn's disappearance slide.

"So what's the hold up? If you're going to get her back, maybe I can help."

This time it was Niall's turn to laugh.

"Absolutely not. You almost ran into the same fate back at the shop. You would have done if I hadn't come for you."

"I mean it," she insisted. "If they are who you say they are, then anything that cuts their wick is fine by me. Besides, I still don't know why they were looking for me at the shop. If they want me for something, I can't have that hanging over my head forever. At least let me help. It's either that or I'll find a way to do it on my own."

She froze as he stalked across the short space between them and sank to his knees beside her, twisting until he was sitting at her side.

"We'll see. I can't offer you any more than that right now, but they'll agree who's going to go and let us know."

She fought the urge to argue more, knowing it wouldn't get her any further. Awkward silence descended, but she had nothing to lose in hoping he'd talk to her. Softening her tone, she sought for the nearest available subject she could mention.

"It's almost possible to believe the world outside doesn't exist here," she mused. "Just the dwelling and the garden with some kind of magic that makes food and supplies appear."

Whether it was a subconscious moment of genius to get him to soften toward her, or residual effects of her childhood memories springing free, she couldn't tell. Niall moved across her line of vision and settled his back against the wooden fence on her other side. In one fluid movement, he slid down until he sat beside her, his wrists resting on his knees.

"That would be Ma Kath's magic cupboard," he joked. "Who says stuff like that can't be true?"

Neri glanced sideways and caught a glimmer of amusement curling up at the corner of his mouth. Shaking her head in wry disbelief, she settled back on her elbows.

"The histories do, facts, official scribings."

Niall chuckled, the sound a dry rolling rumble in his chest, and Neri allowed herself a small smile.

"Who says the historians and the scribes weren't lying? Or bribed? Or misinformed?" he challenged.

"It's a possibility I guess. A well-coordinated one though if that were true."

"All the best lies are well coordinated, because the truth is buried under telling folk what they want to believe."

Moments of silence dragged on after that and Neri wiggled her bare toes through the grass to ease stiffness in her feet.

"Tell me something true." The words came out before she realised.

His lips curved up, his eyes lighting with some kind of wicked amusement.

"Make me."

She hesitated, thrown off-course by his sudden teasing.

"No point, I bet you'd only lie. Besides, I was just trying to be friendly."

She guessed he would make a joke of it again, but he sighed instead.

"I miss my home."

He sounded so distant then, as if his memories were on a different realm entirely, a place she couldn't ever hope of reaching. She bit her lip.

"You're definitely not from around here," she said. "I can tell that much."

She turned her head to look at him and caught his mysterious crooked smile. Despite his amusement, Neri saw a steady thrum of intensity in his dark eyes.

"What gave you that impression?" he asked.

She shuffled slightly to face him.

"You're constantly dressed for winter in the deepest agonising throes of the heat season." She ticked her points off on her fingers. "Your agility is bordering on supernatural and your reflexes are inhumanly fast. I'm beginning to suspect there's something a little bit more than odd about you, and I think I know what it is."

Niall slid his head to the side, his lips still curved in a smile. The dark eyes narrowed an almost imperceptible amount and Neri wondered whether she'd perhaps stumbled on some kind of secret that went beyond her teasing. Feigning nonchalance, she flicked her hand toward the glass ceiling. Then with a small smile, she held her arms out wide.

"You're a *soul-shade*, aren't you?"

Niall laughed, the narrow suspicion draining from his eyes in an instant, as if he couldn't quite believe the ridiculousness of it. Even he couldn't claim *soul-shades* existed, the changeling beings that tales insisted were able to take on the form of anything they chose, be it air, water, wood or the mountains.

"Well done, you caught me," he teased. "I'm your friendly neighbourhood shade. Would you like to see my true form?"

Neri rolled her eyes, the banter dying away from her mind immediately.

"Even if you were, you could probably hide all that stuff from me if you wanted to, so it's all irrelevant. Good thing shades and those sorts of things don't exist, huh."

"You should spend some more time with Ma Kath," Niall suggested. "She tells excellent stories, although you'll no doubt think some of them far-fetched. None about shades I don't think, so sorry to disappoint. She can spin fantasy into reality though, although never as well as Emelyn can."

Saddened by the mention of Emelyn, Neri turned to look at him once more. He was brooding, staring toward the pond with distant, far-away eyes.

"What kind of stories would they tell me?"

She kept her voice soft, almost a whisper, in the hope it would encourage him to answer her. Niall smiled, wistful for once it seemed, and waved his hand over the grass in front of him. She closed her eyes momentarily and sucked in the hazy waft of the *liliam* above her.

"Ocana cats and horcupogs, unicorns and dragons. She'd tell you about the west too, wild tales of where the *air-aerie* walk amongst descendants of folk. Emelyn must still have some of the stories written somewhere."

Neri shuddered through the unexpected chill that stole some of the day's warmth from her bones as Niall mentioned Emelyn again.

"Tell me all you know about the folk that have her," she said.

Out of the corner of her eye, she caught the turn of Niall's head and his almost mocking expression of reproach.

"Or you'll what?" he asked. "We've already established I can outrun you."

Neri nodded to accept that but she didn't feel inclined to back down. Shrugging one shoulder, she smiled as innocently as possible.

"If you won't tell me, then I won't tell you my latest work of wax. It's *special*."

She put emphasis on the last word, even though he'd already seen the crawbird she had carved, and she had absolutely no other idea of what carving could constitute as 'special'. But his eyes widened and she had piqued his curiosity. He slid across the grass until the warm fabric covering his knee bumped against her thigh.

"It's a deal." He took a deep breath. "The Governance believes certain elements of the realm, particular *ways of life* we could say, should be hidden from folk. We are among those who believe the folk should know and should have a right to choose."

His whispered words fell from his lips, shrouded in a quiet sense of urgency and importance. Neri recognised his cunning as he told her nothing of real value, repeating pretty much what he'd already told her.

"I can tell you though, that they are ruthless and believe deeply that these elements should be hidden at any cost. It has to do with their power," he finished.

He leaned back, disapproval falling across his face when Neri huffed.

"It's always to do with power. The more they gain the more they fear losing, and folk don't seem to like the idea of that."

She glanced over at Dog, his head slumbering on his paws with one eye open as she continued.

"Only when you've lost everything you cared about do you appreciate the things you will never have without actually needing them. My gramma used to say that each entity, power and thing was a gift not an object. Gifts can't be owned or controlled but merely enjoyed, no matter how fleeting."

"She sounds wise." Niall's voice echoed softer this

time. "Was she the one to give you your necklace?"

Again with that.

"Why are you all so obsessed with it? You pointed it out, then Emelyn commented and now you're asking again."

Niall shrugged, his gaze drifting off across the garden.

"Where I come from, tokens like those are made for babies when they're born. I never got given one, that's all."

Neri bit her lip. *I really don't need to be feeling sorry for him right now, but I do.*

Niall seemed to shake the sombre thoughts out of his head and turned to look at her with a lighter smile in his eyes.

"So, what great work of art are you carving?" he asked.

She froze as he leaned extremely close to her, his shoulder coming forward to nudge against her own. The heat from his body radiated through the fabric of his shirt, and she realised she could be as vague with him as he had initially been with her.

"It's a figurine, made of wax."

She pulled her eyes wide in a show of innocence and smiled at him. Niall grinned, his chin tilting down as he looked at their legs touching. When he glanced back up, dark pools fixing on her from beneath surprisingly thick, long lashes, Neri realised she was playing with fire by goading him.

"A figurine made of wax, who'd have thought it? What makes it so special?"

Her skin tingled, partly from the sudden gentle breeze that wafted through the otherwise still garden, but mostly from Niall's closeness. The scent of *liliam* carried on the breeze hit her senses and she smiled. The smell had given her an idea.

"It's magic. My gramma used to tell me stories about the meanings of flowers." She kept her voice low so that Niall leaned even closer to hear her. "When I'm done, the carving will offer deep protection to whoever has it."

"Do you believe that?" he asked.

She was sorely tempted to continue teasing him, but she also noted the rivulet of seriousness in his question.

"Ask me again when I've seen for myself whether it works or not."

Niall chuckled. "Cynic."

Neri stuck her tongue out at him, relishing the alien ability to joke and tease.

"Cultist."

She eyed the *liliam* tree. Initially her special figurine had been an idea of fun, an instrument of mockery to tease Niall with, but now she was determined to make it anyway.

"Time's ticking on." She sat up. "I'm supposed to be a candle shop until you tell me what is going on for real, so I better get started."

She kept her words light, with no real bite in them, but noticed a shadow mar Niall's expression all the same. Determined to avoid descending into awkwardness again, she heaved herself to her feet and pointed to the *liliam*.

"Can I pull a few sprigs off to take with me?"

Niall grinned then, his face lighting up. "You can, but if you're worried about its feelings you can always ask it for permission first."

His eyes carved energetic spikes into her back as she turned away from him. She worked three small branches from the tree and walked toward the dwelling. As she turned in the doorway, she held up the branches.

"Thanks for this. Don't stay up in the sunlight, or your shade self will dissipate from the shadows."

Niall laughed and stood with fluid ease.

"Ask Ma for an extra flint stick on your way through then. We shades feed on defenceless young women who go around smelling of flowers."

He made a low bow. Despite the tinge of blush to her cheeks at his mockery, Neri dismissed it as harmless silliness and led Dog up to her room. The comfort of her bed called to her but then she saw that someone had brought up more wax.

With a weary sigh, she settled down on the hard stone slab, setting and stoking a fire to melt the wax. As the fire worked its own sorcery, she set about pounding the *liliam* blooms. To get the colour to meld with the wax, the *liliam* needed to be ground to a powder. She would experiment with flecks of petal to see if it took at all, then she would begin properly in the morning. With the crushed *liliam* stirred into the melted wax, Neri put out the small fire and left it to cool.

She stood by the balcony door watching the suns dazzle the roofs of the abandoned settlement. It took a long while of random contemplation before she remembered the cooling wax and went to test it. The wax warmed her fingers, still soft enough to mould. The *liliam* flecks had taken well, embedded like berry pips in a breadcake.

She moulded a cylinder of wax with her bare hands and then left it on the stone to harden. As she took the remnants in her fingers, intending to make something small, her mind drifted to thoughts of Emelyn out there somewhere, terrified and alone.

CHAPTER SEVEN

When she awoke the next morning, Neri noticed two things. One was that her mould of *liliam*-infused wax was ready to carve. The second thing was that a large plate had been left on the chair at the top of the attic stairs, holding breadcakes with berries and a lump of butter melting in the heat.

Sitting up, Neri tried to work out if she had undressed before bed, even though she hadn't done that fully for at least a year.

I must be getting really careless if folk can sneak in and leave stuff.

She swung her legs over the edge of the bed and kicked the blankets free, rolling her toes against the wooden floor. It only took her a few large bites to finish the breakfast, then she eyed the misshapen lump of *liliam* wax waiting for her.

Sitting cross-legged on the bed with one of the more ragged blankets over her legs, she moved her blade over the wax in slow, cautious swipes. A stem appeared, delicate and spindly, with leaves soon following.

Her mama had always insisted flowers had meaning, and that *liliam* blooms were a sign of trust, but Neri couldn't bring herself to believe in such fancies, even now. A *liliam* bloom with its bulb-like shape would be the sturdiest form to keep in wax without bits breaking off though, so that was what she would carve.

The slaying heat threatened to force her into a faint, but she worked on regardless. By the time the flower was finished, Neri had whiled away a large portion of the morning and her clothes were stuck to her skin.

She wondered what she would do with the charm now and held it up for assessment. Her suggestion to Niall the day before about testing its magical abilities was purely a joke, but it seemed unthinkable now that anyone else should have the charm but him. Uneasy at the thought of what he'd take from such a gift, Neri decided she'd carry it on her instead.

She found a spare bit of string to use as a wick and grabbed the thin end of the tweezers to pierce a hole in the wax. With a make-shift necklace made, Neri tucked the string over her head and the wax charm under her shirt next to her token.

Venturing down the stairs, she found the bathroom empty and stopped to wash. She had no idea when Niall and the others would start telling her things, if they ever did, but until she had a firmer grasp on the situation being clean was such a luxury in the unending heat.

Unable to find a towel, she settled for squeezing the wet strands of her hair with her fingers and left the room to find Niall lounging against the wall as if he'd been waiting a while. She flinched at the sight of him, her pulse beginning to thud.

He frowned, eying her up and down.

"Just waiting my turn," he said. "No need to faint at the mere sight of me."

She pulled a face. "I was up late working actually so I'm tired, nothing to do with you."

"I don't suppose you've finished your lucky charm yet?"

The tease in his voice hung there, lilting in his tone and shining devilishly in his eyes. Neri matched his smug smile and reached beneath her top, pulling out the wax token.

"*Liliam* to banish evil and for protection. If your rescue plan is tomorrow then we'll soon see if it works."

She lied easily about the flower being for protection, making it up as she went along. Her mama always said that they represented trust, but protection fit her previous story better.

Niall's gaze roved over the charm, his eyes wide with wonder.

"Where I come from, *liliam* is given as a sign of trust," he murmured.

Neri's mind juddered and she tightened her fingers around the wick.

Mama must have heard that from somewhere to tell it to me. She knew Hamlin as well from older days. Stop making fates out of coincidences.

She lifted the wick necklace free of her head and held it out to Niall. As his fingers caressed the wax flower, she bit her lip. Her mind, normally clear despite emotions, dipped into unexpected territories.

Heat crept up her shoulders and leapt straight into her cheeks as he took the charm in hand. She dropped the wick and stepped back, bumping against the bathroom doorframe.

Niall's gaze settled on her with undecipherable emotion. A slight furrow developed between his brows, almost a frown. Frantic to find some way of lightening the tense air between them, Neri said the first thing that swept into her grateful brain.

"It's to say thank you for bringing me here. I don't know if that kind of willpower exists, but if it does, it'll keep you safe."

Her words only seemed to enflame the charged space around them.

Niall lifted his chin and tilted his head back so that strands of auburn hair slipped away from his eyes. Neri focused on one of the loose threads of his shirt instead of looking at his face, and he straightened up as if sensing her discomfort.

"You made a good luck charm for me? Anyone would think you cared. Folk will talk."

He winked at her, the tease still hanging on his low, intimate tone. Neri couldn't help but smile. His self-confidence was already irredeemable.

She rolled her eyes at him. "You're addle-headed."

She turned to go down the stairs, aware her hair was still wet and providing a cool soak against her back. Perhaps it wasn't the most appropriate way to go downstairs for food, but waiting for it to dry wasn't an option when her stomach growled loudly.

Something landed on her shoulder before she could move away and she squeaked, stumbling to a halt.

Niall's fingers were warm and dry. He held her still, and she could almost feel the heat of him standing close behind her as he gathered rat-tails of her wet hair in his free hand and squeezed.

Neri focused on keeping her breathing at least going in and out again, trying to hold the ragged heave of her chest from becoming obvious. His closeness startled her but his fingers, strong yet gentle on her shoulder, zinged energy through her skin.

"We can't have you dripping all over the chalk downstairs," he murmured.

His hand left her shoulder and her mind zigzagged through possibilities. She'd prided herself on not letting the more fanciful emotions or thoughts of the opposite sex distract her and hadn't come across too many to take an interest in so far. The few awkward fumblings she'd experienced hadn't left her with much hope or expectation either.

She mumbled something incoherent and shot off down the stairs like a hound in sight of a rabbit, right into the new arrival coming out of one of the doorways. They stopped in front of each other.

Neri quelled a squeak as the mysterious Moonshine smoothed warm, firm fingertips over her forehead.

"You are interesting." Moonshine smiled wide. "Come, sit and talk to me."

Neri glanced back at Niall as Moonshine grabbed her

arm, but Niall gave her the kind of lopsided grin that suggested he wasn't going to interfere. Short of causing a fuss, Neri let the woman drag her through the door into a small, den-like room. Short candles hovered on wooden discs hung from lengths of string. Books were piled lovingly on wooden shelves in haphazard groups but plants dominated everywhere else, from the surfaces to the spare spaces of wall. Moonshine pushed Neri onto a round puff of padded fabric with gentle hands and settled herself onto a woven pink mat nearby.

Neri took a deep breath, catching the strong scent of sweet herbs burning.

"Wow," she muttered.

Moonshine nodded. "Thank you. I will question you, but please do not answer anything you'd prefer not to." Her smile widened. "Tea?"

"I-" Neri hesitated. "Actual tea?"

"Of course. Berry or spice?"

Neri chose berry, amusement tinging through her uneasiness. Moonshine didn't even twitch as Dog padded in and flopped onto a huge pink fabric cushion.

Neri accepted the cup of tea pushed into her hands and braced herself for an interrogation.

"It's not often folk have tea anymore," she said. "Not anyone I know anyway."

Moonshine nodded. "I brew it myself. I'm a great collector of various herbs and spices. Now, I sense a great deal locked away inside you. Do you perhaps have some western blood?"

Neri managed to stifle the snort of incredulous derision

rather admirably. Despite Niall insisting the Governance wanted to find a way through the cursed forest to the fabled westlands, everyone knew that any folk with western blood would have had it diluted over the many hundreds of winterspans since the east and west had been separated.

"I don't think that could be possible."

"You don't believe it's possible at all, or that it's just not likely in your case?" Moonshine asked.

Neri took a sip of the cool berry tea, using it as an excuse to temper her response accordingly.

"I doubt sorcery or the old fables of *aerie*-folk are likely, but then if anyone was suspect it would have been my gramma. I think even genetic magic can skip generations though."

Moonshine laughed. "You must read some of Emelyn's scribings then. I have some here still."

At the thought of Emelyn, Neri's insides plummeted. Moonshine nodded in recognition, her face settling into quiet sadness.

"We will find her," she said.

Neri wanted to agree, or to ask questions, but Moonshine moved to one of the haphazard bookcases before she could think of a way to start. Books started to fly behind her and Neri stifled a grin as Moonshine muttered some extremely non-ethereal cursing. Realising the hunt could take a while and she was still minus any food, she clambered to her feet.

"I should..." Neri inched toward the door. "I have candles to make."

Moonshine waved a distracted hand over her shoulder.

"Go, go. I'll find you."

Neri set her cup down on the nearest available surface and slipped out into the hall, shaking her head. There was no sign of Niall lurking and nobody appeared as she made her way up to her room with Dog plodding along behind her.

"I'm beginning to think I'm the sane one," she muttered. "Not actually a reassuring thought."

She reached the top of the stairs and stared at her room. The candle-making equipment was exactly where she'd left it, the pot hanging over the unlit stone hearth and her blade accounted for. A row of candles lined the wall, right up to the end of her bed but it was the large black scorch mark adorning the wall that drew her attention.

Neri hurried toward it, reaching out her fingertips to swipe through the discolouration. Before she could fathom how something had burned the wall when she knew she'd not had a fire since the night before, a bright glint caught her eye.

The rays of sunslight filtering in and the speckles of dust made light dance over a strange, misshapen object. Neri pressed one hand to the softness of her bed, leaning over to peer at the oddity lying on the blankets. She'd seen glass once before at a market, delicate lumps of it chiselled into candle holders, but it was a rare thing to find and even rarer for folk to afford. Even blade-metal was a pricey trade, and some inherited blades lovingly passed down through families while others made do with wooden blades coated in strong *gar* for chipping with.

"Well, that's untidy."

Moonshine's voice made her jump. She straightened and folded her arms across her chest, eying the scorch mark.

"I didn't make that." She caught the assessing look in Moonshine's eyes. "I know how that sounds, but I didn't. My equipment hasn't been used since yesterday, and that mark wasn't there this morning. Neither was this."

She picked up the misshapen lump of glass, smooth and warm to the touch. She could see a distorted view of her hand through it, and the subtle blaze of what looked like a fiery orange feather.

"A kyne?" Moonshine moved so fast Neri didn't even have time to flinch. "And you say you definitely didn't make that mark?" Neri shook her head. "Interesting. And you've never seen this before. Hmm."

Neri held the glass out, the kyne Moonshine had called it. Wild thoughts of someone framing her with someone else's precious item or trying to chase her out of the sanctuary filled her head.

"I didn't steal it. I've no idea how it ended up here."

Moonshine frowned, an irksome look crossing her face.

"Who said anything about stealing? Don't be silly. This is something you should have. I won't explain why and I don't expect you to ask, but you must take it."

Moonshine reached out to push the kyne back against Neri's chest. When her hands automatically clenched tighter, Neri fought her desire and pushed it back.

"It must belong to someone," she insisted. "These things don't just materialise out of thin air."

Moonshine's eyes glittered and she leaned in close.

"It's yours."

Neri bit her lip. The woman didn't have any sense of bad feeling about her but still she was wary.

She would keep it safe until someone decided to claim it. Perhaps whoever put the mark on the wall had dropped it by accident. She thought of Finn who had been absent for a day or so, a ripple of foreboding sending chills over her arms.

A shadow appeared at the top of the stairs and it took her mind a moment to recognise Niall in her uneasiness.

"Time to discuss Emelyn," he said. "All of us."

Neri bent to pick up her pack and froze at the soft intake of breath.

"Is that a kyne?" Niall asked, his tone reverent.

Neri nodded. "Is it yours?"

He opened his mouth, shaped several undecipherable words, then stared at her like a jumping gob-fish.

"Mine? Of course not."

"It appeared on Neri's bed, along with that." Moonshine pointed to the scorch mark.

"They're very rare, kynes like that," he murmured, apparently transfixed by the mere sight of it. "It's what happens when lightning hits sand. The fable I heard growing up told us that true kynes were made from the tears of a blazing firebird. If it's real, it's very rare. I've never seen one."

That would explain the feather inside then, if such things were actually real.

Neri held it out. When Niall didn't make any move to take it or come closer, she placed the kyne into her pack.

"Firebirds occasionally take charges," Moonshine added. "They only ever leave kynes as a talisman that the person is under protection."

Niall's expression seemed to shake itself off and recover, a remnant of his usual mood returning.

"There's no proof of that."

"*Pfft*, there's always a grain of truth in tales." Moonshine tutted, then held out a small, cloth-bound book to Neri. "I'd like you to take and read this. It's a second copy so don't worry if anything happens to it, keep it as your own. Perhaps it will shine some light on the dark parts of your realm."

She held out a book and Neri took it, knowing better than to argue now. Emelyn's name was on the front, scrawled in what looked like very old dark ink tattooed onto the thick cover. Ignoring the swoop of anxiety, she placed it in her pack next to the kyne.

"Thank you, I'll take good care of it." She glanced up at Niall. "When you said all of us are discussing Emelyn, does that include me?"

He nodded. "That's what 'all of us' means. All of us, including you."

She huffed at his prissiness and followed him and Moonshine down the stairs, wondering if Dog was staying behind to guard her new haul or more likely to pass out on the cool stone hearth for the hotter part of the afternoon.

Her breathing was still uneasy as she entered the den, the room charged with irritable energy. Only Ma Kath looked up to acknowledge her from the sofa before resuming a frantic clicking with her knitting needles.

Matty stood fiddling with a tray of brushes in front of beside a large stretch of stone wall washed white, the smell of paint still heavy in the air. Eva sat on the window seat staring outside and Finn was in the armchair furthest from the door with his fingers tapping on his thighs.

Hoping they wouldn't notice her flushed cheeks, Neri slid to sit on the floor by the remaining unoccupied chair. Niall claimed it moments later and her face burned hotter when he smirked down at her. Luckily, Ma stood to claim their attention, her face grave.

"We all know what's going on," she began. "Rescuing Emelyn won't be easy, but we can pull it off if we work together."

She waved a hand at Matty who raised a thick brush in preparation. Neri could still make out some of the artwork beneath the fresh white coat on the wall, but as Ma spoke Matty started to paint a diagram.

"We believe this is the basic outline of the dwelling they have her in," Ma explained.

The layout of the building they were supposed to be infiltrating took shape. Neri sat cross-legged with her hands on her knees. Each time a new part of the image appeared, she took a steady deep breath and committed it to memory. It would be large, bigger than the sanctuary by far, but she would remember.

"The stairs will be problematic." Ma frowned. "We all know the only way out will be through the second floor window at the back in the stairwell and across the sheds. However we do not know what physical state Emelyn will be in."

Matty daubed a circle on one square representing a room.

"We believe Emelyn to be in this room. Don't be mistaken though, she will be guarded."

Neri frowned. While she had developed her own ways of defending herself, she wasn't exactly practiced at taking on more than one person at a time. Even going beyond scuffles in the far fields of her settlement as a child hanging around those who wanted to join the watch patrols, she'd practiced on her own ever since the Governance came for her family.

"So, what are we actually going to do?" She had to ask.

Everyone turned to look at her. She focused her gaze on Ma, hoping to find at least some semblance of calm understanding from the level-headed matriarch.

"We?" Ma shook her head. "I know you want to go, Neri, and we appreciate that. But while we've placed a level of trust in you, that doesn't mean you need to put yourself in danger. Leave it to us."

Neri's stomach crunched in on itself. She took a slow, controlled breath.

"The Governance has already taken a lot from me. If they've taken someone else, I'll do what I have to so that they don't ruin more families. I also have to find out why they were after me at Hamlin's, which I'm not going to do sitting around here."

She hadn't mentioned the Governance being after her to them but assumed Niall had filled them in already. So she kept her head up high, holding Ma's gaze.

"How do we know we can trust you though?" Finn

asked. "*I* still say you might be one of them."

The slightest smirk curled at the edge of his mouth. Neri folded her arms and twisted to face him square on.

"If I am one of them then you lose nothing by sending me in. If you send in someone you do trust though, and they get caught, you're a person down. A win-win for you I'd say. Besides, if I am who I say I am, and if I can get Emelyn out, that's even better than risking one of your own surely?"

Finn shrugged, his nonchalant face giving her the strongest urge to punch the slim sliver of metal pierced through his lip right between his two front teeth. She struggled to keep her hands unclenched.

"You don't have to prove anything to us," Niall insisted.

"I'm not." She frowned. "I do appreciate the recent kindness, but no, this is personal between me and them."

Niall shook his head. "No, I can't let you. It's too dangerous."

"I wasn't asking your permission." She matched his glare with one of her own.

Ma cleared her throat, a small smile brewing amid the lined worry on her face.

"On second thoughts, perhaps it would be sensible for you all to travel westwards by familiar roads," she suggested. "You can then ask for further advice along the way."

Neri gave Niall a triumphant look, one step short of sticking her tongue out at him.

"So, what's the actual plan?" she asked again.

Matty tapped the wall with his paintbrush. "Um, you

wait until the coast is clear and sneak in. That's about as far as we've got."

Neri stared at him. "O-*kay*, so, you know where this place is. You know the rough outline of where she'll be. Is that all?"

"Not quite." Eva spoke up. "We'll be observing the building until the guards change over. There should be short gap during the rotation. Then we sneak in and get Em out."

Neri rubbed her bottom lip, tracking through the potential pitfalls in her mind.

"Can't we create some kind of diversion to draw them all to the other side of the building at least?" she asked. "The Governance aren't exactly going to give us a slap on the wrist if they find us."

The memory of Hamlin's death threatened to swallow her, but she sucked in a sharp breath and refused to let it take hold.

Eva leaned forward. "What are you thinking?"

Encouraged that at least they weren't ridiculing her straight away, Neri sought frantically for a suitable suggestion.

"Some kind of distraction would do surely, something that would get everyone running to the front of the building if Emelyn is at the back?"

Eva nodded. "That could work. Niall, you can think up a distraction I'm sure. We'll only get the one shot though."

Neri ignored the furious glance Niall threw at her. She listened as Ma explained that they would likely be facing folk who were trained in combat. When all eyes turned to

117

Neri, she cast hers down and shrugged.

"I can defend myself well enough."

She didn't dare look Niall's way as he scoffed out loud, but Ma wrapped up the meeting after that and hurried off to fuss over the kitchen.

Eva and Matty disappeared almost immediately which left Neri with Niall and Finn. Sensing both of them watching her, she clambered to her feet and strode out of the room without looking back. If they were really allowing her to go with them, she would need to carry things. She doubted Ma would miss two blankets if she made a makeshift pack.

Upstairs she greeted Dog, who'd been sitting at the top of the stairs waiting for her. He wagged his tail and she sighed as she sat on the bed. The sensible thing to do would be to leave him here with Ma, but she couldn't contemplate being without him now.

Needing to be busy, she set about folding and knotting one bedsheet until it formed a good enough makeshift pack that she could sling over her shoulder. Then she packed a few candles, Hamlin's pocket watch and his letter. Her old cut-off shorts she slid over the top as well with her blade in its holder still attached to the belt loop.

They might trust me now but that doesn't mean I can automatically trust them in return. She freed the dagger holder to fix it to the pair of shorts she was wearing. *Finn's clearly against me. But Niall was the one to bring me all the way here. Did he know the enemy were coming for me? Did Hamlin?*

Those were all questions she could ask, but she

probably wouldn't get an acceptable answer. Dog huffed a very loud sigh and she smiled down at him.

"We're going on another adventure, Dog," she whispered. "If anything happens to me, I want you to come back here. They'll look after you."

Doubtful he had any idea what she was saying, Neri settled for cuddling his dopey head for a moment before moving to stand on the balcony. The heat coursed against her skin and she despaired as the perspiration appeared almost immediately. Travelling would be tough in the heat, but she couldn't back out now. Recalling Niall's tender treatment of her hair earlier, her adrenalin bubbled. She ignored the internal heat as best she could and strode back into her room to light the physical fire instead.

Setting as much of the wax to form as she could, she made another set of candles and started carving stars into a set one. The methodical swipe of her blade soothed her. She worked on, sweat pouring over her body from a combination of the weather and the close proximity to the simmering flames.

She nodded with a tight smile to Eva who brought up a bowl of soup and bread with an ancient decanter of water but kept working. When she moved a few hours later to eat, she noticed two large lumps of *carana*, a combination of sweet and bitter berries that solidified into a candy when mixed with butter and whipped egg. She considered saving them but they were already half-melted in the heat, so she ate one after the other with indulgent relish and scraped the residue off the plate.

Only when the fire had burnt to ash and the sunslight

had almost faded away, a mere mirage of pale pink and purple on the horizon, did she get up properly and stretch.

Her muscles ached and clicked as she set off downstairs to see if she could get a drink of something to take up to bed. Dog padded quietly behind her and she held her finger to her lips as they tiptoed past the door to the den.

As she approached the kitchen, candlelight flickered in the small gap between the door and the frame. She could hear low voices and didn't want to be discovered eavesdropping, so she peeked through the gap instead. Finn sat at the table, a self-satisfied grin on his face.

"You surprise me," he said. "I take it she's off limits now then?"

Neri bristled at his tone, wondering who he meant. She angled her head a different way and saw Niall standing on the other side of the table with his back to her and his shoulders bunched toward his ears.

"To the likes of you, yes she is."

Finn's quiet laughter responded to the growl in Niall's voice, and Neri took a step back to avoid being found.

"When we find Emelyn and bring her back, I might even ask Neri to come with me for the next step," Niall added.

Neri froze in place and resumed peering through the gap in time to see the cocky smirk wiped from Finn's face.

"That's not right," he said. "She's still not one of us."

Niall shrugged. "We know very little about Eva either, but Matty wouldn't be expected to leave her behind. Besides, Neri could be one of us. There's something about her that we don't know yet, something relevant. I can feel it."

Finn shook his head in disbelief, a scowl creeping across his face.

"We'll discuss this when we return. But if your new toy runs off before we get Emelyn back to safety, I won't stand in their way if they go after her. Then again, I wouldn't rule out going after her myself if she does."

Finn got up and went out to the garden, leaving Niall staring after him. Before Neri could clear her throat to announce herself, Niall smacked his hand on the table with a growl and stood so swiftly that his chair toppled sideways.

Neri shuffled away from the door and retreated back upstairs. She settled on her bed, her mind in a tangle.

What could possibly make Niall that angry? And where exactly is he intending on taking me?

CHAPTER EIGHT

Neri went through her pack for the third time the next morning, more for something to fiddle with than out of necessity. Niall's mysterious words had plagued her all night but she couldn't pull out of the chance to rescue Emelyn now, not if it meant she could find out why the Governance were after her as well.

When Niall came up to fetch her, she shouldered the makeshift pack and followed him down to the den in silence. Eva's eyes were red, presumably from crying, and Matty's weren't far off the same. Neri forced herself not to stare as Ma appeared beside her with a battered hide pack in hand.

"Take this." Ma held the bag out. "It'll support your back better."

Neri took the pack, worn but sturdy fabric neatly stitched at the seams with a proper cinch-tie opening to keep the contents safe. Touched by the gesture, she busied herself with moving everything over. Right at the bottom of her new bag she spied a large hunting blade in a hide sheath. Ma caught her eye and held a quick finger to her lips. Then she moved on to distributing food parcels and Neri's candles among them.

When Finn finally deigned to arrive, Ma smiled around at them all.

"I wish you safety and a successful journey," she said. "We will welcome you home soon and Neri, I hope you'll return to us as well. It's been lovely having you here and I'll keep your room for you."

Swallowing some of her pride and reluctance, Neri nodded. It wasn't a promise or an agreement, but the offer was open to her and suddenly she felt a tiny stirring of hope in her chest. It gave her strength as she, Niall, Eva and Finn left the house.

They walked through the deserted lanes of the settlement in single file, the air silent but for the sweet lulling noise of birds in the trees and their footsteps on the hard earth. Neri kept a sharp eye out but they passed nobody on their way to the fringe of the forest. She followed a few paces behind Eva, aware of Niall at her back and Finn bringing up the rear. With each step, she was grateful for Dog's faithful presence at her side.

The sweat quickly gathered, pooling over her skin from the exertion and the oppressive heat. Neri kept an image of Emelyn in her mind, hoping that it would make her resolve firm when the time came to be brave. She had no idea what they'd expect her to do once they arrived at their destination, but her mind danced over the possibilities. If she returned to the sanctuary, she might even be able to a stay long-term.

The day passed with little to no conversation at all and

the breaks were few and short. Only when the suns were sinking between the trees did they stop by a stream to eat and rest.

Neri smiled as Dog jumped into the stream, splashing back and forth. Without a second thought, she peeled off her boots to run in with him. The water only came up to her thighs but the rest of her got soaked by Dog's energetic swimming.

The other three sat around the beginnings of a fire nearby and Eva smiled in Neri's direction, which cheered her spirits. Finn's intent gaze ranged over her wet thighs and never strayed much higher than her chest. That made her feel uneasy, but it was Niall's emotionless staring into the fire that unnerved her the most. His words to Finn the night before danced back to her and she knew she'd have to confront him about it at some point. He brought her to the sanctuary and she was grateful for that, but she didn't owe him anything and he didn't have any right to take her anywhere without her agreeing first.

When she'd finished cooling off in the water, she joined the others by the warmth of the flames. Dusk settled until the only light came from the fire, the sparks and embers casting dancing shadows behind them all.

"We'll take turns to sleep." Eva broke the silence. "Finn and I will take first watch. Niall and Neri will take the second. We'll wake you."

It seemed Eva was in charge although she glanced at Niall for confirmation. Neri pulled blankets from her pack and spread them out a short distance from the others. When Niall came and settled himself against the tree trunk behind her, she gave him a disapproving look. His lips drew into a tight line as he caught her eye.

"We have to be paired at all times, for safety."

Neri noted a slight catch in his voice and glanced over at Eva and Finn. They weren't close together at all. As she settled and closed her eyes, a more disturbing thought came to her. They probably all saw her as a liability, a flight risk that needed careful monitoring.

Either that or I'm a trade they plan to make for Emelyn's safe return.

The thought slammed through her, the likeliness of it echoing with such force that any tiredness dissipated into panic. She couldn't do anything about it now. If she ran, Niall would catch her. But she needed to keep it in mind. She had no intention of being given over to the Governance.

That possibility and thoughts of Hamlin pestered her as she drifted in and out of sleep, but she managed to rest for a while.

"Neri."

Niall's soft whisper woke her.

She opened her eyes to darkness, her sight taking a moment to adjust to the dim glow from the fire dying nearby. Niall hovered above her like a figure made of shadow.

Without a word she got up, packed her blankets and followed him to the fire. Eva headed straight toward the area Neri and Niall had just vacated. Finn followed her and settled into a pile of leaves a metre or two away. In twos at all times after all.

Niall sat against a tree with his head leaned back but Neri chose to sit beside the fire. She dug in her pack for her carving blade and a candle. Her fingers began to roam across the candle's edge and soon the blade flicked away at the wax. She glanced up at Niall, expecting him to be watching her or the fire, but he was fast asleep. She didn't bother to hide her smile.

I could run. Her fingers stilled over the candle. *I might make it a fair way. But I've still got nothing of value to live on if I do. I can't abandon Emelyn yet either, not until I know they're definitely planning to use me.*

She also had a suspicion that Niall might be an incredibly light sleeper, or he was pretending to slumber to lure her into running if she was planning to.

So she stayed in place, carving away and saving the shavings. When the suns began to rise a long while later, Neri stood as quietly as her stiff limbs would allow. Finn and Eva still slept, as did Niall.

His copper hair had fallen over his eyes and she fought the urge to push it back for him. It would do no good in the long run. She might be developing some kind of ill-advised crush on him, but acting on any such feelings would make things unbearable for the whole group.

Then she spied an apple tree. Most of the trees they'd passed were the usual kind, pale brown trunks with ridged bark and many limbs, towering between the ground and the sky, a mix of silvery leaves and pale green ones. But an apple tree was unusual so deep in the woods and away from others of its kind.

She grabbed one of her blankets and walked over to the

tree, contemplating how to climb it. It only took her six footholds and one near fall before she was secured in the lower branches. She knotted her blanket into a sack and began to load the waxy russet apples into it. She could see their camp clearly from her vantage point and noticed Eva moving. Once Eva had woken the others, she could call out and let them know she was safe.

Eva glanced around and in a few quick strides she was beside the dying fire. Neri gasped as the toe of Eva's boot landed hard against Niall's thigh. He shot up, looking around. Eva pointed at the fire and Neri realised they would think she'd run off.

She shouldered the blanket of apples, gripped onto the tree trunk and slid down. Wincing at the impact, she kicked up leaves and undergrowth to announce her presence.

Eva and Niall both turned in a flurry.

Relief flooded Niall's face then quickly turned to anger, his eyes narrowing as his mouth twisted. She spoke first before he could start on her.

"Don't get your trousers twisted. I saw an apple tree and thought it'd keep us going to have something extra to eat."

She knelt by the ashes of the fire to show them the contents of her blanket.

The amusement on Eva's face was worth Niall's anger. He couldn't tell her off but he obviously wanted to. So he kicked out at the tree he'd slept against and stalked away. Neri packed the apples into her pack and held one out to Eva.

"I didn't think it would annoy him that much," she said.

Eva chuckled. "He's certainly very keen to keep an eye

on you. I thought he was worried about you trying to leave us but perhaps someone's finally turned his head. He's never shown any interest before, unlike Finn who slobbers at anything that moves."

Finn was suspiciously absent but Eva didn't seem concerned so Neri didn't mention it. Eva bit into the apple and Neri smiled to see her savouring the taste.

"Delicious." Eva grinned. "Thanks."

Neri ate her own apple, her mind still stuck on Eva's curious comment about Niall. While Eva covered their tracks and doused the fire with water from the stream, Neri shouldered her backpack and took an apple over to him, holding it out with a frown.

"I didn't realise you'd get so wound up. Did you think I'd run off?"

Niall glanced at her, then at the apple before looking away.

"No, I thought you'd wandered and someone had taken you. If it happened to Emelyn, it could easily happen to you. It's not safe out here even if we're deep in the trees."

"I can look after myself." Neri folded her arms. "Look, I said I'm sorry and we're sort of stuck with each other so you may as well accept the peace offering and stop sulking."

Niall turned to face her, his eyes dark, lips pressed tight. He had no reason to be so furious with her, but she couldn't allow herself to back down.

"Don't look at me like that." She glared back at him. "I honestly didn't think it would be such a big drama. I promise I won't run off anywhere without an escort from now on, deal?"

Niall uttered some kind of curse or grunt. In a swift movement that rendered her speechless, he had her pinned against him with one arm around her waist and his fingers curled tight in her hair.

"This isn't a game," he snarled. "Someone could grab you as easily as I just have and you'd barely have time to scream."

Neri glared back at him, her pulse pounding. She knew a way to disarm him and wriggle free, but it would hurt him and he didn't deserve that. Yet.

"If you don't let me go, I swear I will kick you where it hurts," she warned.

Several moments passed. Then Niall's grip slackened. Neri yelped as he crushed her against his chest.

"I worry about you, okay?" he mumbled. "You don't pull a trick like that again. At least wake me and tell me first."

His sweatshirt smelled of smoke from the previous night's fire and something else, a deeper scent that was sweeter like cake-spice and entirely him.

A tiny buzz fluttered in Neri's chest. When she nodded, Niall let her go with abrupt finality.

"I'm sorry. I got carried away."

He stepped back and Neri reached out to catch his sleeve. She had no idea what to say to him, so she settled for holding the apple out again.

"It's fine. Truce? We probably need to at least be communicating by time we reach wherever we're going."

Niall sighed and a tiny flicker of a smile reached the

corners of his mouth. He took the apple from her and bit into it.

Relieved that they seemed to be on relatively stable ground again, Neri made sure Dog was with her and joined Finn and Eva by the fire. She ignored Finn smirking in her direction but took the smile Eva threw her with gratitude as they set off through the woods. She didn't offer Finn an apple either, still irritated by his general existence.

The morning trek wore on in silence, but after a while they arrived on the crop of a hill. The trees disappeared and the slope fell sharply into level fields.

"We need to be careful here." Niall scanned the area. "Walk fast and don't stop to talk to folk, even if they ask for help. We can slow down again when we reach the next wood."

Neri sensed that the instructions were for her benefit alone as they continued on. The fields stretched toward the horizon, already turning a dusky reddish-brown from the slaying heat, but Eva led them toward the wide lane that ran alongside the fields before it curved away.

Their pace quickened as they walked toward it, the hint of carriages at either end moving both away and toward them. A central carriageway like that would link the bigger settlements and even the grand citadels, so Governance and watch patrols were likely. Neri followed Eva across as they took advantage of a gap in the rumbling carriages and carts clattering past. Safe on the other side, she glanced back to see Niall and Finn now separated from them.

Eva stopped as a carriage rattled to a halt beside them. Large and square painted black, it could have been a watch patrol carriage and Neri tensed, ready to run.

The carriage's driver had no sign of a highborn in his simple clothing and his carriage was serviceable at best. Even his carthorse looked worn, although that could have been due to the heat.

"Can I offer you a ride anywhere?" he asked, his attention fixed on Eva. "I'm bound for the Apeklonian citadel, but I have time to stop along the way."

Eva shook her head. "Kind, but no thank you."

"It'll save you time," he persisted. "Where are you bound?"

His tone was open and friendly but Neri's instincts were resurfacing, dusting themselves off after their slumber at the sanctuary. Open and friendly didn't mean safe. In most cases, it meant exactly the opposite.

"We're just hiking," Eva said.

Niall rounded the back of the carriage and strode across to them. Relieved that the group was whole again and they could continue on, Neri flinched as Niall put his free arm around her shoulders. He didn't hesitate, gathering her against his side, and her insides fizzled with anxiousness on all accounts.

"Well I can offer a lift to a nice hiking spot." The man leaned out over the edge of the driving seat. "There's a river to swim in and barely a soul in sight some days."

Sandwiched between Niall's possessive hold and Dog's bulk firm against her leg, Neri frowned. The others were reluctant to just walk off, perhaps to avoid any suspicion, so she turned to Niall and pouted, going against all of her instincts as she pressed into him.

"Can we keep going? I'm getting hungry and they're expecting us to be on time for once."

She huffed and turned away as if she intended to set off alone. As her hand slid along his arm, Niall caught it and held her tight, his fingers gripping in a warning for her to remain with him.

"We're fine, thanks." Eva nodded to the man. "It doesn't look like it's going to storm for another three days either."

Three days? Neri frowned. *Most likely her trying to sound conversational.*

She doubted there would be any storm for a long while yet given the constant dry heat, with no sense of anything looming other than more of the same. But the man was retreating onto his driving seat and it seemed her performance and Eva's non-committal chatter had worked.

Eva slid into her place at the front of the group and led them on with one final nod in the man's direction. The horse snorted but there was no sound of the carriage re-joining the stream dashing past.

Neri didn't dare look back and none of them said a single word. Only when they'd reached a suitably safe distance did Eva break the silence.

"He's finally gone. I must say I'm impressed, Neri. I was almost waiting for a brawl but that seemed to placate him. Either that or he didn't want to try taking on all four of us."

Neri shrugged, distracted by the ongoing jitter of her nerves. She wondered whether Niall still held her hand tight in his because of their pretence or because he wanted to. Or more likely, in case she tried to leg it the moment they hit the trees.

I won't try to let go if he doesn't, just in case he thinks I'm going to run. The last thing I need is him threatening to carry me.

Her lips twitched at the thought.

The moment they reached the line of the forest, Neri insisted they find the first available stream so Dog could have a drink and cool down. Eva located one easily on a battered old map she produced from her pack and Dog wasted no time diving in.

"We should be on the other side of the river anyway," Eva said. "The banks get a lot steeper but the river isn't too high now. We can wade a short way down stream to get to the next path. Clothing will dry quick enough in this heat."

Niall pressed his lips together and nodded with a hefty sigh, rubbing the back of his neck with one hand.

"We'll be against the current, but it'll save some time if we do," he agreed.

Finn was too busy rolling up the legs of his jeans to give his opinion. Niall dropped Neri's hand, but the unspoken link still lingered between them. She sat on the edge of the riverbank with her legs dangling in the flowing water. It bubbled against her skin and soothed some of the disgruntled uneasiness still hanging in her chest.

She bit back a smile as Dog swam past, a huge panting grin on his face. Without waiting for anyone else, she pushed herself in and squeaked as the cold water wrapped around her legs right up to her waist.

When she looked up again, her breath still sharp, Niall

caught her eye and his lips lifted. Flustered, she looked to Eva instead, but the woman was already in the water and striking out against the flow toward the opposite bank.

Neri flinched as Finn appeared beside her, his irritating grin wide enough to rattle her and barely a breath of space between his arm and hers.

"So, what did bring you into our little fold?" he asked.

She forced herself not to look back and check if Niall was close by or not. The memory of his conversation with Finn in the kitchen the night before surfaced. She shrugged and set off after Eva.

"Hamlin was apparently a friend of my mama's. When she passed, she told me to go find him and his shop, so I did."

The water current surged against her, but she focused on leaning forward into her stride. Finn flicked his sandy hair over his shoulder and gave her a self-satisfied smile that set her teeth on edge.

"That's it?" he chuckled.

Neri forced a fake smile. "Yeah, sorry, were you expecting some kind of fairy tale?"

"Whoa." Finn held his hands up and rolled his eyes. "No need to be hostile, sweet thing. You appear in our midst the day after Hamlin dies, say the Governance is after you and that you want to join us. We have to be cautious."

Neri shoved her hands under the water so he wouldn't see her clenched fists. It screwed with her balance, but she forged on anyway.

"I never said I wanted to join you," she corrected. "I

said I want to find out what they want with me and hit them where it hurts. Emelyn was kind to me briefly so if freeing her ruins stuff for them all the better. I have no actual plans on joining you beyond that, not without being able to trust any of you."

Finn drifted sideways, finally leaving a suitable amount of distance between them.

"I see." His smile had disappeared. "You might want to tell Niall that then."

"Tell Niall what?" The distrustful voice floated between them.

Neri almost groaned out loud and swayed to a halt.

Because of course he's right behind us listening to the whole thing.

Finn shot her a wicked grin and started wading ahead without them. Neri steadied her balance and turned to face Niall.

"I said I never wanted to join your group, just that I need to find out why the Governance are after me. I also agreed to help Emelyn because she was kind to me when she didn't have to be."

She folded her arms and stared him out, daring him to comment. He had rolled the sleeves of his shirt up to the elbow, but the hem was under the surface and the water had soaked halfway up his chest. When he veered closer, Neri almost jumped back out of the way.

"Finn likes to create hassle," he murmured. "I'd say don't provoke him, but I get the feeling you'd do it anyway whatever I say."

The tiniest quiver at the corner of his mouth suggested

he was teasing her. Before she could reply, he lifted both hands and slicked back his hair, dark auburn strands now hanging behind his ears.

"He just reminds me of folk I'd rather forget," she admitted.

Niall nodded, never once taking his gaze from her face.

She looked away. "We should catch up with the others."

She took a step back and almost lost her footing in her determination to get space from him. She flailed her arms, trying to catch her balance. Before she could right herself, Niall's hands were firm on her hips, dragging her upright again. He let go just as quickly but her flaming cheeks were apparently there to stay.

"Thanks," she muttered.

Without daring to look at him, Neri turned around and found Finn and Eva already out of the water up ahead. They stood beside a rotting wooden gate and given the frown on Eva's face, they weren't impressed about having to wait.

Neri eyed the steep, dusty bank. The edge came level with her nose and she assessed a collection of tree roots sticking out nearby. She grabbed one and hauled herself up.

Cool, dry hands swept beneath her arms, stray fingers brushing against the sides of her chest as they tried to haul her up. She reacted on instinct before common sense could reign, squeaking loud enough for anyone halfway across the land to hear.

She dropped back into the water as Finn loomed above her like a leviathan blocking out the sunlight. But she could see the mocking sneer on his face clear enough.

The sound of splashing nearby turned both their heads. She saw the anger in Niall's eyes, the darkness ferocious and glinting. Breathing hard from the shock, she turned to Finn before Niall could reach them.

"Sorry, you startled me. You need to warn folk before grabbing them!"

She searched the bank for signs of Eva, but the girl was nowhere to be seen. She was alone with a possible groper and one very angry pretend *soul-shade*.

Niall's arms surrounded her before she could register much else. His muscles bunched against her, tensed and ready for a fight. She couldn't even gather her thoughts quick enough to shake him off.

"You don't touch her, get it?" he warned. "I don't want any issues between us, so don't put so much as a breath around her."

Neri shuddered as the sound of his threat blasted right next to her ear. Finn glared for a moment, the slip of his easy-going confidence revealing something much darker beneath. Then he smiled, lips curving and eyes glittering as he held up his hands.

"I didn't realise, no harm done. She's yours. Message received loud and clear."

Finn turned and walked away with a jaunty whistle toward the gate.

Neri started to shake as Niall let her go. She turned to face him, rattled by the encounter but also by her lack of anger toward him for basically manhandling her without asking the same as Finn had.

"You didn't have to do that," she said.

Niall shrugged one shoulder, a mischievous, boyish smile inching over his lips.

"I didn't think, sorry. He's got a certain reputation when it comes to girls and I panicked. It's one he's spread himself to be fair, but I didn't think you'd want to get involved in all that. Maybe I was wrong?"

Is he asking me, or telling me?

Neri shook her head. "No, I guess not. But you didn't have to. I can take care of myself."

Niall tipped his head to one side, wordlessly accepting. Neri bit her lip as he continued to hold her gaze. Finn's mere touch had so abhorrent to her but she'd allowed Niall to grab her without as much as a reprimand. Locked in the intensity of their staring match, neither of them heard Eva returning.

"When you've had enough of the deep and meaningfuls, try to remember that we're out here for a reason. Also, Finn's buggered off. He's taken half the food and some of the candles too. He must be moving fast because I can't see him anywhere."

Neri heard the rivulet of foreboding in her tone. Niall glanced around, his shoulders squaring. Eva sighed.

"I left him with my pack while I went to scout ahead," she admitted. "When I came back, he was gone. He can't have gotten far, but we should focus on our own route and go on without him. We've spent too long here as it is."

Neri grabbed the tree root and struggled up onto the bank under her own steam. She paused only to call for Dog, who bounded out of the water with way more agility than she could ever manage and treated them all to a quick shower.

"We'll have to walk part of the night, but we made good time until we stopped," Eva said.

She set off and Neri followed, aware of Niall only a step behind her. His closeness both comforted and unnerved her, especially when not a word was said for a long while after. By the time night fell and they finally stopped to rest, Neri agreed to take the first watch with Eva. Niall would sleep, then Neri, then Eva. To her surprise, Niall fell asleep almost immediately beside her, both of them resting against the trunk of a broad tree. She glanced across the fire at Eva.

"You'd better be good to him." Eva's voice echoed through the trees, crossing over the fire between them. "Don't let him down."

Neri started, surprised by the sound, then allowed the wry smile to cross her face.

"Nothing is forever. I've never been interested in romance much, and no great choice in my youth either."

Eva snorted. "Your youth? You're what, twenty winters if that?"

"Nineteen, and there's been no freedom for it since everything went rotten either. But even if I was interested, it won't be me that hurts him. I won't let Emelyn down either, not if there's something I can do to help her. I keep thinking of her scared and alone."

Eva leaned her head back against the tree trunk behind her.

"That's something then."

Neri glanced up at the snatches of stars she could see through the treetops. They danced their pale multicoloured points of light over the sleeping land and lit the forest like an ethereal wonderland. A rather pointy stick on the ground was poking a specifically personal part of her, but she didn't want to stir too much and wake Niall with her shuffling.

When Eva nodded to indicate it was her turn to sleep, Neri whispered Niall's name and he was awake in an instant. His eyes went from alert to wary until he saw her.

"Thanks," he murmured. "It's your turn to sleep now. I suppose me offering you my shoulder as a pillow would go down badly?"

Neri could make out his face in the dim firelight, amused by his soft smile still dredged with sleep.

"One day I'll say yes just to freak you out, shade," she joked.

Niall tapped his shoulder with his hand. "The shade thing is going to stick, isn't it. Well, it's there if you want it. I won't bite."

Neri tipped her head back against the tree trunk behind her and closed her eyes, not quite able to quell the smirk still on her lips.

Maybe next time.

Too exhausted to worry, she decided she was probably safer with Niall next to her than not and promptly fell asleep. As she slumbered, she had the strangest dreams of fingers running through her hair and of flames and dark eyes dancing around, but they were gone when she woke. She looked up, the remnants of sleep making her feel languid. When she saw Niall still beside her, she couldn't help but smile.

"I'm getting soft if I can sleep this close to someone else without waking," she said. "Folk are going to talk."

Niall chuckled and signalled to Eva she could sleep before turning his gaze back to Neri. Moments passed. She almost forgot to breathe, anxious thoughts kicking up flurries in her head. He could take advantage of her easily if she showed she was softening toward him. Any sign of emotion and she'd be easy to manipulate. She took a deep breath and distracted herself with more sombre questions.

"Why do you think Finn took off?" she asked.

Niall sighed and let his head thump back against the trunk of the tree they shared.

"He's been acting strange for a while now. He went away to find out some information about the Governance and came back all cocky and weird. It's like he's gained some kind of taint that's brought out all his bad qualities."

He lowered his voice and pressed his lips right by her ear.

"I'm starting to think this whole Emelyn thing is changing everyone. I don't know who I can trust these days."

Neri froze, the hush of his breath against her ear sending ripples over her skin.

"You don't seem to sleep much," she murmured. "Maybe you're imagining things."

Niall laughed. "I don't need much sleep. But, if you're offering, I'll take a few more quiet hours now. If anything happens though, and I mean *anything*, you wake me straight away. No wandering off either, not even for apples."

Neri relaxed beside him, conscious of the warm press of his leg against hers.

"If you say so," she grinned. "If I get an itch or have a thought, or an owl hoots or a bat flies by, I'll wake you."

Niall grumbled something very uncomplimentary. Then he fidgeted a few times and moments later his breathing deepened and his arms relaxed, simple as that.

Neri sat there unwilling to move as time passed and the suns began to rise. After a while of dawnlight, she saw Eva's eyes snap open on the other side of the fire. Neri eased herself away from Niall, amused that he grumbled in his sleep, and scrambled up to get food. She woke him and although he smiled at her with enough warmth to turn her to ashes, the three of them ate in silence.

"How much further is it?" she asked.

Eva finished her nugget of bread and stood up.

"We walk all day today. That will get us to the edge of the next settlement. Then it'll be another walk to reach the destination. Niall, you won't have much time to work out your strategy either. When we go in the back, Neri, we just have to hope you're up to it."

Neri sighed. Evidently Eva's friendlier attitude had died out during the night.

CHAPTER NINE

Neri kept silent as they trudged on through the forest. When they hit empty lanes or skirted settlements showing signs of life, she cast a constant wary eye around. Each settlement they passed sent tantalising scents of baking and ripe gardens full of fruit and foliage. Neri's stomach growled and her skin stung with dryness.

Despite tempting distractions, she followed Eva with silent, sure footsteps. Any folk they passed hurried by without so much as a second glance. Neri knew that look well.

Don't draw attention to yourself. Don't get involved.

Her mama and gramma had often talked of a freer east in times past, where you could trust folk while travelling from place to place and always find a friendly fire to eat and warm yourself by. But nowadays folk only talked of the Governance in hushed whispers, and about how restrictions of supply runs from neighbouring settlements were forcing folk to struggle unnecessarily. Healers travelled less. Folk had less to trade. Abundance became scarcity. A bad season of crop could even wipe out an entire settlement.

The lack of healers definitely wiped out Mama, and I still don't believe Gramma just 'wandered off' either.

No sooner had her stomach started to growl did Niall insist they set up camp for the evening. The suns were still sinking but there'd be some daylight left yet. Eva gave him a disapproving look but didn't argue, moving into the trees to fetch firewood.

"We should be safe enough here," Niall said.

Neri nodded. Given the undergrowth they'd hacked their way through for a long while before the forest opened out again, not many folk would choose to venture this far.

Eva returned and Neri helped set the fire, but conversation was non-existent as the three of them settled down beside it.

"We'll move at first light," Eva insisted. "Neri, you sleep first. Then Niall. Then I will."

Neri pulled her blanket out of her pack obediently and settled down on it. The leaves underneath the nearest tree provided some extra cushioning, so she lay on one half of fabric and folded the other half over her. With Dog flopped beside her, she wouldn't worry too much about getting cold.

Sleep played keep-away for a long while, but she was too far from the fire to read Emelyn's book by its light, and too settled to get up and have Eva make a fuss about her wasting her sleeping time. She toyed with idle imaginings instead, of the others back at the sanctuary no doubt in their own beds, the sanctuary dwelling becoming a morphing entity of endless rooms and walls scorched with chalk.

"Neri?"

The gentle voice startled her awake. She sat up, tense until she noticed Niall crouched beside her.

"Eva's going to scout so we'll need you to mind the fire," he said.

She nodded and groaned to her feet, bundling up her blanket and grabbing her pack. Sitting closer to the fire, she tried not to keep looking over as Niall settled on his blanket a suspiciously close distance from her.

Determined not to show she cared by mentioning it, she pulled out Emelyn's book instead.

After the first chapter, she smiled. The tale of a young girl exploring forests of tall trees with mammoth trunks that almost reached the two suns in the sky sounded a lot like Emelyn.

The book detailed such a vivid account of magical lands, encountering unicorns, dragons and fae who lived in the trees, or by the majestic silver waterfalls of *Morlan*.

When Neri read about the digging up of the rails that ran the length of the realm and led through the forest between east and west, sadness swamped her. The little wooden cart wouldn't be able to carry folk back and forth any longer. The thought of the cart growing mould and moss in some woodland clearing tugged tears from her eyes.

Every so often she'd rouse herself from fantasy and check on Niall, amused to find a tiny smirk on his face as he slept. Then she returned to the pages of Emelyn's world and lost herself once more.

She finished and pushed the book deep in her pack as

the first signs of sunslight began to tinge the sky over the trees. Eva hadn't returned from scouting and Neri glanced Niall's way to see sleepy dark eyes blinking back at her.

"Did you know you smile in your sleep?" she asked.

He pulled a face and stretched his arms above his head.

"Did you know watching folk sleep is creepy?"

"It's not like I snuck into your room or anything. You just happened to be right there, and I happened to notice."

With her cheeks burning, she reached into her pack and hauled out a couple of apples, holding one out to Niall.

He produced a small blade and took the apple from her. She watched as he carved a slice off and put the remainder of the apple and the blade down. He held the slice out to her, his eyes dark and shining.

Her fingers brushed his as she took it.

Their eyes met.

With unerringly appropriate timing, the sound of boots crunching closer startled both of them apart. Niall handed Neri the apple slice with a huff, inhaling his in one huge bite. Still uneasy at his sudden closeness, Neri managed an awkward grimace as Eva approached.

"We can eat walking," Eva said.

She didn't wait for them to agree before stamping out the last dregs of warmth from the dying fire. Niall gave Neri a weary look, then smiled as Eva set off into the trees. She couldn't help it; she smiled back.

They walked in silence, keeping a brisk pace. Nobody talked as they passed fields and woods, dipping around silver pools of water that beckoned. Dog stopped to drink every now and then but Neri only slowed her pace for him, not daring to stop completely with the others striding so intently. By the time they skirted the edge of a large settlement, with the dwellings rising higher than Neri had ever seen and the sound of chatter and carriages clattering filling the air, the suns were beginning to fade for the night.

Neri fell into step with Niall. "Is it far, or will we need to camp again?"

"We're almost there," he said. "We'll reach it before nightfall, scope out the area and make sure we know what we're up against first."

Neri nodded, her mind curling around what was yet to come. She had no promise of her own safety, and she didn't know Niall or Eva well either.

They might even be here to trade me for Emelyn. She shivered and tried not to let her pace slow too obviously. *I've asked so little, too distracted, and even if they aren't planning to use me, what hope do we have of achieving this?*

"Did you know the Governance stronghold is on the edge of the cursed forest itself?" Niall asked.

Neri glanced at him warily. "No, how could I have?"

"No need to be prickly, I'm not digging for information." He rolled his eyes, edging closer until they walked side by side. "I'm surprised you haven't demanded more information of us yet to be honest."

So am I.

She aimed for an indifferent shrug of one shoulder and almost elbowed him in the ribs.

"You were so reluctant to tell me anything before. I figured you were either bringing me as a trade or you have no idea what's going on and are chancing it."

She risked a glance sideways, amused to see Niall scowl instantly.

"We wouldn't trade folk," he insisted. "Not for anything or anyone." She flinched as he stopped dead and faced her. "I wouldn't trade you."

Unnerved by the closeness and the determined stare he fixed on her, Neri tried to take a step back but her feet didn't listen. She gazed up at him, half a head taller than her with his chin tilted down. Her heart pounded, thoughts colliding in her head.

A glint flashed between them, a swathe of dazzling light that broke the daze between them. Neri stepped back and lifted a hand to shade her eyes. When her vision settled, she found Niall smirking at her.

"Saved by random catches of sunlight," he said.

"Saved from what, from you?"

She kept her tone light and he shrugged, glancing ahead. Eva had stopped to wait for them and Neri started walking toward her before Niall could answer. He reached her side moments later, striding along.

"As it goes, we're not in such a bad way rescue-wise." He left the information dangling.

She counted to three, then conceded. "And? Or is this more hints you can't tell me?"

"We have a signal we use. If Emelyn's in any state to do it, we'll know which room she's in."

"That's something then. What about once we're inside their dwelling, assuming we get that far?"

"Leave that to us for now." He hesitated. "Don't worry.

I won't let anything happen to you."

Neri snorted. "If you say so. You're lucky my boots are well-worn or you'll be carrying me in."

"I'd be delighted to. I thought I might have to on our journey to the sanctuary. You looked about to drop."

"I thought it was you dragging me by my hair last time you mentioned it."

He shrugged, his easy grin never faltering as he stepped over a huge log in their path, holding out a hand to help her. She ignored it and clambered over, but couldn't do anything about the heat covering her face.

"Ah, there."

Niall pointed as they cleared the trees. Neri gazed out over the land laid out before them, a grassy hill dropping down in front of them until it hit another swathe of woodland that stretched to the horizon. A plume of smoke curled up from somewhere inside the woods, and if she focused her attention she could hear the odd echo of a quiet wailing sound, like wind through a gap or perhaps a bird calling faintly.

"That's the cursed forest," Niall announced. "And that dwelling down there? That's the Governance stronghold."

Foreboding trickled over her skin like icicles as she stared down at the enemy. The Governance dwelling was built with stone, near impenetrable, surrounded by a towering fence of spiked wood and finely woven blade-metal. Neri had never seen anything like it, nor heard descriptions before in all of the fanciful fables she'd heard in childhood. The whole place glowed bright in the evening gloom and she wondered how many candles it would take to light every room.

She wrapped her arms around her middle and focused on controlling the sudden swell of dizziness bubbling up from the pit of her gut as she faced the reality now in front of her.

"We can't hang around," Niall muttered. "Are we sure we don't want to go in now under the cover of darkness?"

Eva flicked a glare at him. "We wait until first light tomorrow, that was the plan. We need to take cover nearby and rest overnight."

Niall glanced at the shadows gathered around them.

"Let's get on with it then."

He strode off in the opposite direction toward a shadowed crop of trees, looking back only once to check they were both following. Neri kept right behind him, focused on not tripping over the wild tufts of grass underfoot, and eventually they reached a suitable thickness of trees to shelter in.

Neri took out her blankets and settled down with her back against a tree. No fire was lit this time as they were so close to the enemy.

"I'll take the first watch," she offered.

She saw the surprise on Eva's face, the twilight not having settled around them fully yet. She didn't dare look at Niall. Eva thought for a moment before nodding.

"You'll need to rest for tomorrow," she agreed. "You and I will be going in to find Emelyn, but you need to be the one to focus on getting Emelyn out if she's unwell or unconscious while I clear a path out. Wake us in a little while."

Neri leaned her back against the tree as Eva and Niall settled down to sleep, her mind racing. Whatever they came up against, the Governance wouldn't let them stroll in and out, she was sure of that. Tuning into the sound of Niall's breathing, she noted the slower, deeper resonance which signalled he was asleep.

The night wore on, but Neri didn't wake either of the others. She pressed her lids shut tight together and opened them again several times to dispel the wave of intense sleepiness that threatened to overwhelm her. They would need all their strength to get Emelyn out again tomorrow and away safe. She forced her brain not to dwell on what would come soon, hoping that avoiding the thought would keep her resolve strong.

Her eyelids fluttered once more, tiredness winning. Only a sudden flickering glow of light brought wary attention back. Without opening her eyes, she tried to tune into her surroundings as the light continued to waver.

A sudden brisk shiver of cold wind blew through the clearing, bringing tantalising scents of frosty promises and ripe autumn fruit.

Neri opened her eyes to a whirl of dead brown leaves nearby, a gust of wind bringing them into the clearing as everyone else around her slept on.

The sky above was an inky hue of twilight, not marred by clouds as it had been a moment before, with shining stars twinkling brighter and with bolder displays of colour than she'd ever seen.

Pulling herself up to her feet, Neri pressed her forefinger to her lips to show Dog he should remain still.

She took a few tentative steps in the direction of the swirling foliage and glanced back at Niall. If she somehow disappeared into a mini whirlwind, would he think she'd deserted them? Facing the mirage of autumn in front of her, the chill now blasting her front while the heat she was used to pressed against her back, she noticed the ball that was creating the flickering light.

The bright golden orb floated in the air some paces away, yellow and orange flickers curling and uncurling.

Neri lifted a hand and stepped through the wind only to find the ball was moving away from her, always a frustrating inch away from her reach. She narrowed her eyes, almost able to see licks of flame in the light. As the orb fully unfurled, she saw a long, slender body with lashing tail and teardrop-shaped head that formed a bird.

It can't be. She inched forward, eyes wide. *This has to be some kind of illusion, or I'm dreaming.*

Her childhood filled her head, her gramma telling her tales and reciting poems of birds with feathers of flame, her mama laughing and saying such a thing hadn't been seen for an age or more, as though the general idea was as real as the suns and just outdated. Neri had drawn many a childish picture of a fiery bird, similar to the one she looked at now.

It must be my imagination. I've gone mad.

The vision solidified, the lines becoming sharper as the bird turned its elegant head to look at her. To beckon her closer.

Increasing her pace, Neri caught her toe on an upturned root. She stumbled and glanced down at her feet in time to steady herself. As her eyes darted back up, she realised that the light, now dull and hardly dawning, came from the horizon only. The illusion with its tantalising scents on the wind and autumnal background, for an illusion is all it could have been, had disappeared.

Neri glanced back, still able to see their camp through the trees. If Niall woke and found her gone he'd assume the worst. After one final check of the horizon to make sure no other visions appeared, she tiptoed back to the others. It took all her muscle power to ease herself down to the ground again without making any noise, but she managed it just in time for Eva's eyes to snap open.

"You should have stuck to the plan and slept," Eva said, eying the dawn. "Wake Niall and I'll get the food out."

"Niall's awake." He lifted his head. "We should be quick and make the most of the early hour for cover."

Neri took the hastily made wrap of bread and meat that Eva handed to her. They ate as they walked through the early morning gloom toward the Governance stronghold, but Neri barely tasted the food, her mind fixed on what might happen. She had the blade Ma Kath had given her still deep in her pack, but she couldn't exactly stroll around waving it without attracting suspicion. She couldn't see any sign of Eva carrying a weapon either.

"How did we know where Emelyn is exactly?" she asked, guessing the question would be rebuffed with some kind of vague dismissal.

Eva glanced back. "We've had folk watching the place on and off, and news travels fast."

She stopped on the crest of the hill overlooking the

153

building and turned to face Niall, arms folded.

"Well?" she asked, her tone demanding. "What plan do you have for a diversion?"

Neri looked from Eva to Niall, alarmed.

He hasn't told her what the diversion is? Why not?

Niall's secretive smile highlighted every inch of the man she was growing inconveniently fond of, and she wondered exactly what he was up to.

"Remember there are meant to be some low-lying barns at the back of the main foundation," he said, diverting the subject. "You should be able to use them to get to the upper levels. Emelyn is in one of those rooms and you'll have to get her out first. I'll draw them to the front."

Eva folded her arms. "And how exactly are you going to do that?"

"With some *soul-shade* magic." Niall smirked in Neri's direction. "Trust me, you'll know when I've done my stuff. After that, I'd say you have a short time to scale the lower levels, find Em's window and get her out. It should be the third one along according to Matty."

Neri saw Eva's scowl but Niall took no notice of it. He stepped back and caught her eye instead. His smile disappeared as he hesitated for a long moment.

"Can I take Dog with me?" he asked.

She frowned, astonished. "Why?"

"It'd help me a lot. I promise he'll be safe the whole time."

Neri bit her lip and looked down at Dog. He sat panting right beside her, his face turned up as if waiting for her decision.

"Okay." She pointed to Niall, her eyes fixed on Dog's cheerful face. "Go with Niall and I'll find you after."

Dog licked her hand, stood with a hufty groan and padded toward Niall's side. Niall caught her eye, the glimmer of a smile on his lips.

"For Hamlin."

Then he was off, jogging down the hill like a shadow. Eva muttered something under her breath but Neri didn't catch it.

"Come on," Eva grumbled. "While he's off playing warrior, we need to get inside."

As she set off down the hill, Neri took a deep breath, then another, and finally she followed.

Counting each footstep helped keep the pounding adrenalin at bay. At the bottom of the hill, they came to the monstrous fence of spiked wood and woven blade-metal surrounding the compound.

"The metal is climbable," Eva whispered. "But the wood shards at the top could provide a problem. We need to be inside before Niall does his thing, whatever that is."

Neri could see the barns Niall had mentioned nearby on the other side. They at least looked easy enough to scale. She couldn't see any sign of guards and guessed this was the reason Eva had been so insistent on waiting until morning.

"No guards?" She had to be sure.

Eva grimaced. "Changeover of guard detail happens first thing, but they tend to get a bit slack on their timing when the powers that be are tucked in their beds."

Neri resisted the temptation to say that Eva had clearly

done her homework on the enemy. She eyed the wood spikes on top of the fence instead, dropping to one knee in the dewy grass and taking two candles out of her pack. Eva didn't move to stop her as she peeled off her boots, threw them over the fence, then started to climb.

Her toes aided her in clambering up, and she balanced at the top for a moment with the candles in one hand. She took one candle and pressed it down lengthways. The candle, fat and round, covered the wire and came to rest on the edge of the fence. She did the same with the second candle and braced one hand on top of each.

Then she pushed with her feet, the beginning kick of fear and adrenalin scoring through her system. She vaulted over the fence, her movements jagged and ungraceful, and dropped to land on the grass below.

Eva copied her, Neri's heart pounding all the while as she waited, looking left and right for signs of any guards approaching.

"Leave the candles there," Neri whispered. "We can use them to get back over."

Eva nodded and slid down the fence with a loud clattering noise. Neri winced but it didn't seem like any guards had heard so she yanked on her boots over damp feet.

They crept side-by-side toward the barns until Neri found a wooden box on the far side, a perfect step up. With Eva's help from beneath, she hauled herself up onto the barn roof. The air sounded far too silent, the inside of the stronghold far too still. Without waiting for Eva, she crept across the tiled roof toward the nearest window.

A cacophonous bang deafened the air, shaking the roof beneath their feet. Neri almost crashed to her knees but managed to hold her balance in time.

"What the-" she realised halfway through speaking what the bang must have been.

Niall's blown something up. She couldn't bite back the smile that spread across her face.

"What is he thinking?" Eva muttered.

She spun around, looking back and forth, then faced Neri with anger twisting her face.

"Keep going, look for Emelyn. Get yourself inside at all costs and I can find you later."

Neri opened her mouth to protest but Eva was off like lightning across the roof. She vaulted with no apparent effort onto the thin ledge that ran beneath the windows and disappeared around the corner of the stronghold.

Left alone, Neri pushed aside the pounding in her chest and assessed the building. The wooden window frames had peeling white paint but the drapes pulled across gave her little illumination into the contents of the rooms beyond.

Niall had said Emelyn's room was the third window along. All she had to do was shuffle forward and not get it wrong.

She inched along the ledge until she reached what she hoped was the right window, heart pounding and eyes darting for any sign of someone approaching below. The shutters were already open so she tapped the frame gently.

No answer.

With every effort at keeping her balance, Neri peeked inside. Keeping the drape around her for cover and holding in a sneeze at the abundance of dust lingering in the folds, she dropped into the dark room.

A shuffling noise in the far corner caught her attention. She tensed, prepared for a fight as a forlorn voice reached her.

"Who are you?"

CHAPTER TEN

The weak voice broke through the otherwise silent gloom and Neri's hope surged.

Emelyn.

She dipped her head around the fabric of the drapes so she was visible.

"It's Neri from the sanctuary. We're getting you out of here. Can you whisper where you are? Are you tied down?"

Silence.

Neri opened her mouth to call again but almost swallowed her tongue as someone heaved her back. She hit the window ledge while still scanning the room.

Wild green eyes lit by the rising light outside glared back at her, sparked with ire and feral vengeance. While the fury in those eyes faded almost instantly, the spark remained.

"It *is* you." Emelyn frowned. "What are you doing here?"

Neri gaped at her. Although she expected some kind of emotional response, this hard-headed tough girl voice and the general shoving wasn't what she associated with Emelyn at all.

"I've come to rescue you. We need to go now while there are still no guards down there."

Trepidation shadowed Emelyn's face. Neri also noticed the dark streak on Emelyn's cheek that looked like a deep cut.

"If there weren't any guards patrolling, it will have been for a reason," Emelyn replied. "We've had folk watching this place for over a winterspan now, bit by bit, and there are always guards there. It means they were expecting you."

Neri peeked out through the drapes. Down below, she could detect shadowed figures moving back and forth. The anxiety bubbled in her gut at the thought of being trapped, and she looked at Emelyn, who smiled back with sad resignation.

"If we go out there now, they'll catch us," Emelyn sighed. "Niall said they were after you when you arrived, and you've walked right into what appears to be a trap."

Unwilling to dwell on that, Neri assessed the room instead. It was entirely empty, no blankets or furniture. She could just make out the odd groove on the floor where a table had once set its roots, no doubt a long time ago.

"Have they hurt you badly?" she asked.

Emelyn shrugged one shoulder. "I take my punishments with good will. I'm learning things while I'm here, or trying to. If one of us gets out it will really help the cause. The guards don't come very often so we have time, for the moment at least."

Neri couldn't succumb so easily to the idea of being trapped and paced the room.

"I'll think of something," she said. "I read your book by the way, about the westlands? You've got an amazing gift with words."

Morning was rising with vengeance outside and Eva might have been caught, or Niall. Neri doubted Eva would come back for them if the mission had been compromised.

"I like words," Emelyn said with a smile. "They come alive for me. There is another route into the west but it's been hidden. That's what the Governance is searching for, the way to move between the two sides of the realm. We need to find it before they do, keep it safe."

Neri considered this, aware that Emelyn was watching her process, then blinked.

"I'm sorry, just so I'm definitely clear, you're saying that the folk, the real live folk holding you captive and hurting you, are doing it because they want to find a way through the forest to the west?"

Emelyn smiled wider and nodded, as if she were willing Neri to have a marvellous moment of realisation and grasp some kind of transcendental truth.

Neri shook her head. "Sorry, but you're saying the Governance believe you, as in the couple of you that are at the sanctuary, are a threat to them finding this way through the forest? There's only six of you."

"Seven, if you count Moonshine," Emelyn piped up. "Eight if we count you."

Heavy footsteps echoed outside the door before Neri could insist Emelyn not count her, chasing away any more madness that might have been brewing on Emelyn's tongue.

Unsure of what she intended to do if anyone came into the room, Neri stepped beside the door and waited. The footsteps passed and faded away. She let out a sigh and moved across the room. To avoid the rumbling sense of being trapped that threatened to make her frantic, Neri focused on placating Emelyn instead.

"So, do all of you believe this stuff? That there's a way through to the west? Is this the whole ancient sorcery thing? Because I'm sure if there was anything in the west, the Governance could muster up all their forces and simply cut their way through, destroy the animals that try to eat them, dodge any mystical bogs that try to trap them."

They had to find a way out of here, and if Emelyn really was being serious then perhaps playing along might keep her more on side to get her out and away than calling her crazy would.

Emelyn grinned. "You mean does Niall believe? Niall is from the west, he was born there. Matty and Finn are descended from folk who were. Ma was only a child when she crossed over and barely remembers much of it now. She's lived longer than most though."

Neri returned to peering out of the window, knowing they were wasting time on myth when they should be planning some kind of escape.

"So, how exactly did you get kidnapped in the first place?"

"I do sometimes go scouting, but not often." Emelyn paused, her expression twisting into ruefulness. "I was too busy thinking about where I'd put one of my books and they saw me before I could run. I have a book of fables, and I wanted to give it to you after we had that confusion over the *Lamentation* wording."

Neri skipped over the guilt that their argument had been part of the reason Emelyn was now here in pain. She sank instead onto the unsettling truth. Emelyn knew not only the words to the poem Gramma had written, but the title too. That didn't prove anything toward the existence of magic ways through woods, but it did suggest that her family had been tangled up in whatever dangers the folk at the sanctuary were involved with.

"The patrol found me before I could defend myself," Emelyn continued. "I didn't think they'd know who I was but turns out they do. I was too busy thinking about the book, then I saw a shimmer. It was a beautiful one too, just a quick glimpse, but it must be winter somewhere in Kirelonia."

She drifted for a moment into her own thoughts, but Neri had to keep on top of getting them out before she entertained ideas of sorcery and other parts of the realm. She was having enough trouble handling everything in this part of it.

"What's a shimmer?" she asked.

Emelyn sighed. "Have you ever seen a flash of something that couldn't be there? Like a painting or projection that momentarily covers what is actually in front of you? You think you're imagining it, but it's so real, the scents and the feelings. Well, they're legitimate. That's a shimmer, a brief moment in time where the veil between different parts of Kirelonia disappears. That's how most folk from the west end up trapped here in the east, by accident. They're rare and that was the first one I've ever seen."

Neri let her chin drop toward her chest, exhausted. None of this was helping them find a way to escape.

"Okay, well, yeah. Let's just put that aside then for the moment. We need to get out of here first as I doubt one of your shimmers is going to pop up and save us. We can't get out through the window without some kind of protection. How often do the guards come in here?"

Emelyn shrugged and winced. She rolled up the sleeve of her t-shirt and Neri gaped to see burn marks on Emelyn's pale arm.

"They haven't come in since yesterday when they left bread and a jug of water for me. The door is always locked and when they do come in, it's always one man with some kind of weapon, like a blade or a club."

Neri focused on Emelyn with critical eyes. The girl was thinner now she looked properly.

No wonder she's pretending magic escapes into the west are real. She's been tortured and starved into delirium.

"What if you need to relieve yourself?" she asked.

Emelyn used the wall to inch herself up to her feet.

"I knock on the door until someone passes. Then that person will get a second guard from somewhere and they monitor me."

Neri grimaced. She rubbed the edges of her mouth with her fingertips and thought.

"I think I'll be able to floor two men if you can get them to take you out, but if they're expecting an ambush or something, they'll be prepared. We can give it a go?"

Emelyn smiled at Neri's suggestion, sagging against the wall.

"We can. Knock on the door for me. I need to pull my mind together."

Neri took a deep breath and stood by the door. She tapped once. On hearing no sound outside, she tapped again a little louder. The third time, she raised her fist but jumped when Emelyn's hands rained down on the door.

"They'll never hear you like that," she insisted.

As they waited, Emelyn's hazy eyes became clear and sharp for a moment.

"If they ask you your name, don't give it to them. They probably know who you are already but we won't help them anymore than we have to."

Footsteps sounded and Neri pressed herself against the wall next to the door hinges. When it swung open to hide her, Emelyn was a perfect picture of female misery and fear.

"I need to go again."

Neri bristled when she heard the guard outside sigh with impatience.

"We're not to let you out today. Maybe tomorrow."

In the wake of his rough, noncommittal grunt, Emelyn flew forward, her fingers bent into claws. With a squeal, she was knocked back and staggered until she hit the window frame. Neri heard the first heavy footstep. By the dull clunk of wood on wood as he took the second step, she estimated he had a wooden club of sorts that had knocked against the door.

The man appeared in her vision, just clearing the door. Emelyn's eyes were clear once more, this time with experienced fear. She shrank against the window as if she might be better off falling out of it than facing him and closed her eyes.

Neri stepped forward, her fingers curling back, her palm flexed. Fury drove her foot as she swung forward, hooking around the man's knee and yanking. He was heavy set, tall and built with muscle. He stumbled but managed to right himself, turning on her.

Neri remembered the blade Ma Kath had packed for her at the worst possible moment, still in her pack and unreachable. She aimed a punch instead. The man caught her wrist in a huge fist, but her foot already connected with his kneecap. He went down onto his good knee with a pained grunt, his eyes watering.

He still had her wrist held tight, but he'd dropped the club. She kicked out once more. Her foot connected with the club and it rolled across the wooden floor toward Emelyn. Neri winced with a yelp as the guard crushed her wrist.

Emelyn eyed the club and picked it up, staring at it. The guard stood, hauling Neri around to face Emelyn, who held the club out as if she intended to hit him. The guard laughed, a low, blood-chilling cackle that boomed and bounced around the tiny room. Emelyn took a few steps closer, her arms trembling as she dropped the club.

Neri strained against the man's strength, but it was

hopeless. Her nails clawed at his hand. She paused with her teeth almost set to bite his finger as Emelyn's hand arced. Neri saw the self-defence move her mama had taught her clear on Emelyn's fingers, fingers curled, palm stiff and hand flexed back at the wrist. The heel of her tiny, pale hand connected with the man's nose and Neri heard a crunch.

He yowled, blood emerging from his nostrils. Emelyn rounded again, this time connecting with the side of his head. He barrelled into her, sending her flying into the chair. As he picked up the chair in the absence of the club, holding it aloft with no effort at all, Neri shunted into his side. Together they stumbled toward the window.

Emelyn might have shouted, Neri couldn't be sure, but she managed to right herself as the guard let go of the chair to catch the window-frame. She turned in time to see Emelyn with the bat held aloft.

A loud crack echoed.

The man yowled as the edge of the wood smashed his fingers and he let go of the window frame. Teetering against the edge of it, he realised his mistake too late. Moments of silence hung as he disappeared, his body tumbling downward and his legs flailing out of sight.

A huge crash rose up.

"I think he may have broken our way out," Neri said.

Her blood was still racing with the adrenalin but she found the bravery to approach the window. The man lay below inside the barn, the roof tiles cracked and broken where he'd blasted through them. Given the wide, vacant eyes and the angle of his neck, he wouldn't be touching

Emelyn ever again.

"Yep, definitely broken our way out." The hysteria bubbled up. "We need to leave now. They'll have heard that. He's... yeah."

She decided in that moment that she wouldn't tell Emelyn about the man's fate. She wouldn't lie if asked, but if Emelyn chose to believe he walked away from her attacking him, then she would let the girl lean on that.

Neri shuddered as she flexed her aching hand. Emelyn held the bat tight now as she indicated to the open doorway.

"He won't touch me again." Emelyn took a deep breath. "I'm not rotten, I promise. But he... did things, and I'm not sorry."

Neri couldn't process that, not when they were still in danger and she felt like she was going to be sick. Her skin flushed hot and her mind raced too fast to be sensible, but the only truth before her was that they needed to get out and the only way now was through the stronghold.

She nodded. "Right. We go on."

"I know they don't have many leads," Emelyn added. "I've picked things up. I heard there's a library downstairs that I'd die for, but I think for now we need to get what I know back to the sanctuary. Lead the way."

The hazy gaze in her eyes had disappeared. Now Emelyn looked sharp and sane, waiting patiently for Neri to take control. Neri steeled herself and pushed her questions aside for later.

She eased the club out of Emelyn's unresisting fingers and tiptoed out into the empty hallway. Despite wearing black boots, Emelyn walked as light as a fairy. The choice of comparison after so much talk of Emelyn's magical forests and lands jarred in Neri's mind.

Practicalities only. She grimaced and wiped a hand over her sweaty face. *Madness later.*

Planks of worn wood stretched underfoot and the stone walls had been painted a stark white that closed in around her. Wooden doors were stained black and the contrast made Neri feel like she was trapped in a nature-less box.

She whispered to Emelyn to keep watch as they reached a door at the end of the hallway. She bent low, glancing through the gap underneath.

No moving shadows and no sound of footsteps.

She stood up and pushed open the door.

Moving with silent ease, she glanced inside. She caught sight of the window first then her gaze moved onto something else.

Someone else.

She froze, her heart skittering a frenzied rhythm.

In the far corner of the room sat a man, comfortable in a plush chair upholstered with rich red fabric. His silver hair was braided back from his face and his long grey beard was swept over one shoulder out of the way.

The mere sight of him sent a shock of warning spiking through Neri's chest, but memories surfaced and anger curled fierce and strong as he smiled.

"There you are. Good. I've been waiting a long time for you."

CHAPTER ELEVEN

Neri stared at the man, horror chilling her right to the bone.

The flashing image of a familiar lane at night-time flickered in her mind, the sound of blades slicing echoing in her ears. She couldn't remember what Hamlin had called the man that night, but the mere sight of him now made her fury boil. The recollection of what had been taken from her at his instruction, by his organisation, cleared her mind.

"I must admit, I didn't expect you to get past my guards," he said. "They let you in but to get yourself out and so quickly shows great initiative. Still, no matter. You have found your way to me all the same."

Neri turned to Emelyn and caught the horror on the girl's face. Turning fully so the man couldn't see her face, Neri mouthed an instruction.

"Run!"

Emelyn took a deep breath, shook her head and stepped forward instead. She grasped Neri's hand, holding on tight, and used the connection to shuffle Neri forward into the room.

"Sensible." The man smiled wider. "Running won't get

you far, not with the power we have. Do you know you have someone unexpected in your midst that told me to await your arrival? We had all the guards indoors planning for your entrance and your friends have the discourtesy to explode our front gates, Ginnera."

Neri couldn't stop her reaction, her eyes widening that he knew her name. It wasn't a far cry to work out her full name, it wasn't that uncommon in the eastlands, but nobody had called her Ginnera in a long while.

She took in the silver hair and the white bush of his beard, as well at the open-necked black shirt that revealed the Governance emblem tattooed under his throat. He leaned sideways and reappeared with a box of flimsy thin wood, nothing remarkable to the eye except for the piece of parchment stuck to the side, the image on it a crude splash of colour.

Neri stared at it, her heart pounding ever faster.

"I am somewhat of a collector of information," he said, tapping the top of the box. "In case you're wondering how I'm aware of you."

He paused to let that sink in, but she couldn't tear her eyes away from the childish artwork on the parchment. Her childish artwork. It was meant to be a field with a horse. Large purple mountains climbed in the background, with just the hint of a palace coloured in pale yellow that was meant to be white on the left side of the page. Her gramma had ground herbs and petals to make powder for paints, so many that Neri hadn't ever managed to use them all. She wouldn't have bothered to save the box, presumably still full of other scribblings, after her gramma and mamma died, but now he had his disgusting, blood-tainted fingers on top of it, she couldn't bear the thought of him being anywhere near them.

When he cleared his throat, she forced her head to lift, to meet his unwavering gaze.

"Now the problem is that you're not one of sanctuary folk, not that we can prove. Nor are you one of us. You don't seem to have information that's of any value, save for the location of the sanctuary, which we will expect you to reveal."

Neri waited, her hand still clenched tight in Emelyn's. This man liked the sound of his own voice and she realised she still had the bat in hand. She kept quiet.

"However, you do know where we are," he continued. "You're obviously sharp to get this close to me without detection, although that was no doubt what your friend's little fireworks were for. Luckily, it was enough to let us know something was going on."

When he paused, Neri pushed her anger deep down. She couldn't risk asking if Niall was okay or if they had caught him. If she did then the man would know she cared and use it against her. She squeezed Emelyn's hand tighter and took a deep breath.

"You know my name, which is unusual. Perhaps you'd at least do us the courtesy of telling yours."

The man chuckled and put his cup down. The almost imperceptible narrowing of his eyes was hard to see, but Neri caught it. He was sizing her up.

"I am Amis. I do the bidding of the Governance, as do we all in one way or another. I am the eyes and ears, although I have many folk as you've probably seen that can be my hands."

You're also a murderer, even if the fatal swipe wasn't done by your own hand.

"I believe you've been looking for me, or watching me at least," she tried. "Creepy, but I still don't know why. You also took my friend here, no doubt because of the cloak she was wearing. Where is the cloak?"

Amis tilted his head to one side. "You don't know why we've been looking for you? How disappointing, but no matter. The cloak can be returned to you provided you're able to see reason."

"And what reason would that be?" She could barely unclench her jaw to spit the words out.

"Your gramma stole something from us long ago, a piece of information. We hunted her for a long time without knowing who she truly was. Then she decided death was a safer choice than giving us what we needed."

Neri's insides swarmed with fire and fury. He made it sound like an accident but now she knew he was the reason her gramma was dead. She clenched her fingers tighter around the bat.

"We need that information now," he added. "I imagine she must have passed it to someone. You perhaps?"

Neri shook her head. "Not that I know of, unless you're interested in how to distil *nejaro* root and make a really disgusting broth. If it's your information she stole, why don't you know it yourself? Or have copies?"

Far from being irritated, Amis smiled wider.

"It is very old information, historical. Still, we will find it one way or another. Your gramma's accident was unfortunate, and your mama's illness- well, we could provide for you now that you have nothing left."

Neri sucked in a sharp breath, holding the wrath steady and controlled. Brewing like the sting of her gramma's *nejaro* root tea.

She cast a quick glance over her shoulder to check if the hall was still clear. If she could give Emelyn a shot at running, it would be worth it.

"They won't come unless I call them." Amis drew her attention back to him. "The guards, I mean. Emelyn is there anything you wish to share with me, perhaps for your friend's sake? I will be keeping you on in your current capacity once she has made her choice."

Emelyn's ragged fingernails sliced into Neri's knuckles. Turning her head, Neri recognised untold horrors in Emelyn's eyes. Whatever Amis had done to her, Emelyn looked like she'd carry the memories for the rest of her life.

Neri struggled to suppress her anger, the monster of fury that curled deep inside her snarling. When Amis addressed her once more, she gripped Emelyn's hand tighter.

"Ginnera, there is always an option of working with us, but I warn you, working against us is not a choice you want to make. Perhaps you need some other motivation. You seem to have an air of the savour about you."

Neri stood firm as he rose to his feet. Emelyn stumbled back, pulling Neri with her as Amis approached. Given the way he was focused on Emelyn now, this wasn't going to be any kind of positive form of motivation.

"What would I have to do exactly? Working with you?"

He stilled but didn't lift his gaze from Emelyn's shaking form, her gaze fixed on her feet, her mouth roving over silent, frantic words.

"You would learn great secrets from us," Amis said. "You may even earn enough trust to go out to research their validity. It would be exciting work, something you can turn many of your assets to if you so choose."

"What do you mean by that, my assets? How do you know I even have any?"

He laughed. "Only that I'm sure you have many special gifts."

Neri nodded, keeping her movements slow.

"So, you're saying if I do this stuff for the Governance, then you'll let me go free?"

She had to clarify. Amis smiled with evident pleasure at her speed of understanding, even as he stood within reaching distance of Emelyn who seemed beyond hearing now, her eyes shut tight.

"As I said, it is good work, a steady job. You will find serving as part of the Governance gives you a very rewarding life. It's servitude of a sort, but we're really like one big family here."

"Okay." Neri took a step forward. "One thing you might have overlooked though."

She had to make sure he understood. He turned his head, the slightest dip furrowing his brow.

Looking deep into his eyes, she smiled wide.

"Servitude is overrated."

She lifted her arms in one strong swing that dashed the bat sideways through the air.

The wood thudded against his head, the force knocking him sideways. Neri rounded the bat again, her monster rising, a fiery dragon chasing the tide of adrenalin through her system, edging her on. The skin on his temple severed. The third time she lifted the bat, she saw the blood spatter on it through tunnel vision ringed with darkness.

"Neri, stop."

Emelyn's soft voice pierced through the fury. Neri stood, the bat raised above her head with both hands, her chest heaving.

"Leave it now," Emelyn insisted, barely able to form the words. "He's not worth getting caught for."

Neri sagged, the bat dropping to the floor with a loud clunk. She barely noticed Emelyn nipping beside her to pick it up. The adrenalin was curving, and Neri knew they didn't have much time.

"We need to get out now," she rasped.

The muttered words felt thick in her mouth, her tongue dry and swollen. A sure sign that the panic would grip her any moment.

I've been so careful, for so long, and now this...

Emelyn took her arm and shakily guided her to the nearest open window.

"Okay, we're going to jump down onto the barns from here. With any luck we can climb the fences before they see us."

Neri nodded. The adrenalin was draining. When it disappeared, the enormity of what she had done would crash down on her and she would lose control. Before the panic could take hold, she grabbed the box of her childhood drawings from the desk and shoved them into her pack.

He can't have them.

She looked back at his body still inert on the floor and fought the bubbling rise of sickness in her throat.

"If we can just get to the trees, then we should be alright," Emelyn insisted. "Folk might still be up there, our folk."

Neri shook her head, hoping to clear the haze of dizziness, and focused on keeping her balance as Emelyn manhandled her through the window frame. Her feet hit the ledge that ran underneath the window and she made sure Emelyn was out behind her before shuffling along the roof. The guards were pacing back and forth beside the fence, but even through her panic Neri could make out her candles still on top.

"How do we get past them?" she whispered, her breathing laboured.

Emelyn grimaced. "Jump down and wait for them to leave. I'll do the rest."

"Are you mad?"

"Probably. Trust me."

Neri had no other choice. She slid off the edge of the roof and onto the grass, keeping to the shadows of the barn. The panic would stay away for as long as she remained on the move but hovering here gave it the perfect chance to swarm her.

A loud shout echoed from somewhere inside the

stronghold, followed closely by more. The guards at the fence hesitated, then broke into a run toward the commotion. Neri shrank further into the shadows but they were gone without seeing her. Emelyn gave her a gentle shove and she broke into a jog, her entire focus fixed on the fence with her candles. Emelyn dashed past her and Neri followed, grateful that the adrenalin was pounding once again. It gave her razor-edged focus and she knew she could make it.

The fence rattled as Emelyn clambered up and over, dropping to the ground on the other side. Neri struggled up, her limbs exhausted from the shock and close to failing her. She slithered down the other side, landing badly on her ankle. She tested it, wincing. It would hold.

Coaxing herself on with encouraging words, promising herself that the woods were almost upon them, she stumbled up the hill and into the shade of the trees. Even though it was still early morning, the suns were determined to give nobody a break from the weather.

Emelyn stopped ahead and Neri staggered up to her with one hand clutching at the stitch in her side.

"How, do you move, so fast?" she gasped. "How did you know the guards would move as well?"

Emelyn managed an eerie smile and splayed her hands out.

"Magic. But time's ticking on so I think we need to keep going."

Neri nodded and took the lead toward where they'd made camp the night before. Eva had said she'd find them in the woods, so they'd check there first. There were no signs of fire to look for, but she happened upon a familiar spot and noticed an apple on the ground and a candle. The tree she must have pretended to sleep against showed signs of activity, the moss being kicked up and the undergrowth disturbed.

She lifted her head and whistled for Dog, the sound piercing through the trees. She listened to silence for several seconds, but heard no barking or movement.

"We camped here last night. Ni…"

She squeaked and almost bit her tongue when Emelyn's hand clamped over her mouth. Wide-eyed, Neri blinked.

"Don't use names," Emelyn hissed. "Never use names, not this close to *them*, just in case. I've heard some gifts can curse or summon with a name."

She jerked her head back to indicate she meant the Governance and Neri nodded. The hand disappeared and Neri gasped for air.

"We camped here last night," she explained. "But we separated from *him* at the top of the hill back there. Me and one other got separated on the barn roof coming in. They might still be behind us."

The idea of a traitor in their midst brought scary possibilities to her mind. Someone had tipped off the Governance that she would be arriving. Amis knew her full name and apparently plenty about her family too. Her mind revolved in a sickening carousel of memories. Niall telling her she had to get Emelyn out first. Niall disappearing to create the distraction. Niall calling all the shots. Niall showing a surprising amount of interest in her. Amis had said someone told him to expect her.

What if...

She flinched as Emelyn gripped her arm.

"We've been doing some research around the area and there are a few dwellings nearby," she insisted. "We can trade for a horse or two. Do you have any coin, or anything to trade?"

Neri shook her head. "No... I don't have anything worth enough for a horse."

"Worth asking. We'll have to borrow some."

Neri gawped after her as Emelyn set off into the woods. Her shaking had disappeared but she walked uneasily, like something pained her.

"Are you okay?" Neri asked, hurrying to keep up with her. "Physically I mean. And we can't just borrow horses. How will we bring them back?"

Emelyn frowned. "We need to get home. Ma is well connected enough so she'll be able to smooth this sort of thing out. She always does."

Neri bit her lip, stumbling over the undergrowth as the forged on at a smart pace.

"What about others?" she insisted.

"They know the plan," Emelyn said. "If separated, we find our own ways home. It's always been that way."

She stopped dead, a soft gasp falling from her lips. Neri fought the urge to cry, the frustration and panic ebbing over as Emelyn turned and grabbed her hand.

"I'm sorry about your cloak. I thought it would be safe. I'll do my best to trade for another one for you."

Neri shook her head, taking a few paces forward until Emelyn followed.

"It doesn't matter," she lied. "It was just a cloak. If you're sure the others will know to follow us, although there they ended up I can't even begin to guess. Ni- he hurried off to cause a diversion-"

"The explosion!"

"I'm guessing so. The moment it happened though, Eva was off like a hound and I have no idea why or where."

Where did Eva go? Doubt settled fast. *If she and Niall were somehow in on things together... but what? Were they planning for me to get Emelyn out, or for the Governance to keep me in?*

She shook her head in the vain hope of dislodging the thoughts sticking like thorns. The Governance would be combing every leaf and blade of grass, so they couldn't linger. Niall was smart, and if he needed rescuing she'd be better planning for it from a place of safety.

Even in the shade of the trees, the heat bore down, unending. Neri risked a glance after a while of walking and had the faintest hint of satisfaction that even airy, pale Emelyn was covered with a shining sheen of sweat.

"I owe you a favour," Emelyn said.

"No need." Neri managed an awkward smile. "You were kind to me when you didn't have to be. I wanted to repay that. Besides, if you weren't wearing my cloak maybe they wouldn't have taken you at all."

She flinched as Emelyn's arm linked through hers, despite both of them being caked in clammy sweat.

"The only folk at fault here is the Governance," Emelyn insisted. "You called me your friend back there, and I won't forget it. I only trust three folk in the whole of the realm, now four. There's you, Niall, Ma and also Moonshine. I used to trust Hamlin too, but I suppose you've taken his place. Oh, and Mik, but you won't know him. So that's five."

Neri grimaced at the mention of Hamlin. She had taken his spot in a way as candle-maker to his friends. But even though she still had stabs of grief at the thought of him, she missed Niall's presence most of all, and she wanted her bed in the sanctuary.

The realisation crashed upon her before she was ready for it, the soft huff of breath hidden in a myriad of breathlessness from the heat, the panic and their fast pace.

The sanctuary was her home, or as close as she was likely to get to one again. The residents weren't family either but they did live like one. The know-it-all, confident face of Amis edged its way into her mind's eye. Ignoring the spike in her anxiety, she focused on her home. He wanted to destroy it and what it represented, what it stood for. He hurt Emelyn, who now called her a true friend. He killed Hamlin. His organisation had everything to do with the deaths of her mama and gramma, she was certain of that now.

The thoughts stoked a different fire inside her, simmering for a time when her planning would need the desire for revenge.

Eva disappeared on me, and what about Finn? He seemed to care at least a bit about Emelyn in the beginning yet he was gone at the first sign of an argument.

His words circled back to her, that she didn't want to see what he'd do to protect those he cared about.

Was that really about Emelyn? Or has he been somewhere on the enemy side all along?

Aching limbs and the throbbing from her sore ankle kept Neri from collapsing. Not having slept the night before seemed like a stupid idea now, but she refused to suggest they stop and rest. Each pain was a sign that she'd gone through the depths of everything rotten to get Emelyn safe and she couldn't give up now.

"Here we are," Emelyn whispered. "Wait, can you ride?"

Neri pulled a face. "A bit. Body between the legs and try not to kick too hard."

"That'll do."

Before Neri could say a word, Emelyn crept away toward the edge of a field where several horses were grazing, along with several rope halters on the fence. Neri followed as Emelyn unhooked two halters, but she didn't hand one over as four horses started ambling toward them.

"Are we sure Ma can smooth this over?" she murmured.

Emelyn shrugged. "She always has before. We don't have time to leave a note. Do you want the white one, the brown one or the golden one?"

Neri stared at each horse in turn.

"The white one looks the steadiest."

Emelyn nodded. "I'll halter her for you and leg you on."

Neri did as she was told, her pulse thudding with an entirely different sort of fear to before as she pressed her hands to the horse's back and bent her knee. Emelyn's attempt at legging her on almost sent her flying off the other side again, but she managed to get herself right and took the ends of the rope halter Emelyn handed to her.

"Stick your foot out for me," Emelyn muttered, leading her horse alongside Neri's uninjured ankle.

Neri did so and scanned the area for any sign that someone was about to come raging at them. She couldn't even see dwellings of any kind, but that didn't mean they weren't there.

She tensed as Emelyn set off and her horse followed, along with several of the herd. While Emelyn handled the gate, she kept watch, but not a single sound of protest followed them.

"We'll have to ride through the night," Emelyn said.

"Do you know the way?"

"Well enough."

With her ankle throbbing, her head dizzy from lack of sleep and her gut burning from lack of food, Neri decided she had to be content with that.

CHAPTER TWELVE

Neri travelled mostly in silence because Emelyn seemed quite happy to do all the talking. She explained about her writings and insisted Neri keep her book. Then she asked for horrifically detailed opinions that took them well through the first night and into the second day. They stopped to rest briefly, but both of them were desperate to reach home, both for food and for safety.

It was only when Emelyn became a bundle of fidgeting energy, to the point she started affecting her horse and sending it into short plunges forward that she then had to rein back, that Neri realised they must be close.

Close to home.

She recognised the lane, her heart lifting even though she barely had energy to smile. Her ankle was pressing painfully against her boot but she was almost used to it now after so long of forcing herself not to think about that. Or the aching, gnawing burn of hunger in her gut.

The sanctuary came into view and front door opened before they even made it off the horses.

Ma Kath hurried up to them with her arms out wide. She

held Emelyn in a tight cuddle for several timeless moments, murmuring her joy at Emelyn's safe return. Neri managed to get off her horse and land on her good leg, but then Ma was turning to her with a shining smile.

Awkward at the display of affection, Neri shuffled forward and allowed Ma to hug her also.

"You came back." Ma didn't sound the least bit surprised. "There will always be a home for you here."

Overwhelmed, Neri allowed herself to be herded through the dark hall and into the den, with only the briefest moments to feel the unwinding of her muscles at the thought of finally being safe.

"Welcome home."

Moonshine sat on a large cushion, her legs folded in what looked like a complicated knot underneath her. She chuckled as Emelyn leapt to hug her, and Neri spared a thought for the horses but Ma patted her arm.

"I'll fetch them some water, don't fret," she promised.

Emelyn nodded. "I'll help."

Nobody said a word about Emelyn's weariness, which seemed to have miraculously vanished. Neri didn't stop to question it as Moonshine followed them into the hall.

Neri hesitated, unsure if that was a dismissal of sorts. She limped toward the doorway as Moonshine returned with a tray and four mugs.

"You've had enough torment I'm sure, so I've made tea," she announced.

She held out a cup of warm red liquid and the moment Neri smelled the berry tea, she drank half in one gulp. Moonshine sank onto her cushion again while Neri drained the entire cup, the warmth soothing through her throat right to her insides.

"There now. Tell me what's on your mind."

Moonshine's voice was soothing and the sudden urge to cry welled up. Neri fought it long enough to get to the sofa and collapse onto it, but she could only get one leg up onto the cushions and curled her body over it.

She was safe, but that meant she had to face the enormity of what she'd done.

"I might have killed someone."

She could barely whisper the words. Panic tickled her chest, threatening to creep in. She bit her lip tight and took several slow, deep breaths, cutting into her palms with her nails.

"If you did then he deserved it." Moonshine kept her voice low. "But you may not have. It is Emelyn's decision whether to tell what happened to her while she was in captivity, but I can sense what he did. If he is gone then I'm glad."

The serenity never left her voice but Neri was not soothed. She always knew the rage-monster inside her would eventually kill someone. She'd spent so long hiding herself in her family's fanciful tales to avoid folk antagonising her, but her caution had made no difference in the end.

"I can sense folk's emotions," Moonshine continued. "I can sense you're on the cusp of a panic right now. I can tell Emelyn will be too exhausted to have nightmares tonight. When folk I'm close to are far away, I can sense the vague positives or negatives if I concentrate hard."

Neri turned her face away. The enormity of what she'd done was dawning on her and Moonshine's cryptic nonsense wasn't going to make her justify any of it.

Moonshine put her mug down and stood up. She pulled the table from the middle of the room into the corner and moved a small spindle-legged wooden stool with a large *frondera* plant on top away from the door.

"She always moves this table," she muttered. "You may think this is all fable and nonsense, but I can tell Niall's getting close and he's extremely angry."

The walls of the dwelling shook in the wake of an ear-splitting slam on the front door.

Neri jumped and dropped her cup. It thudded on the floorboards and rolled away, leaking dregs of dark red onto the wood. She didn't even bother to reach for it when the second slam came, closely followed by something smashing.

Moonshine huffed. "I forgot to take down the painting."

Her words disappeared as the doorway to the hall darkened, a figure filling the space and radiating fury.

Niall crossed the room in two strides, grabbed Neri by the shoulders and lifted her to her feet with effortless strength. She balanced on her good leg and tried to catch her breath as his arms clamped around her. Despite the sudden shock of seeing him, she struggled against the crushing embrace.

"Why didn't you wait in the woods?" he yelled. "Where's Eva?"

His eyes burned dark with savage anger as he yelled at her and something in that woke an echoing part of her. She had saved Emelyn on her own and he was yelling at her. He was furious, but she could match that.

"Someone on our side is on *their* side," she shouted back at him. "The man whose head I caved in admitted as much. He knew I was coming. He knew my name!"

His anger riled up her fury and now she wanted to argue, if only because anger was less painful than guilt.

The information seemed to catch Niall's attention through the rage and hints of brown showed around his pupils. Her chest heaving with exertion, Neri calmed a bit too.

"They weren't expecting us to be there that soon," she explained. "But they were expecting us."

Her worries about him dissipated immediately, but she remembered Eva's mysterious disappearance and Finn's absence too.

Before she could mention it, Niall loosened his grip on her and rearranged his hold, pressing her tight to him instead so her cheek was smooshed against his shoulder. She let him hold her for several moments, bewildered at the frantic pounding in her chest. She couldn't help smirking when she heard Moonshine's flippant attempt at regaining some semblance of sanity.

"Men are marvellous when they're raging, but for now we all need food and more tea. Then we talk."

Neri cleared her throat and wriggled free of Niall's arms, her cheeks burning. Dog padded across to her and she took solace in ruffling his ears, unable to look at Niall again until they'd both calmed down.

Moonshine glided from the room as Niall heaped down

on the sofa as though he belonged there, grinning up at Ma and Emelyn as they came in.

"You passed us in rather a rush, dear," Ma teased. "But glad you're safe."

"He shot past us so fast we weren't even sure it was him," Emelyn added. "But Moonshine will probably want some help with tea."

She grinned and danced out of the room, Ma right behind her muttering about the safety of her kitchen.

"That girl is relentless," Niall said.

Neri frowned. "She's my friend."

Silence drifted between them. Neri hovered until Niall rolled his eyes and tapped the cushion beside him.

"You don't need to look so nervy. I promise to behave myself, no more manhandling."

Neri snorted, knowing full well it was her emotions causing the nerves as much as his behaviour. She sat beside him, perched on the edge of the cushion.

"They'll be back any moment anyway," Niall groaned. "If they're not already eavesdropping at the door."

Neri looked up at him, hesitant to discuss his behaviour. She should be demanding answers, threatening to tear bits off if he ever grabbed her like that again, but she couldn't dredge up any energy. He caught her expression and sighed.

"I'm sorry for shouting. I was so worried. I managed to create the explosion and got back into the trees, but then you never showed up. That's why I asked for Dog. He was sniffing and trying to get me to go with him, but the plan was to wait where we parted. I knew if all went wrong, he'd be able to find you again."

Neri looked at Dog now passed out on the floor, his tongue lolling onto the floorboards.

"Emelyn said the plan was to make our own ways back. He led you all the way here?"

Niall shrugged. "He led me this direction out of the forest and I figured this would be where you'd try to get back to. It was only on walking up to the front door that I realised I hadn't once considered you might have run away."

Indignant, Neri twisted to face him. "As if I would!"

The thought of grabbing one of the smaller cushions and whacking him in the face with it occurred to her, but she was saved by a loud rattle from the hall.

Emelyn came in with a large wooden tray that contained a large plate of bread, cheese and slices of apple, Ma and Moonshine right behind her with another tray of plates and more tea.

"Right, let's get down to business," Moonshine said.

She balanced on the cushion with her legs folded elegantly beneath her while Emelyn sat beside Ma on the second sofa with her legs crossed.

"I know who the traitor is." Emelyn's lively face became sad at the thought. "The only way I know for sure is because it can only be one of two folk we know and I overheard that man talking through the open windows."

Neri leaned forward. Emelyn sipped from her cup and surveyed them all calmly before continuing.

"It had to be either Finn, which I couldn't believe to be true, or someone else at the sanctuary. He said that 'she' had been watching us for months, digging her way into our inner circle. It has to be Eva."

Neri frowned. For a single moment she feared they would suspect her, although her treatment of Amis should have proved otherwise with absolute clarity. She shivered.

"I thought as much." Niall sighed. "She's been different since Finn returned. I couldn't believe she would be with him romantically when she obviously loves Matty, but then Finn's been different too. I mean, he's never been an absolute delight, but he seems tainted somehow. I wondered if they were in it together."

Neri sagged, her relief bittersweet as she thought of Eva and the scant interactions they'd had.

She flinched as Niall sat up straight, the movement jarring her ankle.

"Wait until we find her," he seethed. "If she has betrayed us, it won't go down well, I can promise you that. Anything could have happened to either of you."

Neri forced unwelcome thoughts of what had happened to the back of her mind.

Emelyn rolled her eyes. "Don't bother with the bad boy act, Niall, it's only sexy when you're joking."

Neri choked back a giggle as Emelyn winked at her.

"Eva is here." Ma said.

Neri squeaked in alarm as Niall sat up fast enough to dislodge cushions.

"What?!"

He got to his feet but Ma was in front of him with her hand firm on his chest before he could take a step.

"Not yet. We need to discuss this between us first. We

also have no proof to throw at her either yet."

Niall sank back down with his arms folded and a furious look on his face. Neri wondered if he had noticed he was a lot closer to her than before but decided not to point it out. Moments later, her mind dragged her back to what Niall had said before. She twisted to stare at him again.

"How on earth did you make it back here so quick then, if you were waiting around? We didn't."

"I stole a horse," he admitted, rueful impishness lifting the corners of his lips. "Dog led me out of the forest and I recognised the direction. The Governance had left the door to their livestock barn wide open so I helped myself."

He exploded a building and stole a horse, all in one day. Neri grimaced. *But we stole two horses and attacked two men. Our tale is probably the worse one.*

"That would explain the beasts currently tearing up the edible foliage outside?" Moonshine asked, amused.

Neri bit her lip and smiled guiltily, amused to see similar contrite expressions on Emelyn's and Niall's faces, all three of them too relieved at being home to be truly sorry.

Home. It was a strange thought because Hamlin's had never felt like home, but somehow the sanctuary did. Perhaps because Ma had shown her the photo of her mama and gramma, or perhaps because knowing they were against the Governance aligned with her own needs. Definitely not because of Niall, who'd gone back to smiling hopefully at her.

"I'm just surprised they didn't catch you," she muttered.

Niall's grin widened. "I'm uncatchable. No, they were

chasing me but luckily I've learned a thing or two in my time. Remember when we took Dog out and you climbed that tree? I did the same. Put Dog in a bush and climbed the tree above it. They just kept going without looking up once. Then I ran back to the barn and found the fastest looking horse they had."

As Neri flushed at the memories of their first few days of knowing each other, the conversation turned onto their inevitable return to the sanctuary.

"I have to rescue my garden from all these horses," Ma said with a broad smile. "Moonshine, perhaps I could use your assistance in getting them to the neighbouring field?"

Emelyn shot with a conspiratorial glance at Moonshine, who rolled her wise eyes and waved her arms toward the door. Emelyn got up too, apparently determined to accompany them.

Left in silence, Neri couldn't think of a single thing to say to Niall, who sat watching her with equal trepidation. Instead of returning to the shouting and manhandling topic, she forged on with another issue that was plaguing her.

"Emelyn seems to think you were born in the west, which still sounds entirely addle-brained considering there's meant to be a cursed forest in the way. Did you somehow find a way to cross over, despite that being something nobody in living memory has managed according to most?"

Niall's eyes widened. His bottom lip dropped, a sharp breath whistling in. He didn't respond for several moments, serious apprehension scrawled across his face. Recollections of fiery visitors in the night filled Neri's head.

"I also saw something that's been bugging me." She forced herself to look right into his dark eyes. "The night before we went into their stronghold, I saw something. It's impossible but it felt so real. A bird of fire came to me and led me through the forest, or tried to. A wind picked up and it smelled like autumn, the same scents and chills."

Niall remained completely still so she carried on, unsure.

"The bird was glowing gold like fire, or I thought it was. Then Emelyn mentioned shimmers into the west and she seems so convinced. I can't believe it but I can't help wondering why you'd all be saying the same thing about the west, even the enemy, unless there's something in it?"

She waited, desperate for a believable answer, but Niall took his time finding one. When he did, he took the less honourable route.

"I don't suppose I can use my superior distraction skills to stop you dwelling on it?" he asked.

Neri snorted but her indignation settled immediately. It wasn't her place to demand answers, not really. They might have accepted her as one of their group, but she'd not made any actual promises to stay.

So why does the mere thought of moving on now that Emelyn is safe bother me this much? Where would I even go?

"You could try." She kept her tone low. "Although if you lot believe something, who am I to doubt it until it's been proven wrong?"

Niall leaned forward, a flood of some uncategorised

emotion in his dark eyes. A hot tinge jumped to Neri's cheeks. She gulped when Niall's hand settled firm over hers, forcing her eyes to meet his.

"I have something I'm supposed to do," he admitted. "It involves finding something and that may take me somewhere untoward one day."

The words appeared to stick in his throat and his voice faltered.

"This is to do with this whole way into the west thing the Governance is seeking, the secret path through the supposedly magic forest?" she asked.

Niall watched her for a moment. Slowly, he nodded. The awkward fear in his eyes, the anticipation that she'd move away or patronise him, made him look so vulnerable.

He believes it as much as Emelyn does. Maybe Moonshine and Ma Kath really do too. Can it really be harmful to humour them? The desire to belong swelled, to return to the sanctuary with the door always open to her. *They aren't bad folk and I'm lucky to have found somewhere safe and kind.*

"Who am I to doubt what I haven't seen disproven?" She shrugged. "I actually thought of the sanctuary as home on our way back here. If someone real wants to destroy it, like the Governance, then all the cursed stuff is just part of the background."

Niall rubbed his chin with his free hand, reminding Neri that his other one was still curled around hers. She slid her fingers free, forcing herself to face the awkward truth still swilling in her head.

"I overheard you talking to Finn before we left as well,"

she added. "You said I could be one of you and that you might ask me to go with you. Why, and where?"

The tip of Niall's boot started to tap as he grimaced.

"You heard that? No wonder you've been wary of us. The Governance is after you but we don't know why. What I have to do next involves finding out more about them, as well as *other* things."

"Things like your magical mystery woodland path?" Her brow rose in disbelief.

He chuckled. "Yeah, that. I thought that if you came with me, you might get some answers for yourself as well."

"I got some." She hesitated but he didn't press her. "He hinted they had something to do with my family's deaths, and that my gramma stole some kind of ancient information that they want back. He had artwork I'd done as a child as well, and hinted they might have had something to do with my gramma and mamma dying."

He sighed. "That's a lot to deal with. I won't ask what information, but if you want payback you're with the right folk for it now."

"I don't want to think about it, not yet. I need time. But yeah, payback will be a start."

Niall raised his arms above his head with a groan, so comfortable in his surroundings while she sat like a flighty bird beside him.

"Then again, I've seen how dangerous it will be now." He smiled. "And how easily you cause chaos. Maybe it'd be best if you go stay at the sanctuary with the others instead."

Neri sat up, glaring at him. "Oh please. You can't invite

me to join you then say 'actually, no, stay behind'. If there's a way to find out what they want from me, I'm taking it."

"Okay." His soft laughter filled the room. "Somehow I imagine it'd be safer for me to have you with me rather than against me."

As he leaned toward her, the neck of his sweatshirt gaped and Neri saw a length of pale string nestled against his skin.

"You still have the charm?" she asked.

"Of course, you gave it to me." He pulled the *liliam* wax out and let it hang from his fingers between them. "You still don't believe in the mystical stuff, do you?"

Neri faced him. "Does it matter?"

"I guess not." Niall tucked the charm away again, but she could see a flicker of disappointment marring his face.

"Perhaps you'll just have to prove otherwise," she countered.

CHAPTER THIRTEEN

Neri was still sat with Niall when the others came back. Despite the lack of sleep, Ma insisted they eat before retreating upstairs and Neri's gut growled its agreement for everyone to hear.

"So, what do you think, Neri?" Emelyn asked. "Now you've seen them at their worst and been near the cursed forest, do you believe us?"

Neri grimaced "I've spent my whole life being told that folk are getting eaten or possessed by going into the cursed woods. Now you're telling me that there really is some ancient sorcery that keeps the east and west apart?"

She smiled with affection at Emelyn, who for once looked sulky and frustrated. Moonshine unfolded her graceful legs from the chair to intervene.

"We need to focus more on the events in our part of the land first," she said. "Tomorrow we will have a conversation about all this. Then Niall, your time will come soon to do what you must."

Neri glanced over in time to see Niall nod. He caught her eye and she knew that his next journey would be to find the magic way through the supposedly cursed wood. Still unable to believe it, Neri realised she would follow him regardless of myth and magic if it led her to information on what the Governance thought her gramma had stolen.

More time in Niall's company just happens to be part of the deal.

She flinched as Moonshine's eyes bored into hers.

"Your time is soon to come too," Moonshine announced. "You've already made the choice without really knowing it, but your part in our tale is just beginning. Never believe you aren't important because you definitely will be."

Her voice, suddenly deep and eerily quiet, hit a quivering part of Neri's soul. She gulped against a catch in her throat and nodded. Moonshine softened again as she turned back to face the others.

"I think we need to inform Neri of exactly what we're up against."

A flicker of doubt passed across Emelyn's face and Niall's shoulders rose with tension. Neri glanced at Moonshine's knowing smile and nodded her head to confirm herself ready. There would be nothing they could throw at her now which she wouldn't handle.

"Emelyn, I think it best if you explain," Moonshine decided. "You are the resident scribe after all."

Neri settled back against the satisfyingly supportive curve of the sofa and waited as Emelyn cleared her throat.

"The land was once whole, governed by three brothers with ancient blood tied to the entire realm of Kirelonia. But the east and west were very different in their natural resources. Arguments began over who would benefit and soon fighting broke out. Both sides had massed great fighting forces, so to avoid carnage the three brothers bid the land separate the east from the west. The forest grew and nobody has ever been able to breach it. There were ways through, but nobody on either side was told what they were. Some folk tried to follow the old cart tracks but none who were known for it ever returned. Some said that they reached the west and decided to stay there, but most believed that there were simply too many perils put in place to stop folk strolling through."

"What, like magic creatures?" Neri asked, her tone sceptical.

Emelyn shrugged. "We can't be sure. Maybe. Knowledge of the three brothers disappeared into myth. Some say they're still out there biding their time, watching over us. Others say they must have died by now. But the forest is there, and those who have gone in never return. We have someone inspecting as many old texts as he can, and I overheard a few things in captivity."

Emelyn shuddered at the thought and fell silent, her expression grim. The flicking tail of the story beast curled away and allowed Neri to regain her sense of reality.

The suns waned outside and cast the pale golden hues of summer evening through the window. The fabric covering the window picked up the light, bathing the whole room in a pink glow. For the length of the story the world outside had drifted away, and Neri could easily entertain the fantasy as reality. All of her mama's worrying and her gramma's careful lectures about kindness and fighting angry urges had been steeped in pretty imagery, but the firebird had been one of their favourites. The thought of the monster curled deep inside her rose up and Neri bit her lip, forcing her mind to focus elsewhere.

"So, you're really suggesting there's a magic path through the woods to the west, but it's conveniently been lost for centuries, and that's why the Governance are making so much trouble?"

The wary looks that passed amongst the others only made her feel worse. Even with the strange she remained the outsider. She pressed her fingers to her eyes in frustration.

"They don't need that as an excuse to make trouble at all," Moonshine said. "But they pride advantage above all else, and access to the west would open them up to new resources and powerful allies. It's always to do with gaining power."

Neri nodded and lifted a hand to swipe errant strands of hair behind her ear. She would need to sleep but the thought of washing first became irrepressibly enticing.

A firm warmth closed around her arm and she jumped at the touch, wincing as twinges of pain radiated through her wrist. Niall held her arm closer to his face, baring the bruises that resembled fingertips on her skin.

"What are these?" he demanded.

She pulled her arm free with a frown.

"Bruises, what do they look like? We had a couple of near misses with some of them. My ankle's worse off now I think about it."

All eyes dropped to look at her boot and she leaned

forward to pull it off. It took a few delicate moments and several anguished faces, but she had no time to worry about the potential smell as Ma appeared with a serving tray of food and huffed loudly.

"Look at you!" She shook her head. "That'll need cooling. I have a tincture of *ungbry* that will bring that swelling down."

"I'd imagine brindle root would fare better," Moonshine added.

Both women looked at each other, expressions descending into identical cool glances.

"The *ungbry* is fresh. Brindle root takes longer to brew."

"Brindle root is more potent for swells."

"I don't think so."

"I know so."

Niall groaned and hid his face behind a cushion as the argument drifted into the hall and echoed down to the kitchen.

"I'd better go and hide the cutlery," Emelyn muttered, apparently serious in the face of two matriarchs about to go to war over a couple of herbs.

Left alone with Niall again, Neri huddled herself small.

"It's probably not as bad as it looks," she tried.

Niall chuckled. "Too late. They'll be fighting it out until one of them either concedes or your foot is healed. But you've not told me your story yet. What happened while we were separated?"

Neri shook her head. She didn't want to dwell on it, or what she'd done, but he'd given her the diversion she needed and proved that he was one of the honest ones.

"I managed to get into Emelyn's room without any trouble, conveniently so, but the moment your explosion went off so did Eva."

She took a deep breath. *I don't have to mention what I did, not yet.*

"Em was in a bad state, but we managed to get a guard to come in. There was a scuffle and she- we- he went out of the window. Then we tried to escape but we came across-"

She huffed a choked breath, the memories swarming. *Blood, the unyielding press of the bat in her fists.* She shook her head.

"We met the man who killed Hamlin, the one who was speaking when he died. His name is Amis and he- I-"

She couldn't continue. When Niall folded his arms around her shoulders, she struggled but he pulled tight until she was pressed against his chest.

"We're safe here," he murmured. "Whatever happened, it's done now."

Neri shuddered and clenched her eyelids against the hot tears. She took comfort from his closeness, aware he was holding her without any fear of what she might do to him, what she might have done to others.

"I had a bat," she whispered. "I hit him, hard. I don't know if he's still alive."

Niall froze. She waited for the inevitable loosening of his arms, the subtle chill that would come with him letting go and inching back.

"You did what you had to." He nestled her tighter

against him, her head pressed to his shoulder. "I won't tell you it's going to be okay, but if it was either you or him surviving, I'm glad it's you."

Neri couldn't summon up any response to that.

"Look, you're exhausted," he continued. "Close your eyes and sleep if you can or rest a bit at least. I promise you'll be safe."

Neri snuffled and twisted her head away from him to wipe her eyes.

"Even with you?" She didn't dare look up at him.

"Especially with me."

She settled her head back on his shoulder and closed her eyes, assuming sleep wouldn't come. A few more moments of embarrassment, then she could find some reason to excuse herself. Her mind circled but already the upheaval was taking its toll. Her last thought before dreams ensnared her was that she could feel Niall sighing into her hair.

Her only dream was of Niall beside her, but the details were so hazy that she wondered on waking again if she'd dreamed the whole thing. She lifted her head and relaxed the moment she recognised the den around her. A quick glance down at her leg propped up on a padded stool and she smiled to see two separate poultices bound to her leg, one with an ominous yellow colour seeping through the rag binding it, and the other smelling distinctly of aged milk.

Even more excruciating that being a healer's minion, was the lump of man currently folded over her. She tried to shuffle without disturbing Niall, but he'd apparently seen fit to stay sleeping on the sofa beside her and had slumped on top of her. The grumble of sleep in his voice as she shifted suggested he wouldn't wake, but it was the sudden onslaught of folk coming through the door that made his eyes snap open.

Neri managed a weary smile at Emelyn, then at Ma and Moonshine both giving each other frosty looks before rushing over to inspect her ankle. She sat meekly while they fussed and prodded and argued, her attention drifting past them to an unexpected face.

Finn sat himself in the armchair and fixed his attention on his fingernails. Neri eyed him warily but he didn't as much as glance up at anyone, not even Emelyn.

Matty appeared moments later and Neri twisted to see Eva right behind him. Matty didn't look troubled, but Eva had a faraway look on her face, her mind elsewhere while she worried at her bottom lip with her teeth.

So astonished to see Eva acting like nothing had happened, Neri didn't have time to register Moonshine's vicelike fingers gripping her sore wrist and pulling her downwards, let alone struggle.

"Hold back, but don't let him go too far."

Before Neri could question it, Niall leapt up and crossed the den in three leaping strides and loomed over Eva with his fists clenched.

"You're one of them, admit it."

"What are you doing?!" Matty jumped between them, his eyes wide with horror.

Eva eyed Matty first, then her expression flickered once and any sign of emotion faded. She bobbed her head in Niall's direction.

"Evie?" Matty blinked, confused. "What does he mean? You're one of who?"

The desperate note in his voice suggested he knew exactly what Niall meant deep down, even as his wide eyes searched her face for any other answer but that one.

"How long has it been?" Niall pressed, ignoring Matty. "Since you came here?"

Eva shuffled back against the wall and her eyes lost any sense of shock, making her look dead with stillness. Niall started to pace back and forth in front of her.

"I didn't think you'd actually escape them." Her voice sounded dull now, timeless. "Otherwise we'd be long gone by now. I used to be one of them, but I gave that life up before I came here. Then I met Matty. At first I thought it wouldn't hurt to be on this side, to watch everyone scrabble about pretending to be some great resistance against the Governance. But then I met one of them about two months back. It was by chance, but he reminded me how strong they are. You won't win against them in the end. Nobody will. All I want is a secure life, and that's something you can't offer me hiding away here."

Niall growled but didn't interrupt.

Bewildered, Neri noticed the sadness of realisation in Ma Kath's eyes and the resignation in Moonshine's and Emelyn's. Only Matty seemed to still be in shock. His entire body quaked and he stared at Eva as though she were a stranger that he was supposed to know but couldn't recall.

"Was that why you were trying to get me to leave earlier?" he asked, his voice frail. "Evie, how could you?"

Eva didn't look at him. "I didn't expect anyone else to get back so quickly. Didn't think Niall would at all to be truthful. We were meant to be away from here and off on our own adventure before anyone realised."

"I'll bet." Niall scoffed. "What do they know about us? You owe us that much at least."

"They asked me for information, but I didn't want to give them the location of this place."

She glanced just once at Matty with sad eyes before the emotion drained again. She returned to watching Niall's progress as he started pacing the floor in front of her.

"They already had names and pictures of us all, but they told me it was Emelyn they wanted. I watched and explained where they could likely catch her alone. It was only after that I realised they'd get the general idea of where this place was."

Neri looked over at Finn during Eva's pause. He was still absorbed in the surface of his fingers, rolling his hands in idle contemplation. She had no idea if he came straight back in a huff after leaving the group in the forest, or if he was in league with Eva and ran on ahead to warn the Governance they were coming.

"When everyone suggested sending Neri after her, I told my contact what they needed to know. You met him, the man in that carriage that stopped us on the road. I didn't expect them to remove the guards at the stronghold either but they wanted you inside, Neri. I suppose they hoped you might convince Emelyn to see sense as the word-weaver."

Neri's confusion grew. Her mind jangled over Eva's term 'word-weaver'. What could Emelyn's gift for writing be that they considered it of such great value?

Niall flicked his hand in the air, throwing a palpable wave of irritation out with it. Everyone turned when Emelyn spoke.

"They wanted me to create a pathway to find a route through. I refused. I heard various useful things too but perhaps this isn't the time."

Neri heard the words but looked back to Eva quick enough to curiosity light the woman's eyes.

"How did they know we were coming then?" Niall spat, eying Finn now. "You were with us the whole time once we left here. Suppose the two of you were in it together and you took off to warn them?"

Neri flinched as Finn flew out of his seat, his shoulders hunching.

"Are you serious? As if I would ever betray the cause or our folk. Not for her, not for anyone."

Niall turned back to Eva for confirmation. She shrugged.

"That man we met on the road in the cart, I warned him. We use weather as a communication system so they knew when to expect us."

The storm. Neri bit her lip. *I thought it was weird she mentioned it storming in three days. Very specific, not 'a few' or 'soon'.*

Niall seemed to think that was the end of the interrogation either way. He leaned down and grabbed Eva by the arm. Eva sensed something final and began to struggle, scratching his hands and kicking out at his legs.

Neri remembered Moonshine's words. Eva's struggling

was losing strength fast and becoming frantic flailing as Niall shook her, his hand stealing toward her throat. Images of Amis flashed through Neri's head. The memory of panic spiked in her chest.

"Niall *stop*. Not like this."

The trepidation in her voice seemed to carry some weight. Niall's shoulders lowered. He opened his fingers and Eva staggered back as Neri hurried forward. Niall had protected and guided her so far. Now it was her turn to be in control. When she placed her hand on his arm, he didn't react.

"What will happen to her?" she asked.

She looked to Ma but it was Moonshine who stood. In those few moments, Neri found out who really ran the show.

"She'll remain here. There may be a time when she'll be useful and we're not going to act as they do."

"Aren't you going to try and reason with me?" Eva asked. "I'm surprised you're not trying to change my mind."

She didn't sound overly bothered by the idea. Ma shook her head and took a step forward.

"There wouldn't be much point. You've made your views quite clear. You may tell us why if you feel the need to, but it won't change our opinions of you. Not now."

Eva shrugged. "When I was little, I used to wish the fables of great ancient gifts existed, those that could move mountains and wield flame as easy as breathing. I think a lot of folk do deep down. Things changed after a while and when I found out what the Governance were doing, I wanted in. Wasn't too keen on the way they did things back then so I ran. I met Matty and this resistance nonsense seemed so much fun at the time.

'But a few months ago, I got talking to someone during my last scout mission. We recognised each other from older days. At first, I didn't want to draw suspicion by being rude and brushing him off. Then when I explained, little by little, he convinced me that I was being deceived by folk who were obviously dangerous. The more I spoke to him, the more it made sense. Finally, he asked me if I would help him. He'd ask the Governance to give me a proper role and we could convince Matty to come around too."

Eva sighed and picked at her fingernails.

"I knew they'd expect information in exchange for what they offered me, I'm not naive. But Niall would bring information from Hamlin and I'd feed any of it I could back to them. Then I mentioned your name a week or so ago, Neri, and that *really* took their interest."

Neri froze. Eva looked up at her, curiosity burning in her narrowed eyes.

"They sent guards to watch you at Hamlin's shop," Eva continued. "I said I'd never give them this location while Matty is still here, but I confirmed Hamlin was involved. I don't want to spend my life in hiding for the sake of some misguided attempt at goodness or kindness. Sometimes the realm is a harsh place and tough decisions need to be made. I can't go against that, not when they're offering me freedom."

Neri snorted. "Oh yeah, the freedom of your very own

cage, being at their beck and call because you owe them. And you'll always owe them, because they're the ones with the resources for the cosy life you want so badly."

Eva sat up. "A pretty philosophy, *Ginnera*. But you, they have a real interest in you. They wanted to know all about your history. They asked me if the name Amoria meant anything, or if you'd ever mentioned it?"

Neri's breathing stumbled and she huffed a few breaths before it seemed to desert her entirely. The name shouldn't affect her so badly, not when she already knew that the Governance were after her family. But to hear it spoken out loud hit a nerve. She took a step backwards, almost falling over the arm of one of the chairs.

Eva leaned forward with a hungry gleam in her eyes.

She's not collateral damage of a power war. She's one of them by choice, despite what they've done to folk. What they did to Hamlin and Emelyn, my family and countless others.

Anxiety rose, clawing its way up her throat. Hearing her gramma's name after so long hit a long-buried nerve, and coming from Eva's lips it sounded like a curse.

Neri turned, pushing past Niall who had no time to react or catch hold of her. She made it out of the den and into the hall, Niall's determined voice echoing after her. She dashed through the kitchen before she could gather her senses, leaving herself with no escape route.

As she burst out into the garden drenched in late afternoon light, fingers gripped her elbow. She spun around to see Niall staring wide-eyed at her in horror but his hold made her panic worse. Hauling her arm free, she stood with her chest heaving, looking around for some kind of escape route. Amis had mentioned her gramma stealing information from them, and the Governance had known enough to raid their flat. But still, hearing that name spoken aloud after all this time, and by a traitor to everything her gramma had represented...

"Neri, what is it?" Niall asked, his tone laced with warning. "Is there something you've not told us, something we should be aware of?"

His voice bit further into her angst. Indignation at his assumption cleared her mind, slicing through her panic.

"Wow, you hear something that upsets me and you assume I'm withholding things? What, do you think I've lied to you?"

Folding her arms across her chest, she glared pure acid at him. The shock Eva had hit her with still resonated but instead of panicking, her blood kindled with frustration. Niall opened his mouth, presumably to argue back, but no words came out.

After a moment or two he turned away but rotated back again just as quickly. He tried to speak but didn't manage anything more than a nonsensical noise. The shock on his face at her vehemence did nothing to bridle her rage. She gave him the dirtiest look she could manage and whirled away from him, coming one step short of falling into the pond.

Amoria. She hadn't expected to hear that name spoken ever again, except in her head. *Amoria.*

It wasn't a common name, not that Neri had ever heard. She'd met one Ginnera before and several Pelias, her mama's name. But never once in fables nor in passing folk had she heard of another Amoria. The void of shock in her mind had heightened her perceptions to the area around her. Swirls of spicy scent tugged her to turn around and face Niall, who now stood right in front of her.

"I'm sorry, okay?" His voice was barely audible. "I overreacted. You just looked so panicked and I thought- I'm sorry."

Still rankled, Neri bit her lip. "It was the name that shocked me. But I see you don't trust me, even now after everything with Emelyn. Thanks."

"I was all shaken up over what happened with Eva and I made a mistake. I am sorry."

His cut-up tone and the defeated sadness in his eyes began to have an effect on her.

"Amoria was my gramma's name," she relented. "There's nobody left alive that should really remember that besides me and possibly my father, who is in the back end of nowhere and has been since I was born. And apparently the Governance, which is another confirmation of this not somehow being a big show somehow."

Niall nodded, his dejected expression tugging on her heartstrings, his shoulders slumped like he knew he'd already lost out.

"You've talked about her before," he said. "I thought a couple of times she sounded like she could have been one of us. Apparently she used to know Ma so she probably was at some point. We'll figure out why they're interested in her."

Neri shrugged, glancing sideways to avoid being

swayed by his kicked puppy expression.

"Will you forgive me?" he pressed. "I'm not used this, but I worry about you."

Without looking at him, she nodded. "You don't have to worry. I can take care of myself."

"I know you can, but you can't help it when you have feelings for someone."

Flutters burst over Neri's skin, turning to heat across her face as she processed what he'd just said. She had to take a quick glance at him. Given his wide dark eyes and the sudden stillness, the admission had shocked him as well.

Feelings? I guess he's proven that he does care, but actual feelings, or just as part of the group?

Deciding that she wouldn't focus on his comment about her gramma being 'one of them', Neri took a few deep breaths to dispel the uneasiness in her mind.

"I suppose, in a twisted way, it could be considered, by a complete and utter addle-brain, as a sign that you care," she conceded.

Niall huffed a ragged breath of relief. "I do, more than you know, and not because of any information you might have or what you might be mixed up in. You shouldn't have had to see me like that though, with Eva I mean."

All thoughts of awkwardness or reticence leapt out of Neri's head as they stood facing each other, mere inches apart. She took his hands, ignoring the bewildered look her gave her.

"You didn't do it in the end though."

"I shouldn't have grabbed her," Niall whispered. "I shouldn't have gone in raging like that. It's not okay."

"You didn't do anywhere near as bad as you could have done," she insisted, conflicted by her own reassurances. "You stopped yourself. She betrayed us. Nobody knows how many folk have been hurt by her actions. She could have told us all she knew to help us find Emelyn, but she didn't. She chose a side and it wasn't ours."

Niall sagged, his chin dropping to his chest. Neri put one hand on his shoulder and the fingertips of the other on his chin, desperate to make him feel better.

"Jolly up, big *shades* don't cry."

Niall looked up, hope widening his dark eyes.

"I promised Hamlin I'd keep you safe," he insisted. "I was only supposed to bring you here and that was the end of it, but by the time we got here you'd made a pretty fearsome impression. I'm not used to worrying about others, not like this. I grew up in a home where nobody really cared and I've spent my entire life looking out for myself alone."

Neri bit her lip, aware that this was the first time Niall had shared anything real about himself or his past. He sighed again and dredged up a woeful smile.

"So that's all the emotional shade stuff you're getting today."

She nodded, still touched by his trust in her. Before she could turn their focus to more unsettling matters, like what they would do about Eva or the imminent return attack that would no doubt come if the Governance found them, the sound of laughter filled the garden.

Finn lounged in the kitchen doorway, his eyes narrowed at them both.

"What do you want?" Niall asked. "Finally worn out your charm on the locals?"

Finn's lip curled as he winked in Neri's direction. "It sounds like you're keeping family secrets after all by all accounts. Maybe you could shed more light on the mysteries than you're admitting to after all, add some flames to the dark between our trees perhaps?"

Neri froze. She remembered the ball of light she'd followed through the woods the night before entering the Governance stronghold.

Did he follow us after all? A chill swept over her, and she shuddered despite the humid air. *Or is he saying more cryptic nonsense to sound pretentious?*

"Leave her out of this." Niall's words barely made it past his clenched teeth.

His shoulders hunched higher as Finn's grin widened.

"I take it she doesn't know what you are yet either. I'll tell you now Neri, my sweet thing, you're walking into a dead end if you think following him will make you happy in the long run."

His words were obviously meant as a taunt, a parting shot to get the last word. Niall moved before Neri could catch hold of him and all of the pent-up anger he'd reigned in when dealing with Eva spilled out.

Finn made it through the kitchen door by the time Niall's fist collided with his jaw. Neri panicked as Finn stumbled back and hit the doorframe, wild thoughts of him dashing his head on something filling her mind.

Niall flexed his fingers as his shoulders lowered.

"I doubt you know how it feels to love someone other

than yourself," he growled. "I actually pity you. Don't think any of us have forgotten your mysterious disappearing act either. Convenient considering Eva's treachery."

Finn pressed a hand to his cheek. "You'll regret that."

He turned and barrelled into the kitchen, the sound of a door slamming inside echoing moments after. When Niall returned to her side, Neri stood floundering in a swamp of hesitant curiosity.

"Sit down."

Niall's sharp tone brought her heavily down onto the grass as he started to pace back and forth. She didn't want to condone his anger but there was a part of her that recognised it. She smothered her own fury and frustration with thoughts of goodness and kindness, but those intentions rarely made the feelings fade inside. Niall needed to bark at things and let off steam now. She could find time to stand her own ground later. Even with him raging at her, she had the overwhelming sense that she was safe.

"Finn's right," he said eventually. "There are certain things you don't know about me that might affect the situation. I'm not going to explain because it comes from the stuff you won't believe."

He sighed, frustrated, and shoved his hands up to push his hair back. As suddenly as it appeared, his irritation ebbed. He turned face her, his frown lifting into a rueful smile.

"I don't suppose these are the best ways to tell a girl how you feel."

With the suns prickling at her skin and her eyes forced to squint up at him, Neri decided to cut the dancing around and confirm it outright. It did sound like he had said what she thought he meant.

"You mean the whole, what you said to him?"

He dropped to sit on his heels in front of her, his wide, dark eyes showing a swirl of nervous anticipation.

"I mean the whole 'caring about you' thing, yes. It's utterly mad considering we barely know each other. I'm not really the sort of person who gets involved with anyone either, not ever. Too dangerous, and I'm guessing you're the same."

Neri nodded, frightened a single untimed noise might scare him off. He'd said it as 'having feelings' for her originally, and then he'd used another, deeper word to Finn. She couldn't be sure if the thumping inside her was panic or hope.

"I like you," he admitted, his voice almost inaudible. "You probably guessed that much but if you don't feel the same just say so. I mean, I don't expect declarations or anything, I don't know."

He groaned, turning his head away so she couldn't see his whole face. Neri bit her lip, looking over his copper hair that desperately needed washing and the dark eyes ringed with shadows. He had wisps of beard growing around his mouth too and she had the strangest urge to run her fingertips over it.

Probably not the best idea right now.

"I'm not great with words," she started. "I say the wrong thing a lot. I guess I probably do the wrong thing a lot too. This definitely isn't a declaration, it's honestly not."

Niall nodded, chastened.

"But," she continued, averting her gaze to the broken lace on his left boot. "I think I like you and it scares me. I don't trust folk easily, so this is hard."

Niall swung his head up so fast that she flinched and accidentally looked at his face. She stared, unable to fathom the sheer bewildered hope in his eyes.

About drown in an ocean of awkwardness, Neri growled at him instead and threw a light-hearted slap against his chest, almost knocking him backwards.

"You could have just told me," she added. "It's not like I'd have laughed at you or run off crying. I don't really have feelings for folk though."

"What, not normally?"

She shook her head. "Not ever, not like that. I mean, I'm no innocent but there wasn't really anyone in my life before that lingered. Then my family disappeared. I figured survival was all I had left. You were a huge shock to be honest."

Niall laughed as she fixed him with a stern look and issued her final shot.

"But no more going around punching folk, okay? He may have deserved it but that's no excuse."

Grinning with what he no doubt thought was pretend obedience, Niall nodded.

"Whatever you say. I'm happy to be your huge shock, for now, and I promise no more punching unless it's absolutely necessary."

Neri tipped her head sideways, looking away from him. He'd said he liked her so perhaps he would be willing to share things with her now. Then again, she didn't want to cement such wonderful sentiments with sour prying either.

"Why is the Governance so desperate on finding a way through?" she asked. "Why now? And what will they do if they find it?"

Niall dropped to sit beside her, the last knots of angst loosening from his shoulders.

"I'm not sure why now. We reckon they've always been searching, but if your family did have something to do with any of it then you appearing would have sparked them hunting. If we find it first, I'm supposed to eventually travel through to the west and make contact with folk there."

Neri nodded. It sounded so simple, in a very addle-brained and imaginary sort of way.

"Do we know what the pathway through the forest will look like?"

Stories of ancient tunnels through mountains and little wooden carts on rails filtered through her mind.

Niall chuckled. "You sound like you almost believe it's possible this time. There are more accidental ways to travel but it's near impossible to do on purpose."

Neri recalled the vision of autumn and the flickering bird of flame she'd seen in the woods. Emelyn had explained a shimmer to her.

"But someone can travel by shimmer accidentally?" she asked.

He leaned back, surprise wiping across his face.

"You've been doing your research. A shimmer is one of those strange times when the springtime air smells of currents, dried fallen leaves and bonfires. Winter has a waft of a warm breeze bringing you the scent of brightly coloured flowers and heat. That is a shimmer, when the parallel between two different parts of the realm collide and a haze mars the gap."

His voice softened, his mind drifting to places Neri had never been. She kept quiet, awed by the faraway look in his dark eyes.

"You walk through the scorched long-grasses, and you see carriages ahead of you even though there are none around and no lanes for them to travel on, rushing through wintery chill. Only by accident do folk pass through the haze and end up on one side of the forest or the other. Old tales say that ancient folk used to be able to shimmer at will though."

Niall's words, possibly somehow borrowing some of Emelyn's power of creation, invoked a strong sense of delight in Neri's mind. The tiny kernel of childhood still hidden deep inside her cracked, allowing a tiny green bud to grow out and latch onto the visions he created.

"Moonshine says I should leave tomorrow morning," Niall announced. "We can't risk the Governance getting ahead of us, and they probably know more than we do already, them taking Emelyn and coming for you says as much."

Neri twisted her fingers together in her lap. The thought of leaving when she hadn't even seen her room yet sank like a stone in her gut.

"We have the horses now at least," he continued. "That's assuming you're still set on joining me as part of your anti-Governance vendetta, but it will involve travelling further west. With them aware of who we are, it'll might be dangerous."

Neri shrugged. "Wouldn't be the first time we've done something dangerous. What is in the west that we want to risk it for?"

She watched as Niall hesitated, a bashful smile creeping across his face. His eyes picked up a mischievous shine. When he smiled, it made her do the same, even though there was little for them to be cheery about other than Emelyn's safety.

And the fact he apparently likes me.

"There was a reason I wasn't waiting for you in the woods," he said. "Straight after the explosion, I was doing a bit of prying through one of the windows once I'd given everyone the slip."

Neri laughed at the vision of him crouching to peek in random windows.

"I now have a name and a settlement that is of great interest." He straightened his legs out in front of him with a groan. "We'll go have a look around, then there's a friend we can visit who will know more afterwards. He's a scribe of sorts."

When Neri asked how Niall knew this mysterious friend, he winked and tapped the side of his nose secretively.

"I do have friends outside of the sanctuary you know."

Neri snorted. "That makes one of us, I don't have

anyone at all."

"Well, now you have Emelyn and the others." He nudged her shoulder with his. "You have me. We'll leave first thing in the morning. The Governance wants to find the way to the west and we can't risk them making acquaintances over there, or being able to march any kind of fighting force through."

Neri opened her mouth to agree with him but flapped it shut again when he continued, determined strength lacing his tone.

"I didn't realise how important it was until recently, not really. But now I have something and maybe even someone, I hope. I want a world where there's no need to always be looking over our shoulders."

He slid his hand over hers and squeezed, setting the fluttering free inside her belly right up to her chest. The thought was an appealing one.

They'd need to ready themselves for the next journey, but she intended to spend the rest of the day chatting with Emelyn. If Niall honestly believed there was some magical way through the cursed woods, then she wanted the entire history. It might come in handy somewhere along the way.

Niall got to his feet and pulled a wry face.

"Ma and Moonshine will want to throw a party before we go. They knew this would happen eventually and they'll want to give us a proper send-off. I do however have to pick some stuff up first, so I need to disappear for a while, if that's okay?"

Neri gave him a doubtful smile. "You're asking my permission? Not like you."

"Not exactly." He chuckled and held his hand out to her. "But I don't want you to think I'm being unreliable."

She took his hand, her chest fizzling as he hauled her to her feet. Given the triumphant glimmer in his eyes and the mischievous smile, she decided not to comment on exactly what she thought of him.

He doesn't need the ego boost right now.

"Okay," she sighed. "You go off and do your pretend shade thing. I want to talk to Emelyn about some stuff anyway."

Niall groaned and covered his face with his hands, peeking through his fingers.

"The shade thing is actually going to stick, isn't it?"

Neri grinned. "Absolutely, wouldn't want me to think you're being unreliable."

Niall swung a swift arm around her shoulders before she could tease him any further. The closeness chased any words away and the feather-light kiss he dropped onto her cheek moments later removed any hope of coherent thought. Neri could only stand there and stare as he smiled at her and darted into the house.

I left here to rescue a girl I barely knew and came back with a friend and, what, a boyfriend? She took the first steps toward the kitchen, her mind reeling. *Okay, I can cope with this.*

CHAPTER FOURTEEN

Neri stepped into the kitchen, still bewildered by the abrupt change in her relationship with Niall. Fleeting thoughts of coming across Finn darted through her head but disappeared when she saw Emelyn sitting on the counter, her bare heels drumming a soft, uneven beat against the cupboards.

"Niall said he had something to do," Emelyn grumbled, her fingers twitching as she braided her long sunny hair. "I think he just wanted to avoid helping us set up for the party. Oh, by the way, we're having a welcome home party for Moonshine, or maybe it's a welcome home party for me. Then again, it could be a welcome to the family party for you. Why are you all red and flushy?"

Emelyn hopped off the counter, her eyes glimmering as she realised the exact reason for Neri's blushing.

"Ohhh, I see," she grinned. "I'll say no more for the moment, but I did want to talk to you. I heard something while I was captive and it's not something I've ever come across."

Neri frowned and dithered in the silence that followed.

She wasn't sure if this was the kind of information she wanted to hear. When she received no answer, Emelyn continued.

"Does the Tallow's Eve festival mean anything to you?"

Neri shook her head. The words sounded more like Emelyn's mysticism than anything real. They had festivals in the settlements of course to celebrate the harvest or when the signs of the weather turning warmer came. Various places celebrated local achievements of history, but she'd never heard of any Tallow's Eve festival.

"That man was arguing with someone." Emelyn sighed. "He said Tallow's Eve would soon come around again and they were running out of time. He said it had to be then, but they needed to find exactly where the Tallow's Eve festival was being held because it wouldn't be at or near the inn."

Neri looked away, her gaze settling on the door to the hall. She rubbed an idle finger over her bottom lip and sighed.

"Tallow's Eve means nothing to me. Tallow is the stuff they used to use for making candles before we started unearthing tree wax."

She wondered whether to confide in Emelyn about more emotional matters. Emelyn had known Niall longer and might be able to give her some idea about him, but Ma Kath bustled in before she could find the right words.

"Right." Ma eyed them both with uncharacteristically stern determination. "We need to get this party organised before Moonshine has another one of her little *opinions*.

Neri, if you can whip the eggs please, they're in that bowl over there ready. You need to be nice and light with them. Emelyn, you know how we make the breadcake batter."

Before Neri had anything to say on the matter, the bowl appeared in one arm and her hand had been forcibly wrapped around a wooden fork. She watched as Ma Kath's fingers directed hers in acceptable motions until she appeared suitably well trained to continue alone.

"How do I know when these are done?" she asked.

Emelyn laughed. "Ma will be back before then. She and Moonshine love each other but they're a disaster under the same roof. Ma always prays for a shimmer to come and get her by the end of it."

Neri thought about her last possible shimmer and bit her lip. She hadn't mentioned the specifics to anyone yet but Emelyn was her friend. Even though the likelihood of it having happened at all was unbelievable, it would be good to share her more addle-brained moments with someone who wouldn't think she needed serious help.

"When we were camped out on our way to getting you, I saw something. It's probably my imagination playing tricks on me, and maybe a large jot of wishful thinking now, but it's been bugging me all the same."

Having caught Emelyn's attention, Neri lowered her gaze and focused on the monotonous sweeping movements of the wooden fork in her hands.

"The night before I found you, I was the one keeping watch and I saw a fire between the trees. Now this stuff you're all saying about shimmers has clearly gotten to me, but I thought I saw taller trees and there was a sudden chilling wind."

She turned mid-whisk and leaned against the counter next to where Emelyn perched.

"The leaves on the trees became autumnal, red and gold, and the scent in the air changed to currants and harvest. Then I saw what looked like a curling flicker of firelight. Only for a second or two, but I couldn't mistake the fire for anything other than the shape of a large bird. The wind was fierce too even though the heat season was still right behind me."

Her hand picked up the pace, her vicious whisking sending splatters of egg onto her arms. Instead of waiting until the bowl skittered from her vigorous ministrations, she turned and set it on the side.

"I can't believe that a firebird actually exists but it felt so real. I hadn't slept properly for a while or eaten well enough, but for that moment it seemed like the bird was calling to me. I thought it was a crawbird. It looked like one, jagged wings and all, but then it caught alight."

She left the counter and paced toward the back door. She turned and paced back, unable to meet Emelyn's intense gaze.

"The kyne Moonshine says you found in your room is a symbol of firebird protection," Emelyn frowned. "It's unbelievably rare."

Neri paused her pacing and whirled back around. Any hint of ridicule, if it existed, remained completely invisible on Emelyn's face. She had no doubts about her diligence when it came to controlling indoor fires, but she'd left the room for hardly any time at all and yet there the kyne was when she returned.

"Where we come from, to be visited by the firebird indicates you've been marked, blessed," Emelyn insisted. "That's why crawbirds are a symbol of eternity. They're meant to be kin in the old tales."

Neri shook her head. None of it made any logical sense. She began to doubt whether she could handle any more revelations and focused on the bowl she'd been whisking, pounding the egg with furious vigour as Ma came back into the kitchen. The woman's re-appearance reminded Neri that she was supposed to be looking forward to a party, not agonising over fantasy paths to the west and mythical creatures appearing in visions.

Ma peered into her bowl and nodded.

"Good. Emelyn pour those into your bowl and keep mixing. Neri, will you go and help bring the cases in from the front? Be quick and don't let yourself be seen."

It wasn't really a request, more of a good-natured command, but Neri took the opportunity to escape. In the hall, she realised that the front door was closed. Last time she'd looked at that door with any kind of attention, Ma had coerced her away from it.

"You won't find any more doors here that are locked to you."

Moonshine's ethereal voice sounded like meditative floating, but it made Neri jump all the same. She swallowed and placed her hand on the latch. When she flicked it up, the door popped open. With a sudden sense of childlike insecurity, she opened the door wide and turned back to see Moonshine's radiant smile.

"Is all of this real?" she asked. "The path to the west stuff?"

There was a sense of mischief in Moonshine's smile and sparkling eyes, but instead of making Neri feel ridiculed, it settled some of the discomfort in her mind.

"What is real?" Moonshine philosophised. "What matters is that, in the fleeting lives we all lead, we need to make our choices of wrong and right, up and down, forward and backward. You can decide to accept what happens, what you see and feel with your own body and mind, or you can deny it. It is as simple as that and always your choice."

Neri nodded. She couldn't bring herself to voice gratitude but she did manage a small smile. Then she turned and walked out into the blast of dry heat that hammered down.

Matty stood in the middle of the front garden, his legs mired in a mixture of long, brown grass almost dead and wilting wildflowers amongst the briars that snagged at his skin.

He didn't look up when Neri cleared her throat or make any attempt to straighten his slumped shoulders.

Six small wooden crates were piled against the stone wall separating the garden from the lane, so Neri edged forward, skirting round him and wincing as brambles snatched at her bare legs. Seeing his scrunched up face, she knew she should at least make some attempt to rouse him.

"Um, Ma asked me to bring the boxes in?"

Matty turned to face her, his eyes unfocused. Realising she'd not get much sense out of him, Neri picked up the first box. The hefty weight surprised her, as did the clink of glass from inside. She turned to take the box back into the dwelling and faltered.

Matty fell, kneeling in the middle of the grass with his head hung low. Not knowing what else to do, Neri hurried inside. She took the box through to the kitchen and wondered who would be best to deal with Matty. Emelyn was engrossed in mixing the contents of her bowl and Ma was stirring a large black pot over the flames in the fireplace.

"Matty's just sitting out there," she announced. "He didn't seem to register when I spoke to him. Someone might want to make sure he's okay."

She decided it best to broadcast the fact in general and let other folk nominate themselves. Nobody said anything for a moment until Moonshine came into the kitchen, hustling Matty along in front of her. She bodily pressed him into a chair at the table and Neri couldn't stem the flow of pity for him.

Each time she went out for another crate and came into the kitchen to see him looking so defeated, it made her wonder whether the pains of true devotion were worth it. Trying not to dwell on the idea that Niall might one day live to hurt her, assuming she could even keep his interest for that long, she brought in the last crate and used her shoulder to push the front door closed.

Perhaps a party was exactly what they needed. It would serve as a reminder that there were still simple pleasures. The company of friends who cared in a place that could safely be called home. The sense of belonging whizzing through her, dredging a smile to her lips.

Even if I wanted to leave, I have no coin, nothing to trade and nowhere else to go. Nobody to look for. These are good folk, so why can't this be as good a home as any other?

She put the final crate on the kitchen table and stared with no small amount of trepidation at the thick blade-metal bar Ma gave her.

"It's to open the boxes, dear."

Neri blushed as Ma laughed at her surprise. She levered the wooden lid off of the first crate and peered inside. She found a pile of bulging sacking pouches inside and pulled one out at random, staring at the hand-scribed label on the side. *Regarla* wine. She couldn't remember the last time she'd seen wine.

Dark nights and the swipe of blades filled her head. Yes, she could remember.

Poor Hamlin.

The sense of occasion the alcohol brought to the afternoon reminded her strangely of Candletide. Ever since her mama's death, she hadn't celebrated a Candletide or even marked her span-day. Hamlin had tried with Candletide but she hadn't been there long at that point and her grief drove any hope of festivity away.

Pushing the memories aside, Neri pulled the pouches out at random, noting various infusions of elderflower, blackcurrant and perglebry. The next two crates contained mead and apple cider. Ma managed to grab the bar off of her with amused chastisement dancing in her green eyes.

"We will save the rest," Ma said. "Just put the crates in

the corner by the door."

Pleased with her short burst of manual labour, Neri hovered in the hope she would be given something else to do. She wanted to stay involved in the atmosphere of lively jollity that passed between them all.

By the time the heat had abated outside a little and she had set out a large wooden table in the garden, Neri realised she hadn't seen Niall for a long while. She stood in the kitchen instead and tried not to get in the way as Ma and Moonshine circled territorially around discussions of how best to prepare things. She ended up standing in the doorway to the garden, trying to hang up a banner of ribbons that Emelyn had hurriedly strung together.

As she pinned the last bit of ribbon into place, a sudden shift of air around her brought the familiar scent of spice. Her insides burst with a tremor of excited fluttering. Arms wrapped around her waist from behind and she didn't even have time to flinch.

"Did you miss me?" Niall asked.

Remembering his sudden mysterious disappearing act, Neri turned in his embrace to face him.

"I've been too busy."

He didn't ask her what with, just took her hand and led her into the garden. His sudden easy confidence startled her, the hug and the hand-holding a wholly new phenomenon. She worried her hand was clammy but then noticed that his was caked in grit. Niall had clearly taken her acceptance of his feelings as confirmation that they were together, something she was still finding hard to get her head around. Determined not to spoil the moment, she eyed the garden instead.

Moonshine had put her candles to astonishing use. They hung on disks from every available branch and bush, while the sky cast a glittering blanket of shining stars above that swayed with harmonious movement in the flickering shadows thrown up by the soft candlelight.

Neri guided Niall to the long table set on the middle of the grass and gave him her best attempt at a determined stare.

"So where did you disappear to, and don't give me the 'shade stuff' excuse."

He grinned, his lazy smirk and spirited dark eyes suggesting secrets.

"Hamlin gave me instructions before he died that if we came close to finding the pathway, I had to go and get some of his personal things. I went back to the shop to find where he'd hidden them."

Neri smiled, feeling the sadness tug at her heart when she thought of Hamlin. So much had happened and changed since then. She hadn't noticed the horse missing either, but now it was dozing on the other side of the garden fence, just visible through one of the narrow gaps.

"I also had time to look around and I found this."

Niall reached in into his back pocket. He smiled so tenderly that a thousand ridiculous thoughts tumbled through her mind.

"Close your eyes," he insisted.

She did as she was told, anticipation jittering through her skin and making her limbs buzz. With her eyes closed, she couldn't tell what he put in her outstretched hands. Her fingers roved over the surfaces and it felt like a very slim book.

Before she could give in to temptation and open her eyes, a delicate floral scent swirled nostalgia through her. Her eyes snapped open. She didn't notice her body dropping like a stone, or the whack of her knees against the grass. She couldn't even comprehend the sudden tears that blurred her vision as she stared at her gramma's poem book.

The binding, just a simple stitched notebook felt so familiar under her fingers. It even had her crude childhood painting of a firebird rising free from between two trees under a starry night-time sky. It was stuck on with *gar*, but her Gramma had asked for the picture specifically and Neri had spent ages on it.

She raised her head to look at Niall. His uncertain expression of hope and worry only brought further tears to her eyes. She struggled to her feet with the notebook clamped firm between her fingers, her tears falling freely onto her cheeks.

"Hey, I thought it'd be a good surprise." His concerned murmur brought a choke to her throat. "I almost didn't find it but that little girl with the curly blonde hair ran up and asked me if I'd seen you. When I said yes, she said Hamlin told her to keep it safe, threw it at my feet and vanished. I thought it would make you happy?"

Neri had no idea when Hamlin would have found time to get the book from her and ask the girl to hide it, or how the girl had known to wait around for Niall to come back, but it was a kindness that couldn't be ignored.

"I never thought I'd see it again. It's the only thing I had of my gramma's." Glancing down once more to ensure it was definitely real, she smiled through her tears. "I'll *never* forget that you found this again for me. Never."

Niall's worry faded and his relief mixed with a bemused smile. His thoughtfulness filled Neri's head with a thousand buzzing possibilities, but there was one truth she could settle on without too much lingering doubt.

If I'm going to go with this whole me and him thing, I might as well do it all in.

She threw her arms around his shoulders and held on tight.

"Niall put her down, she's not going anywhere." Emelyn tittered nearby.

Neri let go but his arm slid around her hips, holding her close to him.

"Do you want a drink?" he asked.

Neri glanced over at the pouches she'd unpacked on the table. A motley assortment of wooden cups stood nearby, highlighting just how homely the sanctuary felt now. She took the most battered cup and held it out as Niall poured some kind of wine into it, then she peered into his cup.

"I didn't think shades needed to drink."

He rolled his eyes. "I still can't believe that's going to stick."

Neri grinned and settled to sipping her drink. The first sweet tang of the fruit followed by the swift burn of alcohol made her splutter. The gentle shaking of Niall's chest indicated that he'd noticed and was laughing at her but she didn't care.

Only the gentle sway of fear that the evening would turn out to be a miraculous dream could mar the euphoria that her tipsy mind swam in. Even as her thoughts turned towards their inevitable journey, she couldn't muster any excitement or trepidation.

She settled on the grass beneath the fragrant haze of the *liliam*, amused that even in the peace of the garden Niall was quick to stay by her side. Ma provided blankets and cushions to sit on and they lounged in lazy comfort, Neri with her shoulder pressing into Niall's. Matty barely stayed. Niall avoided Finn, whose bruised cheek from the recent punch had been explained away by some mysterious accident shrouded in hurt pride. Finn didn't hang around long either, muttering something none of them caught before he disappeared.

When night had fallen and even Emelyn looked ready to drop, Ma suggested they could leave the clearing up until the morning. Everyone looked up as Moonshine came out of the kitchen, her mouth pressed thin.

"Eva is gone, Matty too," she announced. "He must have helped her out. No Finn either but that's not entirely unusual."

Ma groaned to her feet. "We should have seen it coming but there's little we can do tonight. Come on, Emelyn. Neri and Niall need time to discuss things I'm sure."

Neri flushed before realising that by 'things' Ma must have meant their upcoming journey. She nodded goodnight as the others formed a solemn procession into the house.

"I'm about ready to drop right here," Niall murmured.

"As Ma says, nothing we can do tonight."

"You're not worried about Eva telling the Governance exactly where to find this place? I didn't even think to ask, but wasn't there someone watching her, or Matty?"

"Her door was bolted from the outside. I suppose Ma and Moonshine thought they could trust Matty. It wouldn't be the first time we've had to relocate though. The worst part will be Ma and Moonshine under the same roof longer than a few days. Their arguments are legendary."

Neri sighed. She couldn't be as laidback about losing the sanctuary as he seemed to be, but the evening had swept an irrepressible languor through her limbs. As if he sensed it, Niall inched his arms around her.

"Everyone will be safe until morning," he promised. "As it is, I'm more than satisfied if you want to continue using me as a pillow until then."

Neri knew she should make excuses and go up to her room. She hadn't even seen it since leaving to rescue Emelyn. But Niall was comfortable and she trusted him.

Much more than I trust myself right now. She smiled.

"How can I refuse such a self-deprecating sacrifice?"

She twisted to curl her side against him, her legs over his, and smiled as he flinched at the bold move. They would have to deal with issues and dangers in the light of the new day, but for now she had a brief moment of peace, a rarity. Without a word, she dropped her head against Niall's chest and tiredness stole her consciousness some moments later.

CHAPTER FIFTEEN

Waking up with a boy wasn't the dramatic scandal Neri had somehow imagined it might be. The light had just broken over the garden, the purple sky turning to gold, and the warm air was still. She lifted her head to find Niall already awake, his fingers curling idly through strands of her hair. When she sat up, he let her go.

"We'll have to leave straight away," he said without greeting. "I'm always packed ready but there's time enough for you to get whatever you need to bring."

Neri stood, uneasy. His matter-of-fact manner and the lack of any smile sent rivulets of dread racing over her skin.

Does he regret things now he's had time to think?

She nodded, turning to slip away into the house, but he launched to his feet and caught hold of her hand.

"Are you sure about this?" he asked. "You'd still be safer here with the others."

Neri pulled her hand free and folded her arms.

"You'd rather I didn't come with you after all? If the whole thing with me and you- if you've changed your mind, don't use my safety as an excuse."

Niall stared at her. Instead of the concerned frown or defensive scowl she expected, his lips lifted.

"You're pretty when you're annoyed at me."

Neri blinked. "What? How does that have anything to do with anything?"

She froze with her insides skittering as he stepped closer and grabbed both of her hands to hold her still.

"I don't want you to feel like you have to do this. I do, but you can still back out. Nobody would think badly of you."

"Do you want me to stay now?" she stared at his shoulder, too afraid of the answer to meet his gaze.

"I do and I don't."

"Wow, amazing clarity, thanks for that."

He chuckled. "I want you here because you'll be safe. That's the sensible thing to want."

His arms crept around her waist, stealing her breath with the lightest of holds as her hands settled on his shoulders.

"And the non-sensible part of you?" she asked, her voice sticking. "What does that part want?"

He pressed his forehead to hers. "Your sparkling company, it turns out, or whatever parts of it I'm lucky enough to have. I should insist you stay here but I value my extremities and your nose is going all scrunchy again. Go, get your stuff."

Neri ignored the mention of her scrunchy nose and stepped back.

"This isn't your attempt at doing a runner while my

back is turned?"

He grinned wickedly. "You know, I never thought of that. Go on, I'll be waiting for you in the hall."

Still not entirely trusting, Neri walked into the kitchen with a purposeful stride. The moment she was out of his sight, she dashed through the dwelling and up to her room.

Someone had put her box of paintings and her pack on her bed, and she rifled through to check the contents, making sure Hamlin's effects were still in her pack along with the rest. She threw in some blankets, candles and her gramma's notebook, then pulled a handful of aged parchment from the box, closing her eyes as the subtle ghost of *liliam* and *meadowsweet* wafted out with them. It was frivolous to take space in her pack with them, but she folded them as best she could and slipped them in beside Emelyn's book.

Only then did she notice Dog sitting beside the bed, doleful brown eyes watching her. If by some insane chance they did find a way through to the west, it wouldn't be fair to drag Dog through with them. Whatever stuff Niall had planned would also likely take them closer to danger. She dropped to her knees and wrapped her arms around his furry neck.

"You know you have to stay here. You can't come with me. Behave and do what Ma, Emelyn and Moonshine tell you. If I can, I will come back for you. You've been my best friend."

She held on for uncountable moments until Dog huffed and shuffled free. Neri grabbed her pack and walked to the door, turning back to look at her room.

I'm going to miss this place, but I will end up coming back. She clenched her fist around her pack strap and huffed in a deep breath to stem the threat of tears burning her eyes. *When we don't find a way through the woods, we'll come home.*

Niall looked up as she came down the stairs, Ma, Moonshine and Emelyn waiting behind him in the hall.

"You will always be one of us and one of the family." Emelyn sniffed, folding Neri into a tight hug. "Never forget that. We'll see you soon. This won't be a proper goodbye."

Neri patted her friend's back, concerned that Emelyn seemed to be fearing the worst. She glanced at Moonshine. The woman smiled and nodded but there was a glint of sadness in her eyes.

Even she doesn't think we'll make it back. Neri couldn't help the shiver of panic that ran through her. *But I have to trust Niall. Mama said to trust Hamlin and he said to trust Niall, who hasn't exactly steered me wrong or betrayed me yet.*

Niall led the way outside to two waiting horses. Neri swallowed a choke in her throat as she took the reins he handed to her. He seemed to be continuing on with the large black horse that had pulled the cart before, but the stocky grey mare now standing alongside him snuffled at her fingers and gave her such a lazy glance that Neri had no fear of riding her.

Ma, Moonshine and Emelyn stood in the dwelling's doorway to wave them off, so Neri forced a smile in reply.

As Niall set off, her horse followed his with a loud huff.

She held the smile successfully until they reached the end of the lane then allowed the true sense of desolation wipe through her.

Niall rode alongside her and reached out to take her fingers in his. Even without him saying another word about it, Neri knew going with him was the only option. To stay at the sanctuary without him would have turned her home into a prison once more, and she still had to find out what information the Governance thought she had of theirs. If dreaming of an actual future with Niall was becoming a possibility, she wanted to do it without any catches. She took a slow, deep breath and steadied herself to be at least half useful for what might lie ahead.

They let silence reign throughout the journey. Neri wanted to ask questions about Niall and his past but knew that would bring up the supposed truth that he was originally from the west, which went against everything she'd ever known and been told.

After a short distance, Niall had her wrap her hair in a large deep red cloth, insisting she would be too easily recognised.

"Why don't you have to wrap yours then?" she asked irritably.

He grinned. "I can hide well enough when I have to, and they haven't caught me yet to know I'm of interest to them."

Neri grumbled under her breath as she wound the thick fabric around her hair and they rode on. She put up with the itch it cast over her scalp, relieved beyond belief when the suns started to wane again. They'd exchanged the wider lanes for narrow ones and thin paths through woodland, and Niall smiled when he said she could remove the covering.

Sweaty and irate, she hauled it off and resisted the urge to drop it into a deep ditch alongside the lane.

"*Finally*. So, are you going to bother telling me where we're going now?"

"We'll be there in another hour or so, I think."

"Where is there?"

Niall sighed. "Somewhere information could be stored. Could have gotten there in half the time but some lanes are more forgotten than others and we can't risk being seen."

Neri nodded and cast her eyes back over quick flickers of golden-brown fields through the high hedgerows and trees. Autumn season would be with them soon enough and her sensibilities always became conflicted when the night air began to bite again, the trees aging to shed their leaves with glorious fire-bright colours.

To her, autumn felt like her old settlement, like kicking up drifts of leaves on the walk home from the watch training fields, picking the plump, ripe berries from the bushes she passed and trying to remove the tell-tale blue stains from her fingers before getting home.

Her gramma had disappeared in autumn. Mama had died in autumn. Now, a winterspan later, Neri's sheltered life of fable and daydreaming had been shattered to splinters.

"Emelyn mentioned overhearing something when she was captive, the Tallows Eve festival. Do you know of it?"

Niall shook his head. "It's a weird choice of wording,

Tallows Eve. It's definitely not a celebration I've ever heard of."

"The only thing I can think of is that tallow has something to do with candles. It's probably just the name of some obscure little settlement celebration in the middle of nowhere that has nothing to do with anything."

She sighed, sagging over her horse's neck. Niall smiled with fond affection, one side of his mouth hitched up with amusement. The mere hint of such a dedicated stare made her pulse leap. Flustered, she let the first thought in her head tumble out of her mouth.

"So if you really are from the west, what's it like there?"

Niall's face froze for a long moment. When he glanced at her, there was no smile, only nervous hesitation.

"You don't believe it."

She shrugged. "I have no reason to believe it, not when everything I've known says otherwise. But convince me. Or lie to me if you have to. Paint me pretty tales of this magical place hardly anyone has ever seen."

"If you want. The west is slightly cooler than the east, vast fields of lush grass so nutrient-dense it's almost always a golden green, not like here with the browning greens and yellows. The earth is softer too, the trees much taller. They tower up to the skies, some with pale pink trunks that would take actual time to walk around."

Memories of vast trees and burning flickers of flame between them fluttered into Neri's mind.

"Well, it definitely sounds magical. Is it hotter there then? You're always wrapped up in shirts and cloaks while the rest of us are dripping from the heat."

Niall's lopsided smile reappeared like magic.

"It is colder in the winter there, but we get heat seasons too. Would you prefer I didn't wear the shirts and cloaks at all?"

"I'm just trying to learn, nothing to do with you so calm your ego."

"Of course," he grinned, not fooled. "You know how I first thought you might have a certain interest in me?"

Neri rolled her eyes. She couldn't pinpoint the moment she realised she liked him in that way, but she didn't intend to spoil his fun.

"Girls don't give boys apples just for the fun of it. Seriously though, you want to know how I figured out what I felt for you was more than just curiosity?"

She nodded. The sky had dimmed now, the suns sinking low behind Niall's head, causing speckles of soft light to shine on his copper hair. Soon they would have to go sneaking around somewhere, most likely in the dark, on what she guessed would most likely turn out to be a potentially dangerous dead end.

"I knew because when I first thought you were so ruffled at meeting Finn, I was jealous."

Neri shrugged. "I probably stared at him because I wanted to work him out. He acted so confident but always I felt wary around him, even right from the start."

"That and you didn't want to make it obvious that you were totally crazy about me."

Neri decided not to dignify that with an answer, mainly because she didn't have one to hand that would be suitable for denting his ego. He accepted the small smile she gave him though without teasing her any further, and sank into the silence that followed as they rode on.

Night soon fell around them and Neri's anticipation rose. She tried to keep herself steady and awake, even though an explosion and the end of the realm probably wouldn't liven up her horse up any, but with the distorted shadows looming around them and fatigue tugging at her eyelids it was impossible.

"Are we riding through the night?" she asked.

Niall nodded. "For a bit longer. We're not far off now though."

"And what exactly are we hoping to find? Other than the wonderfully vague answer of 'information'." She rolled her eyes when he hesitated. "It's a bit late to start getting squeamish about honesty now. Here, I'll share something with you if you're honest with me."

Before he could answer either way, she pulled her pack forward to rest between her thighs and her horse's neck, pulling out a handful of pages.

Niall squinted at them in the echo of starlight above.

"This one looks familiar," he murmured, tapping the top one. Then he lifted his head and caught her astonished gaze. "Not as in I've seen the drawing before, but what it's of."

Neri frowned. Her gramma had asked for several specific paintings even though she had very little artistic talent back then. Even so, the paintings in her hands were surprisingly detailed, much more than she remembered being capable of. She sorted through the pile, the memories swarming.

"When I left our home after my mama died, I couldn't take much with me. Just the poem book you saved from Hamlin's." Neri pulled her necklace free of her top and let the charm dangle between them. "And this. I had to keep room for clothes and food but still travel light. I left these drawings back at the dwelling along with everything else. But then I go to Hamlin's and the Governance come looking for me. They take Emelyn because she's wearing my cloak. Amis knows my given name, and my gramma's. They're looking for a way west and so are you. Now you recognise an image my gramma asked me to paint. I'm struggling."

Niall laid a hand on her shoulder and squeezed, before reaching out and plucking the entire handful of pages from her. As he leafed through them, Neri let her mind unspool. It all pointed to one inconvenient, astonishing truth, that everything folk were saying about the west might be real.

"What's this?"

Niall held out something small and Neri took it, a small scrap of thick card lacquered with *gar*. She pulled it close to her face and frowned at the tiny words beneath the small drawing she'd made of a barn with a large candle alight inside it.

"It says 'tallow' and 'grain', I think. It's too small to make out the second word," she murmured.

"It's almost like a calling card," Niall added. "Inns use them often to recognise returning customers and welcome them back."

"Frequent inns often, do you?"

He chuckled. "If I have to."

"The words have been added later. I don't remember them, but that could be my gramma's scribing. Tallow could be the candle, could be linked to this Tallow's eve Emelyn was talking about. Then again, it could be pure coincidence."

"It's not a million miles away either from my friend's dwelling," Niall said.

Neri took the rest of the drawings back from him and placed them inside her back before flicking her fingers at the dark forest ahead.

"Well by all means, lead on. Although I don't see how we're going to make it all that way without finding some proper food or water for the horses."

To her surprise, Niall smiled.

"You let me worry about that. We're not too far away now."

He pointed, and Neri squinted at the tangle of dark wooded trees in the far distance.

"Isn't that…"

He nodded. "The cursed forest. Why do you think the sanctuary is based where it is? We're further south than the Governance stronghold, don't worry. But our destination is on the boundary."

"And our destination is?"

"We're going to meet a friend. He's a bit illusive but don't worry, I'll keep you safe."

They carried on, skirting around wider lanes and tracks, keeping to the shade of the woods mostly. Neri's mind wandered, but never far from the Governance, her family and the cursed forest as they drew closer to the dark edge of it, waiting for them like a set of jaws ready to snap.

Even putting the whole cursed forest thing aside, the Governance has always been interested in my family. Why else would they have a box of my childish drawings?

She scanned her memory to mentally walk through their old dwelling, but the recollection dusty and resistant to form clearly. Other than her gramma's poetry book and the box of drawings, she couldn't remember anything that might have interested the Governance enough for them to take. The kitchen had always been full of pouches and some of her gramma's herbal remedies, but mostly just her mama's jams and breadcakes. She'd left her small collection of raggedy toys behind in the tiny room that had been hers and her small collection of clothes. Even the larger room split by curtains and wooden boards that her gramma and mama shared had held nothing secretive, no hidden floorboards or panels, not even any tradables or stash of coin.

Why only the drawings, what's so special about them? Could there be something in what Gramma asked me to draw, some kind of story that hid a secret about the Governance or this supposed mystical pathway through the border forest?

When she sighed, her eyes blurring on the endless rows of trees they rode past, she realised Niall had been glancing at her worriedly every minute or so.

"Go on," she sighed. "You're dying to ask something, I can tell."

"Okay, but don't shout at me or anything. How much do you know about your papa?"

Neri hadn't been expecting that. She didn't even bother thinking about him nowadays, the man who had found out about her existence and quickly admitted that he wanted nothing to do with them.

"Enough to know he's not around. He left straight after I was born, and he and my mama were never officially united. I had a picture of him, or Mama did. She never knew that I found him two winterspans before she died. Then she got sick and I couldn't bring myself to tell her. Gramma *hated* him."

"You found him?" Niall asked, surprised.

"I did some digging with the locals, checked some old settlement records and things. I even went to see him but he had a new life and didn't want to know me."

Niall seemed to struggle with his thoughts for several moments, his lips twisting back and forth.

"I thought maybe, given that he had your drawings and stuff back there-"

"You thought *Amis* was my papa?" Neri snorted. "This isn't one of Emelyn's fanciful fables. I'm not some secret lovechild of a Governance leader. I guess I can see why you thought it, but no."

She froze as Niall pulled his horse to a sudden halt, her horse happily copying, any chance for a break. Neri waited, thudding beginning in her limbs and her chest.

Then she heard it, the unmistakeable rattle of wheels on hard ground.

"Patrols," Niall whispered. "Or worse. Nobody else would be mad enough to be out here that late."

Neri tensed as he turned his horse and set off at a

plunging pace into the trees. Neri urged her horse after him, her hands tight around the reins as the pace turned bumpy.

She ducked one low branch and dodged sideways to avoid a huge clump of leaves. Crouching low over her horse's neck, she glanced back at the darkness looming behind them.

Sharp pain broke across her face as she turned forward again, her agonised squeal lost to breathlessness. She couldn't uncurl her hands from the reins, unsure if the branch that had caught her square in the face had left some kind of sap or dew, or drawn blood.

The slightest hint of day lit the skies above, giving Neri more illumination to see with. The carousel of shadows blurred around her, but she could see Niall and that was enough comfort to keep her moving forward without bursting into frustrated tears.

As Niall slowed up ahead and turned his horse sideways, his eyes roved over her face and he grimaced.

"Your head's bleeding," he said.

Neri forced her fingers free of the rein as her horse snatched at the nearest available bit of greenery. She touched her fingertips to her temple.

"Have you got some water and a bit of cloth?" she asked. "No sense stopping, and I can patch this up myself on horseback."

Niall shook his head and pointed forward. A subtle trickle of water filled Neri's ears and relief swelled. The horses could drink while she cleaned her wound, then they would continue on to whoever Niall was taking them to see next.

Her horse huffed when she insisted on following Niall, but the sound of the stream grew louder and almost immediately Niall was stopping again.

Neri hesitated as he swung down from his horse. Her limbs felt heavier than mountains but she tried to swing her leg over her horse's neck. Niall appeared beside her before she could manage it, firm hands sliding over her thighs to her hips. She tried not to grumble when he helped her down, but the shadowed amusement on his face showed all the same.

He led both horses to the edge of the stream and left them tethered for a drink and a rest, then found her a large rock to sit on. Neri shivered, wishing she still had her cloak. The days were scorching but now the nights were hinting at the colder weather yet to come. Before she could work to hide her shivers, Niall swept his cloak around her shoulders.

She sat obediently while he got a strip of cloth from his pack and dipped it in the stream, dabbing at her forehead.

"There, almost as good as new."

Neri blinked, caught all of a sudden by how close he was leaning, his fingers now moving over the uncut side of her face, warmth stroking down her cheek.

We haven't even kissed yet, not properly, and I'm following him halfway across the realm on some mad mission.

Niall seemed to be frozen in the same timeless trap as she was, his eyes fixed on hers. Her pulse began to pound a slow rhythm as he inched closer.

Neri heard the loud beating of her heart in her ears moments before irritation flashed across Niall's face. Then the beating sound became the rhythmic clop of hooves somewhere nearby.

The suns were beginning their assent over the horizon given the slightest tinge already growing across the sky, but Niall's gaze lingered on her face a moment longer before he helped her up and untethered their horses. This time he held out his hand to give her leg a boost so she could mount, and she did the same with her foot for him.

"We'll have to risk it," he whispered. "Wrap your hair again and keep your head down."

Neri grabbed the dark red fabric and bound her hair, careful not to aggravate the cut on her forehead. In the pre-morning stillness they rode at a steady walk until they reached a lane, the echo of hoofbeats still somewhere behind them.

"It's a common route and curfew is over now the suns are on the way up," Niall murmured as they rode along the lane. "Don't speak to anyone. Don't make too much eye contact."

Neri rolled her eyes. "Obedience, got it. Where are we going anyway?"

Niall glanced across with a broad grin. "I'm not sure I like the sound of you being obedient, much less entertaining. Also not convinced you could manage it. But before you get all grouchy again, we are on our way to visit the wisest scholar on all things Governance-related, of course."

Neri frowned, the pull of sleepiness dragging at her

eyelids. She focused on her hands around the reins but the gentle roll of her horse's gait was convincing her to lean forward and have a little rest. If she fell off, so be it.

"Is there anything I need to know about them, or where we're headed?" she asked, hiding a yawn behind her hand.

"His name is Mikael. We just call him Mik. He's very wise."

She nodded. "I think Emelyn mentioned him once. She said he was one of the five folk she trusted."

"They've been friends for a long while but don't get to see each other often now. Was I one of the five?"

"Yep, me too apparently. Look at me having a real friend for once."

She turned her head with a smile to look at him as he chuckled and reached for her hand. Having gone from a life of hugs in as a child to a whole winterspan without any contact at all, Neri found that Niall's easy habit of touching her still made her insides go all unnecessary.

"Well, aren't we blessed," he said.

Neri nodded, keeping one eye on him as he focused on the lane ahead.

Blessed in a couple of ways, for now at least.

She considered the information she had so far. If there really was a magic path through to the west then the Governance had a head start with unlimited resources for searching. But if they truly didn't know where to start looking, then at least they were running as blind as she and Niall seemed to be.

She thought of the kyne that lay in her pack under the pictures of fantasy lands and creatures. Moonshine and others insinuated that a firebird had arrived in the room and left the kyne for her. Whether that was some kind of clever ploy to involve her deeper in their beliefs, she couldn't tell. Her gramma's *Lamentation* poem began to circle her mind, tugging at her to lose herself in the possibility of the impossible.

The vivid scorch marks she remembered on the walls of her room at the sanctuary suggested the legitimacy of it, but then she still couldn't be sure. Wishing she'd had more time to learn any secrets her family may have held, Neri sighed aloud.

"You're deep in thought. Want to share with me?" Niall asked.

Surprised by the sound of his voice, Neri shifted in her seat to face him.

"I'm thinking it all through. Moonshine was insistent that I take that kyne and Emelyn said it was a sign that a firebird had taken me under its protection. I'm struggling with the whole idea of it."

Niall opened his mouth then shut it again. His fingers tapped an irritated rhythm on his reins and she caught the subtle repetitive bounce of his toes against his horse's side.

"I know you're not going to like it," he began. "I think your family came from the west, or at least they would have been descended from someone who was. You may still not believe it, but that makes you one of us too."

Neri let that sink in. She had to at least consider it was a possibility. While folk often had gifts from the land, they were small skills left over from the suggestion of a much older, more magical age. Magic wasn't even mentioned much anymore, except as fables and tales. There weren't any ways to study the supposed sorcery of old, no lessons or old books that she'd ever seen. Some even believed the west itself was a myth and the forest simply full of beasts and traps until it dropped away into endless water.

Carefully aiming for a non-confrontational way to phrase her question, she took the plunge.

"So, Emelyn talks of magic and shimmers and mythical creatures, I get that. There's the west out there somewhere as a whole different part of our realm, and I get that too. But can anyone actually do magic beyond the normal sorts of land-gifts most get born with?"

She paused, a thousand previously forbidden questions running riot.

"Are you going to tell me that things like *soul-shades* actually do exist?" she continued, her voice catching. "And if firebirds do, then what about horcupogs, or unicorns, or dragons? Do they all exist too? Can folk fly, or wield fire or bring down mountains with their bare hands?"

Surrendering herself to the absurdity of the idea that the whole situation now felt alarmingly real, Neri took a deep breath and tried not to laugh at the alarmed wideness of Niall's eyes.

"Sorry. Let's start somewhere simple," she suggested. "Did you come here on purpose?"

"I found an unexpected opportunity. I took it and followed instructions until I found Hamlin. It was chilly here then, and unfriendly. I didn't know what a real home felt like though, not really, so I didn't miss much from the west."

Neri caught the bitter lilt to his voice as he assessed his memories and looked up. Frowning, she sought for a way to ease the pain twisting on his face.

"I'm sorry, it's not my place to ask."

Glancing away, she rotated back in one swift movement when she felt Niall's fingers tightening around her hand. Strange that the sensation of his hold felt so normal, so right.

"Don't say that," he insisted softly. "This is all stuff that I know I'll have to tell you eventually. I'm no scribe though, and you'd be best off asking Emelyn or Moonshine, or even Ma, about the complexities on the other side."

Neri waited, her throat constricting. He might give her some kind of brush-off still or tell her to wait until they got back to the sanctuary. Or perhaps he hoped his mysterious friend Mik would tell her instead.

"I didn't want to tell you any of it in case you weren't ready," he continued. "But now I don't know, perhaps it would have been better to drop it in gradually. I keep thinking you're going to dash off in disbelief and leave me."

Neri scoffed and allowed herself a weak smile when he frowned at her.

"It's just strange that I even believe any of this," she admitted. "It only just dawned on me that maybe I *could* believe it, although I'm not saying I do, yet. But I am curious, I guess."

She flushed and wondered whether the time would come where she could see Emelyn again and ask her some avid questions. Catching the brooding frown leaving Niall's face, his shoulders lowering slightly in relaxation, Neri tried to lighten the mood.

"So, to clarify, you're not actually a *soul-shade*, are you?"

She smiled and stuck her tongue out a little, hoping that would communicate her ebbing mood. Niall regarded her for a long moment, his expression unreadable and his eyes still dark as the day dawned fast around them. Then he lifted her hand and laid a tender kiss on her palm. He let her fingers go, but not before giving her a flicker of his devilish smile, the one that made his eyes crinkle. Any good intentions she might have held onto went *squish*.

"You'll have to wait and see," he teased.

Neri chuckled as he winked at her. She wanted to make some witty retort but exhaustion removed any hope of wit from her head. Every bone in her body, especially the ones she was sitting on, were screaming with protest.

"We're almost there now," Niall said, as if he could read her thoughts. "Mik's quirky but you can speak openly with him and he's always good fun."

Neri forced her eyes to stay open and fixed her bleary gaze on the lane ahead. Niall led them through yet another swathe of woodland until the meandering lane became a steep hill of dirt, carpeted over with tree needles already dropping.

Neri leaned forward as the horses laboured up the steep incline and soon a dwelling came into view up ahead. The stone cottage had been thatched with a straw roof and wide windows still firmly shuttered, an abundance of bushes growing either side of the door.

"I feel like we've come to see some kind of sorcerer for a spell," she whispered. "Like something out of one of the ancient fables."

Niall laughed as he dismounted and this time Neri succumbed to letting him help her down. Her ankle spasmed with feeling as they hit the ground and she winced at the ache in her hips.

Niall slid his arm around her waist before she could even draw breath, simple as that. Instead of shrinking away from the contact like she might have done with anyone else, Neri nestled against him instead. Niall wasn't just anyone. He nudged her and leaned close to whisper as they approached the door.

"Oh, you're not far off actually with the sorcerer thing. Mik's as magic as I am, in his own way."

CHAPTER SIXTEEN

The relaxed hang of Niall's shoulders and the steady roll of his hips told Neri that she had nothing to fear, but the habit of wariness was a hard one to curb, even with him around. He walked right up to the wooden door and knocked three loud raps that rang out through the silent morning.

Neri rolled her teeth over her bottom lip in nervous anticipation as the door opened a crack to reveal two large blue eyes peeking at them. The door swung open and a waft of airy lightness swept out. When her gaze did settle on their host, Neri got a surprise. She'd been expecting some wise old man, grey and grizzled with piercing eyes, not a serene young one with messy pale gold hair sticking up at all angles.

"Well, Niall, it's been a long time since you came knocking at my door, and you've brought a friend."

The young man leaned forward, plucked Neri's hand free from her side and swept a deft kiss onto her knuckles before she could react. She caught the almost instinctive stiffening in Niall's posture and tugged her hand free, flushing deeply.

"Now then, I'm surprised by you." The man winked at her. "Niall always travels alone, rarely speaks to a soul, and yet he's anchoring you so tight your pretty head will pop."

Neri frowned at his booming laughter and glanced sideways in time to catch the rueful smile on Niall's lips.

"You'll have to forgive me." The man grinned wider. "I love to tease folk and I so rarely get any visitors. Niall's especially fun to torment because he reacts so easily. But I'm being rude. My name is Mik and you're welcome in my home, come in."

Mik turned and headed into the long hallway. It ran all the way to another wooden door at the end which might have led to a garden or into the woods surrounding the dwelling. Wooden stairs led up the side of the left wall and two doors stood on either side of the hall.

She looked down in surprise to find bare dirt beneath her boots instead of floorboards. Niall pushed her in front of him and she took cautious steps after Mik as he headed through the doorway to their left.

"I'm surprised you haven't tried to insult me yet, Niall." His voice floated back to them. "Is this young lady dimming your defensiveness somewhat? I'm intrigued."

Neri paused to look at Niall's smile, sheepish with resigned embarrassment.

"Would it be so hard to believe I'm just glad to see an old friend, and that I don't want a verbal sparring match?" he asked.

As they followed Mik, Neri failed to hold in a low

breath of awe. The room was entirely covered underfoot with earth and sprouting plants from every spare space. Trees grew in large pots, towering up the walls and across the ceiling, flowers growing here and there from the floor. The overwhelming ambience of nature made Neri's wary defences flutter away on the tiny breeze that stroked past her face from the wide, unshuttered windows.

She looked around in awe before turning to Mik. His tall, bear-like stature made him look almost cuddly, but the twinkling blue eyes revealed some hint of a fiendishly intelligent mind that worked within.

"Now, tell me." Mik faced Neri with a broad smile. "First, what is your name and second, how many deep dark secrets do I have to spill in order for Niall to feel uncomfortable?"

His eyes danced with a burst of naughtiness and Neri glanced at Niall, who watched the exchange with wide-eyed bemusement.

"My name is Neri. I have no idea how much I don't know about him so you can start, and I'll let you know when you hit on something interesting."

Raising his eyebrows, Mik watched her with renewed interest. He waved his arm at a mattress decorated with a stylish woven throw that served as a seat.

Neri curled onto it, relieved that Niall dropped down next to her with no sense of ceremony and that Mik sat opposite them.

"We will leave the necessary discussions for later, I think," Mik decided. "First, tell me news. How's the family doing?"

He turned his attentions to Niall, leaving Neri free to get a better look at the room. She couldn't see anything that indicated this was a Governance scholar or even a mild enthusiast, but then she supposed he would want to keep such things hidden. Her gaze snagged instead on a cluster of tomato plants extending from a plastic growbag in the corner of the room, heavy with ripe offerings, and a hanging bag of muslin pockets from which spilled over with small red berry plants. Famished, she tried not to stare too hungrily.

"Moonshine has returned to the sanctuary for the moment," Niall said. "We'd urge you to do the same but of course you'd give it no attention."

Mik nodded his agreement and Neri crossed her legs on the mattress. She couldn't admit her sudden immense hunger at seeing natural produce, but she flushed when her stomach voiced the issue for her loud enough to carry down the hill and on to the nearest settlement.

"Ma and Emelyn are safe too," Niall continued. "Although Emelyn had a brush with the Governance. They had her for a good span of days before Neri managed to get her out."

Neri turned at the sound of her name and caught his affectionate smile. She bit her lip and tried to smile back, ending up with a grimace. She didn't want to think back to that day.

"Is Emelyn okay?" Mik asked. "Other than being safe I mean?"

Neri regarded him a little more critically. The undertone of anxiety sounded out like a bell and she wondered whether there was something there other than just acquaintance between this eclectic hermit and her first real friend.

"She seems to be, yeah." Niall looked to Neri for confirmation. "Dippy as ever. Finn is being an absolute arrogant arse as usual, doing nothing of value to anyone."

Neri smiled properly then and almost managed to hold back the quiet snort. Both men turned to look at her and she assumed herself in safe enough company to be a little playful herself.

"That's not exactly a good enough reason to punch him though, is it?"

To her surprise and delight, Niall's cheeks tinged pink and he looked ruefully at her through lowered eyelids. Despite Mik's presence, he leaned over and took her hand, his thumb rubbing across her knuckles.

"He deserved it, but I did promise, no more punching."

Neri turned her attention back to Mik then, aware of Niall's fingers still clinging onto hers.

"Well I never. Is this emotional growth, Niall?" Mik asked. "Punching folk to defend a lady's honour?"

Liking the bashful side she was seeing to Niall, Neri watched them argue good-naturedly for a while until Mik again apologised for his rudeness and offered food.

"I hope you'll both stay a night or two. I have a room upstairs for you and there is much I feel we should discuss."

He disappeared through the doorway and moments later there were clanking and thudding sounds from across the hall. Niall took the opportunity to shuffle closer.

"Colourful friends you've got." Neri smirked at him.

He murmured an agreement, but his eyes were relaxed and dopey. The overwhelming sense of safety, of being hidden away from the horrors of the realm outside, filled her with a warm peacefulness.

Mik returned with a large wooden tray which held honey-bread that smelled fresh, pale cheese that crumbled at the touch, large root-bulbs flush and red, and a small bowl holding a mix of chopped foliage. With restless hunger, Neri struggled to keep her eyes from staring at the beautiful sight.

Niall showed no such politeness, leaning forward and breaking off a chunk of bread, cutting cheese and grabbing the salad he wanted. Neri glanced at Mik who grinned and inclined his head in mock chivalry, indicating she should tuck in. Wine was produced once they'd eaten, with fruit and breadcakes that Mik insisted he'd baked himself.

"I love the natural life and it rewards me well. Now we should discuss what brings you here."

Niall quickly detailed Hamlin's death, skirting over it with rapid pace. Mik admitted he had heard the news, his face pensive. Then Niall told of Emelyn's capture and finally of Eva's betrayal. The first real shake in Mik's expression came when Niall explained about Matty's desertion. His face fell, his eyes widening with shock. Eventually he sighed sadly.

"With any luck, he will remember his allegiance before it's too late."

Niall shrugged. "Maybe. We know the Governance is looking for a way through the cursed forest, we've always known that, but now they're hunting Neri too."

Mik's sandy eyebrows disappeared under his fringe. "Explain?"

Neri sighed as Niall squeezed her hand.

"It's a long story, but they were swarming around when my mama died, and my gramma. Then I insisted on helping get Emelyn from them, but we ran into the same man who watched while his firing squad killed Hamlin." She clenched her fists, a flash of rage balling in her gut. "His name is Amis."

Mik seethed through his teeth before she could go on.

"He is pretty much as high up the Governance chain as they go," he said.

She nodded. "I thought he would be. He had my old drawings as well, and they should have been back at the dwelling I grew up in, or burned as useless fire-fodder. I don't know why he thought they were worth keeping."

Silence drifted as she paused, her mind flashing back through the drawings to the smaller one with the barn and the candle, and the odd inscription.

"Emelyn mentioned something she overheard while they had her," she added. "Something about a Tallow's Eve festival? The Governance are convinced it's soon apparently, but they don't know where. She said something about it not being right near the inn as well, wherever that is."

Mik sat back with an astonished huff.

"They're trying to find the summing ceremony."

Neri turned to Niall but he looked as baffled as she was. Mik shook his head, instantly irritated.

"Sorry, I forget folk don't know the histories like I do. The summing ceremony, or Tallows Eve festival, is an ancient attempt to summon a shimmer. They use tallow from animals to create a big effigy. It's mostly been an excuse for a party in older times but there are those that genuinely believe it will work one day. If the Governance are interested, then we should be too."

"Sorry, let me just get this straight." Neri couldn't hold back the doubt surging forward. "You're saying the Governance are looking for a festival of animal fat to try and summon a shimmer through the cursed forest to the west?"

Mik eyed her for several moments. "I'm saying they'll likely try to stop anyone else summoning it by any means necessary. They also won't want the west warned of their existence, not if they plan to plunder it eventually. But if they're hunting you, then you must have some use to them. He didn't mention anything?"

His eyes were suddenly alight with curiosity and he fixed her with a serious look. She ignored the rankling sensation of being potential collateral.

I just have to hope that's not what's inspiring Niall to keep me close.

"Nothing that makes sense. My gramma apparently stole some information from them long ago. She was always telling me tales of myth and fable, about firebirds rising from a single flame. Our whole settlement thought we were a bit odd."

Once she began, the initial words sprung a deep-set well of secrets and truth.

"I'm not sure when I realised it, that we were seen as different, but we always were. Gramma was known all around for being especially good with herbs, and Mama could charm pretty much anyone. Then my gramma disappeared. Her body was found in a river and they said she must have gone mad and wandered in. She was the sharpest person I knew. After that my mama got ill."

Neri sniffed and rubbed her nose, taking a second before ploughing on. Niall's arms wound around her waist and pulled her close, but she couldn't let that comfort stop her admitting the rest. He deserved to know all of her, especially the dark parts. She turned to face him.

"When she passed, I had no idea what I was going to do. Before I even had a chance to process any of it, the Governance came to our dwelling. Everyone in our settlement knew that meant trouble and I had no reason to stay, so I grabbed all I could carry and left. Mama had told me to go to Hamlin if they died, so I did. Then when I went in for Em, Amis said that with my family gone they could look after me. Made it sound like they'd had something to do with it after all. So I hit him."

She ignored the tears that trailed down and dripped from her chin onto her bare knees. She paused, waiting for Niall to release her, to edge away. When he didn't, she forced herself to continue.

"It's not the first time I've let my anger get the better of me either. There was a girl in our settlement and she was always taunting me. One day I snapped and lashed out. Her family was important locally and Mama got into trouble over it. I promised myself I wouldn't let that happen again.

Then the Governance came calling and Emelyn looked so scared and we had to get out. I just started swinging."

She wiped a rough hand across her eyes as Niall's grip tightened.

Mik sighed. "It's admirable that you've shared that with us. I believe I know Niall well enough that I can speak for both of us and say we don't judge you for a single bit of it."

His resonant tone brushed away a few dregs of the fear that had accumulated in her head. Niall shifted, pulling her closer still, his cheek brushing against her ear as he murmured his agreement.

"We will leave our more serious discussions for today I think," Mik said.

Neri couldn't fight the tiredness much longer but she wanted more time to talk. So many questions about the west plagued her and she wanted to learn more about Niall, knowing instinctively that Mik could provide answers to all.

"Kirelonia is a very bemusing realm," Mik explained. "East or west, north or south, no matter how long you travel its lengths, no matter how much you see, it will never stop surprising you."

Neri raised her head, not aware that it had slumped against Niall's shoulder since her almighty confession.

"The east is all I've ever known. All most folk have ever known."

Mik nodded with a smile. "Except for the folk who don't live in the east perhaps. Still, I can be as outrageously honest as I choose and you will either believe me or not, but I refuse to lie to folk."

He fixed her with a serious stare even though his eyes twinkled with amusement and Neri had the sudden urge to surprise him and unseat his unshakeable confidence.

"I'm more intrigued to find out how far the creatures go to be honest. I've heard of firebirds and I'm guessing unicorns and dragons are commonplace over there. Do *soul-shades* walk in the night or the day, and do folk over there have actual magic rather than simple land-gifts, or is it a case of some lucky some not?"

Mik laughed at her enthusiastic questioning, tilting his head as he regarded her. His gaze flickered to Niall momentarily before he shrugged.

"I commend your imagination. Unicorns, to our knowledge, keep away from settlements and, without wanting to get into the entire history of our lands, dragons are not enslaved in the west as they are here in the east."

Neri bit her lip. She'd heard tales of enslaved dragons being used beyond the Apeklonian citadel, but that was further north than she'd ever been.

But she liked that she could be entirely herself with Mik and that he would tease her in return. She already felt at home in his dwelling, talking to him like an old friend.

"I think a long rest would do you both good." Mik stood and clapped his hands. "I'll ask you not to overexert yourselves, purely because the dwelling is old with thin walls and I don't want to even think about that, much less have to hear it."

Neri flushed at the insinuation but it was Niall's mortified grimace that sent her into quiet giggles.

"You only have the one spare room," Niall said. "Neri can have that and I'll sleep down here."

Mik raised one eyebrow but didn't respond, turning to wait for Neri's input instead. She heaved herself to her feet with a groan.

"You've been leading us this far and doing most of the work, so you take the spare room and have a proper sleep."

Niall stood and faced her with his arms folded, his brow furrowing.

"You've hit your head so you should take the proper bed."

Neri matched his stance. "You'll be leading when we move on and your horse is more tempestuous than mine. I can probably have a nap on mine, she's so lazy. You take the room."

Mik's quiet laughter drew their attention.

"Then either you both take it or neither of you do, but no unsavoury activities under my roof either way."

Neri eyed Niall and tried to keep her stern expression going with great difficulty. The corner of his mouth lifted.

"I can make a wall out of cloth or something if you're worried about being left alone with me," she offered drily.

"Let me show you where the room is," Mik suggested. "Then you can spend the night arguing about it without me."

He beckoned them with one finger and led the way out of the room. Niall grabbed both their packs before Neri could reach hers and hustled her into the hall.

Mik stopped at the top of the stairs, indicating they should take the door to the left. He smiled and wished them a good morning before disappearing into his own room. Only then did Neri realise it was morning, yet Mik was going to bed.

"He's a night-bird and sleeps very little," Niall murmured. "We're safe here either way."

He led Neri inside and she smiled to see a large wooden bed with an invitingly thick mattress, a simple set of drawers and a red rug centred on the floorboards. Niall chuckled when Neri faced him once more, hands on hips.

"Are we going to have a spat about this then?" she asked. "You look completely done in so I'd rather just make do."

"Either we're in the bed or you are, your choice."

Of course he would leave it down to her. She watched him busying himself with setting the packs down. His awkwardness badly covered in false nonchalance gave her the confidence to do what she probably wouldn't have done in any other situation.

"We've shared small spaces before. Let's not overthink it." She faced the bed but then turned back. "But also don't expect anything."

Niall watched her with his lips twisted in a contemplative frown.

"Are you afraid of being left alone with me?" she asked.

The words were intended as a light tease, but her mind flickered back to her earlier confession about hitting Amis. She looked away. Before she could move back toward the door and go to sleep downstairs after all, Niall appeared beside her. He tucked a knuckle under her chin and lifted her face.

"Don't think that your past or what you've had to do to survive changes anything. We all have dark bits and secrets we keep. Come on, you choose your side and promise to keep your hands to yourself."

Her eyes met the glinting darkness of his. Breathing deep and harsh, she couldn't help a distressed chuckle.

"I won't seduce you don't worry," she retorted.

Blushing with age old embarrassment she expected some pithy comeback, but Niall's attention had drifted. She followed his gaze which was now captivated by a small painting hanging on the wall by the window.

An enormous white-walled dwelling dominated the middle of the scene, surrounded by a backdrop of cliffs and a golden-green hill. A waterfall surged down the rocks on the left side of the dwelling, ending in a large pool at the base. It was more reminiscent of the palaces lauded in the fables of ancient times, and Neri stared in awe. Winding down in front of the palace there were hints of a settlement, haphazard dwellings built of stone or wood or both on either side of a long, mostly straight lane.

In the painting, torches burned to light the viewer's eyes and the houses were shown growing abundant plant life from cracks in the walls, trees spurting up around gaps in the stone.

"It's like my drawing," Neri murmured in awe. "The one on the side of the box."

She joined Niall and glanced sideways at him. His eyes were alive with emotion, the darkness encompassing them until they were black. He stood with his nose almost pressing the canvas, his fingers raised as if he wanted to stroke his way into the image itself.

Realising she was intruding on what appeared to be a personal moment, Neri cast her gaze away and stepped back. Niall's hand snaked out lightning quick, gripping her fingers.

"This is Jakiris," he said. "It's the seat of power for the whole westlands of Kirelonia. The Jakida, who should still be in rule, governs the land from here."

Neri stilled. "It's beautiful."

She had no other words she could possibly say to him. The painting showed a place in the west, and she couldn't bring any other thoughts or soothing litanies to mind. Instead she monitored the gradual decrease of darkness from his eyes, waiting until the brown irises returned and he allowed his gaze to move from the painting toward her.

"Tomorrow morning we'll have to get all the information we can from Mik," he sighed. "Tonight, all I want to do is forget the whole thing."

She caught the remnants of some kind of inner torment in his tone and heaped herself onto the bed with a shrug.

"We're not in any rush and at least the bed is comfy. Get some sleep and we'll face everything later."

Niall crossed the room as she slid under the covers fully clothed, lying on her side so they'd be facing each other. They would have to share the blankets but Niall seemed more afraid of the idea than she was now and that made her smile as he inched in beside her. The morning glow from the suns outside gave the room a gentle light without being overpowering, and Neri noted that Niall was keeping a very healthy portion of the bed's middle clear between them.

"We'll face it, whatever 'it' ends up being, together?" he asked, his voice almost inaudible.

Neri nodded. "Together."

Niall's fingers curled around hers. After a moment, he murmured a gentle rumble of contentment and his breathing deepened. Neri settled and let her mind swim back to thoughts of the sanctuary. She wondered whether Dog had chosen someone else to sleep by. She thought of Matty out there somewhere and pitied him, but the idea of Niall plagued her more. If he had decided to join the enemy, would she follow him? She shook the thought away.

Even if I have to live my life on a wild chase, I apparently can't be without him either way.

CHAPTER SEVENTEEN

Neri woke to the late afternoon light stealing in through the window and smiled when she remembered where she was. Niall's heavy breathing told her he remained locked in the deepest throes of slumber, and he didn't even twitch when she cautiously creaked her way off of the bed. She opened the bedroom door and snuck out onto the landing, leaving the door ajar. Memories of creeping through the sanctuary during her first few days there swirled in her mind and a hefty pang of homesickness hit her.

Once downstairs she poked her head into the plant-filled sitting room but found it empty. She paused in the hallway, wondering if perhaps Mik wasn't up yet and she'd taken a liberty by creeping around his home on her own. A second later, a clatter from the room opposite tempted her to sneak a look through the gap in the kitchen door.

Mik stood at the kitchen counter, his hands in a large wooden mixing bowl and his arms caked up to the elbow in what looked like dough. She eased the door open wider, the hinges whining her arrival. Mik whirled around, saw her and relaxed in an instant.

"Couldn't sleep too long then? It appears Niall's standards are slipping, however. It's nice to see him relax himself properly, all thanks to you of course."

Neri blushed and shrugged one shoulder. She still had questions for this man in the bright light of day but she didn't want to appear rude. When he asked her to help him mix more ingredients to make fresh bread, she washed her hands and set about following his instructions. By the time her mix vaguely resembled bread dough, Mik had launched into a full account of his experiences of the sanctuary and its residents.

"It's not all trickery of course. Moonshine really does have an innate knack for coming in at the right moment, and if anyone else wrote Emelyn's words exactly they wouldn't have half the power hers do. She can't move mountains but her writing that you find the odd lost item is a blessing, which she only does *if* you stay on her good side."

He turned around, causing her to copy his movement, and she caught sight of Niall in the doorway. His disgruntled frown looked nowhere near as impressive as he intended whilst he was still drugged with remnants of sleep and his hair stuck out in messy straggles.

Mik moved Neri's dough out of the bowl and onto a floured wooden chopping board. She watched for a moment as he kneaded the dough with quick, deft flicks of his hands then set about putting more ingredients in the bowl.

"I've not slept that deep in ages," Niall murmured.

Mik laughed. "Dear me, I never thought I'd see the day

that Niall gets his head turned by a girl. Let Neri finish her task then and we'll have a quick chat. I'm sure we all have things to discuss when she's done."

Niall followed him, somewhat reluctantly Neri could tell, and she completed the next lot of bread mixture. She had a go at kneading the dough as Mik had done, then wrapped it in the clean cloth on the side and set it in the sunslight next to the ones he'd already made. Tempted to go for a quick look around the room, she busied herself with folding up the excess cloth when she heard voices in the hall.

"Come and have some food, Neri. You must be ravenous," Mik called.

She left the counter and hurried across the hall. Niall sat on the mattress and patted the small space beside him, indicating she should sit close to him. She obliged and happily accepted bread, butter and fresh jam from the plate Mik offered her. He left the room while they ate and Neri settled back against the cushions.

She doubted they'd get any further information from their visit, nothing of value anyway. But after having met a friend Niall obviously thought highly of, she considered their journey a success all the same.

A moment later, the strong, unmistakeable aroma of frying egg wafted through to them and Niall chuckled to see her sniffing the air.

"I do love visiting Mik because the food is amazing," he said. "He's got birds out the back."

Neri waited as patiently as she could but on seeing the egg that was held out to her on a plate, she took the food, tore off a hunk of bread from the main tray and ate with no thought for manners. Once she had cleared their plates away into the kitchen at her own insistence and washed them, she returned to the living room to find both men staring at her.

"I want to show you something," Mik announced. "I think it may open a few doors as it were. I got to thinking last night when you mentioned Tallow's Eve, and I think I may have hit on something useful."

His tone was shrouded in mystery, his eyes hooded with secrecy, and Neri bit her lip. If all the craziness was somehow true, then could it be possible he knew how to cross through the forest?

Mik stood up to lead the way out of the room and up the stairs. On the second-floor landing, he opened the door to the bathroom and ushered her in. Niall appeared behind them both, his face pensive.

Mik stood on the edge of the huge wooden bathing tub and faced the wall. With one almighty heave, he dragged his body to the side with theatrical effect and the wall disappeared.

Neri's jaw dropped in astonishment. The wall had to have disappeared on a runner or some kind of hinge behind the bit that still remained, leaving a dim darkness beyond.

Mik leapt with agile grace off the tub and into the gap. Neri glanced at Niall who nodded to urge her forward. Stepping over the tub, she stared into the gap and saw steps leading up. On reaching the top of the stairs she only saw clutter, but she didn't want to be rude and aimed for an expression of polite interest.

Niall scoffed in amazement. "What is all this junk?"

Neri bit back a smile as Mik started to laugh. He held his hands up in acceptance and started ferreting around behind a pile of boxes.

"I figured a day would come where my historical prowess would come in useful. I just need to find where I left it."

Neri glanced at Niall. He shrugged and blew a swift kiss in her direction while Mik wasn't looking, grinning all the while.

"Aha!" Mik emerged.

He held up a dusty old book covered in cloth with a broad, triumphant smile.

"This is an account written long ago," Mik explained. "The woman wrote a lengthy biography, and I mean it's absolutely huge. This is only part of it but there's mention of a summing ceremony and the need to travel by fire. If you're to believe the stories, there are four elements that were cast down by the entities that even predated the ancients. Air, earth, water and fire. The summing ceremony is a ritual conducted to summon a shimmer using the fire element."

Neri took tiny breaths and tried not to sneeze but the dust was tickling her nose. She rubbed her wrist across her face as Mik continued.

"Now, the festival is held each winterspan on the tipping point of the nights turning colder. This means it must be very soon."

Niall's head shot up. "We're in luck then."

Mik nodded, his expression grim although his eyes were

sparkling with eagerness.

"It is indeed very fortuitous, but one thing many accounts have mentioned is that summing ceremonies don't actually summon anything. They speak instead of needing the firebird to appear and open the veil between worlds."

Neri realised she was on firmer ground there. "Emelyn said that firebirds sometimes give gifts to folk, or they honour someone or something."

"A kyne appeared to you at Moonshine's house," Niall reminded her.

Mik shot upright, his eyes sparking. "A kyne? Really? Neri, you may have been given other signs, think carefully. Perhaps an image of the firebird has come to you while your sleeping? Or awake?"

Neri frowned, knowing she'd have to admit to her vision in the forest.

"It's probably nothing," she hesitated. "I did see something a while back, or at least I thought I saw a crawbird that burst into flame. It tried to lead me through the forest. I can't be sure though because it all seemed too ridiculous at the time. My mama and gramma did tell a lot of stories about them though when I was little."

This kindled the fire in Mik's eyes, enough that unbridled nerves jittered in Neri's belly. Mik and Niall exchanged a look, laden with hidden meaning she had no knowledge of. Niall rubbed his chin, his foot beginning to tap.

"We don't know where the festival is being held though," he reminded them.

Mik opened the huge book in his hand, his eyes scanning lines quicker than a flash of lightning. He started muttering words to himself, flicking through the pages at a feverish pace.

"A-ha!" He held the book aloft. "I knew there was mention of a riddle of some kind. There used to be an ancient meeting place, an inn at the border of the forest on both sides. To know which one, folk made up a riddle."

"Well that's handy." Niall sighed. "No chance the riddle is actually in that huge pile of dust?"

Mik nodded. "It is, as it happens. Find the feast where the wick meets the grain."

"Er, what?" Niall scratched the back of his head.

Neri's mind rippled, the echo of memory filling her head with the same image of the small drawing. A candle with wick burning bright amid a barn full of grain.

"The drawing gramma asked me to do." She caught Niall's eye. "The smaller one. The barn, the candle. Tallow Grain it said, but what if that wasn't what it said? She coated it in *gar* for a reason. None of the others were treated to keep them safe like that. "

She pulled the drawing out of her pocket, flinching when Mik yanked it from her fingers.

"Yes!" He did a little leaping dance. "Grain is, of course, made in a granary, also known as a grange. Wick, well that will be-"

"-from a candle, and old candles were made of tallow." Neri grinned.

His enthusiasm was catching and a buzz of anticipation rippled over her skin.

"This must be it. Tallow Grange is an inn not far from here. That must be the meeting spot that will lead you to the Tallow's Eve summing ceremony." Mik hurried past them toward the stairs. "This could be the break we've been waiting for."

Neri pressed warm fingers to her neck. Her mind lurched back and forth over possibilities, all ridiculous to consider, but the childlike excitement inside her wouldn't dissipate. She curled her fingers around the small stone token hanging against her chest and tried to calm the flutters of anticipation.

Mik led the way back down toward the bathroom and she followed in his wake, her mind thundering. He directed them into the plant-filled sitting room but Niall went back up to fetch their bags while Neri paced back and forth by the plants.

"Ready?" Niall appeared in the doorway.

Neri nodded. *Wherever he goes... Magic pathways aren't real, they can't be. There's no proof of any of this, or any kind of magic I've ever seen. There will be some kind of explanation for the things I've seen, even if it is only chaos in my head.*

Mik reappeared and held out a large loaf of bread with a box made of blade-metal to Niall. Neri caught the solemn, knowing look that passed between the two men and bit her lip. She needed time to consider what they'd told her and what they possibly weren't telling her. The journey on horseback would provide that.

"I'm very glad I met you, Neri," Mik insisted. "Look after Niall and keep him out of trouble."

She thanked him and shouldered her pack. He came to the door to wave them off and Neri mounted her horse with a sinking feeling. Niall set off first, leading the way back down the hill, but Neri twisted to stare at the dwelling as it disappeared from view. Rotating until she faced forward once more, she looked at Niall's faraway frown.

"So, now we go to Tallow Grange," he said. "All these references to tallow can't be a coincidence. There will be someone there who knows where the summing ceremony is to happen."

Silence descended as they rode through trees and across stretches of browning grassland, squinting against the dazzling glare of the suns. Neri wrapped her hair once again and was glad now of the partial shade it gave her eyes. Niall set a faster pace than the day before, but they stopped for a while to rest once the dusk fell around them again.

With their horses tethered beside a fast-moving brook, Neri eased her stiff muscles by pacing up and down. Niall delved into his pack and came up with some breadcakes to share.

"A far cry from the first walk we did together," she said.

He smiled sadly. "That was a worse time. We were both grieving and I had no idea who you were or whether I could trust you, at least not beyond Hamlin's word."

"And now?" Neri stopped pacing beside him with a grin. "You think you can trust me now?"

He stared back at her, his lips curving upward with mischievous intent. Realising how close this put them, she blinked back, unnerved by the sudden increase in her pulse. His eyes caught the waning sunslight and fed sparks through the dark brown depths, entrancing her as he drew closer.

"I hope I can," he murmured.

She tensed as his fingers caught an errant strand of her hair beside her cheek. He pushed it behind her ear, his fingertips lingering down the curve of her neck and turning so his knuckles brushed featherlight against her collarbone.

So sick of thinking and worrying, Neri lifted her face that little bit further, giving wordless permission.

"Can I trust you?" he asked.

The question washed a hefty chill of doubt right over her. Chaotic thoughts of him seducing her to keep her on side leapt to her mind, and of Finn questioning her motives.

Niall sensed the change in her, straightening slightly to give her space.

"What is it?"

Neri ignored his worried frown. He'd mentioned love to Finn after only knowing her a handful of days, which was ridiculous, but then Mik had noticed a change in him before either of them explained a thing. She had to decide for herself whether she could trust him and he had to do the same for her. Taking a steadying breath, she looked him directly in the eyes.

"You need to decide that for yourself," she insisted. "I can tell you that I have nothing to do with the Governance, and I'm not entirely convinced by this whole magic path to the west thing yet either. But whether you trust me or not-"

"Neri, stop. I trust you. Enough to let you come all this way with me, to meet Mik who doesn't socialise with the outside at all. To let you go in and rescue Emelyn rather than doing it myself. I trust you completely. I didn't realise you'd take it seriously."

"Then why ask?"

He sighed and ran a hand over his face. Glancing over his shoulder, he pulled a rueful face.

"I thought you were teasing about the whole thing. Do you trust me?"

Neri hesitated, aware of his hands now clasping hers between them and his thumbs rubbing soothing strokes over her knuckles.

"I want to."

He nodded. "It's a lot to take in, I get that. But you must trust me at least enough to follow me into the unknown. Unless you're into the whole potential death, risk-taking thing."

He smiled at her, soft and fond and full of amusement. He wasn't judging her for doubting him, and she had to take him at his word when he insisted that he trusted her already.

Neri found herself smirking back at him. She wasn't too keen on the whole potential death type of risk-taking, but perhaps she could be bold for once in other ways.

Niall flinched in surprise as she rose onto her tiptoes and pressed her lips to his. Nerves burst inside her, her entire body buzzing with adrenalin. She dropped back down to her heels, intending to pull away, but he followed her. His arms snared around her waist as he deepened the kiss, and she let her hands wander the front of his shirt up to his shoulders. His tongue wisped over her lips and she reached out to meet him with the same caresses, desperate to get as close as possible. Caged desire kept them gripping at each other, until one of the horses snorted loudly and they broke apart panting.

"That was..." he chuckled and pressed his forehead to hers.

She nodded. "Yeah."

"We should get going."

"Yeah."

"Not that I want to, I'd be quite happy-"

"Niall? Stop babbling."

He grinned and gave her one last lingering kiss before dropping grabbing her hand as they approached the horses. He set the pace as they rode on but she barely noticed her aches and pains, her mind too tangled up with excitement.

Somehow, even with his previous declarations, kissing moved them from something possible into something actual, but she couldn't find her usual wariness when she thought about the worries she'd had.

Gramma said to live life wherever I have the chance, and Mama said to trust my instinct. With him I'm doing both.

"I can't believe Mik has been so close to this all along, and we never knew," Niall said a long while later.

They were moving steadily through the darkness, following lanes lit only by the dancing flicker of the stars. Neri had no idea where 'this' was meant to be, but she guessed they were close.

"It may not lead us to anything useful," she reminded him. "Are we near now?"

Niall nodded and pointed ahead. Now that she focused, she could see the flicker of firelight and a large dwelling up ahead. The horses seemed to notice it too and put on a fresh spurt of energy until they arrived in front of the Tallow Grange inn. It stood as two levels of rambling stone and wood, illuminated by candles in the ground level windows against a backdrop of shadowed trees.

"We need to make a bit of an impression." Niall frowned. "We want to hint we're here for the festival but not actually tell anyone. Then we can scope out any likely folk and follow them."

Neri turned around in her seat and yawned wide.

"I guess I could pull my hair into a side knot and try to look dippy?"

Niall's eyes twinkled. "I'd like to see that."

He grinned as she set about braiding her tangled hair into one messy line so that it hung more on one side, the natural fall trailing down over her shoulder. Despairing at her efforts, she slid off her horse's back with a grunt and gave the trusty mare a gentle pat. Niall had shouldered both packs already, one on each side, and they led the horses around the side of the dwelling to the barn.

Nobody appeared so Niall settled the horses into two empty stalls at the end nearest the door and led the way toward the inn. Neri offered to carry one of the packs, but he quelled her with a look and drew her close under his arm instead.

The inn door stood open and sounds of hushed

conversations drifted out despite the lateness of the night. As they stepped arm in arm into the dim recesses of the bar, the conversation hushed. A few lingering drinkers regarded them warily before returning to their own business.

A black-haired man about thirty winters young glanced up at them from behind the bar. He finished wiping a glass and braced his hands on the counter, staring at them. Neri noticed the small scar shaped like a crescent moon on his chin and a collection of small dragon tattoos on his right arm. His eyes glowed amber in the firelight but there was a carefully practiced aura of unwavering dullness to him. This was a man that put a lot of effort into being unremarkable, despite the tattoos. He looked like he could be the type who was into hiding the location of secret festivals.

Niall started bargaining for a room and Neri settled closer against him, wondering why she hadn't thought to check if he had any coin on him before leaving the sanctuary.

"I can spare you a room for a night," the man said. "After that we'll have to see if anyone decides to vacate."

Neri balked at the cost he asked but tried not to show it. Niall nodded his agreement and shook the barman's hand, tipping a handful of wooden coins into the man's palm along with it. Then the innkeeper's amber eyes drifted over Neri. He seemed to be giving her a thorough once over.

"You have a lot of wax on your hands," he said.

It was a simple comment, with no discernible hint of intention or suspicion behind it. But the vibe was there all the same. Neri tried momentarily to channel Emelyn's inner sunslight.

"I dabble in making our own candles at home, just a bit of tallow from the leftovers."

The explanation and her gushing tone seemed to placate their host. He turned his gaze back to Niall, one side of his mouth curving up.

"I've got to be careful," he said. "Lots of strange folk moving through last few days."

Niall nodded, his amenable expression never once twitching.

"Strange folk, you say? We heard tell of some celebration, but it could just be silly talk."

The barman lifted his hand up to the hollow of his throat and inched his thumb under a leather lace around his neck, his gaze never once leaving Niall's face. Neri thought she heard the rest of the bar dim, as though voices had been dialled down.

"I imagine there'd be safeguards in place if there were," the man replied. "What with the wrong types of folk always sniffing around."

Several seconds passed. Neri eyed Niall, wondering what he was hesitating for.

The barman frowned then and pulled the leather string out from under his t-shirt. A flash of grey glittering silver and gold caught Neri's eye. The man's charm was made from the same type of stone that hung around her neck. He stuffed his back underneath his clothing before she could make out the shape, but it was smaller and rounder than her own.

Niall shook his head and took a step back.

Celebration. Safeguards. The situation swilled in Neri's head. *Niall said these tokens are given to children when they're born in the west, but that he doesn't have one. What if they're some kind of symbol folk from the west use to identify each other?*

Her mama had insisted she not show anyone her token, not unless absolutely necessary and only to someone she trusted. The thought had seemed ridiculous then but now Neri wondered.

She tugged her token out from under her shirt and let it hang from her fingers long enough for the man to notice. His suspicious expression cleared in an instant and he turned his head to bark through the door that led behind the bar. A young man came rushing through.

"Show these guests to room seven," the barman barked. "They'll be staying a few days."

"Room seven is taken, remember?" The young man grinned wide. "I'll go for room three."

The barman returned to cleaning glasses as the young man hurried off toward the hall. Niall swept his arm around Neri's waist, pulling her close and guiding her after him.

"I'm glad you catch on quick," he murmured. "I would have figured something out but now I don't have to."

The young man continued to beam at them as they joined him, and Neri imagined him like a sketch of an excitable puppy. His ash-grey hair was peaked up in spikes with grease and his pale green eyes never seemed to focus on one thing for more than a second. His jittering energy began to make her feel queasy, but at least his enthusiasm distracted her temporarily from the damning realisation that all these folk might believe in the same fables of the west as Niall did.

"Room seven isn't really taken," he whispered, not bothering to introduce himself. "That's just what Alex says to let me know you're our kind. I thought you looked like the type straight away though. Have you been to the festival before?"

Neri almost halted in surprise that he was mentioning it so openly, but Niall's arm dragged her on alongside him like a paper anchor being towed by a ship.

"We came once winterspans ago, separately then, but now we want to see it one more time," Niall lied easily.

"It's going to be special this year," the boy said. "I'm sure you've heard. It's quite hard to get to if you've forgotten the way. I can always come and find a bit later. Then you can join one of the small groups making their way to the site. I'm Tongue by the way, because Aelon keeps threatening to cut mine out if I keep talking too much."

Given the wide grin, Tongue had no actual fear of having anything cut out. Niall nodded, sliding effortlessly into comfortable companionship.

"Thanks for that. Where should we meet you?"

Tongue opened his mouth to reply but it wasn't his voice that filled the hall. Neri tensed as a familiarly mocking drawl drifted over them.

"I should have guessed you two would turn up here."

CHAPTER EIGHTEEN

A shadowed figure moved out of the doorway and into the hall. Neri slid a hand onto Niall's arm in pre-emptive warning.

"What are you here for?" he growled.

Finn still had the mark of Niall's punch yellowing on his cheek. He sauntered toward them but wisely stopped a few paces short of being within reach.

"I roam wherever I'm needed," he said. "I'm a flexible soul, unlike some."

"Where are Matty and Eva then?" Neri asked, if only to distract Niall's temper.

Finn frowned and folded his arms across his chest. "At the sanctuary, I'd have thought. Or did you bring them? No, probably not."

"You didn't help them escape the night you left?" Niall pressed, his tone drenched with cynicism.

Finn's eyes widened. "No, I didn't! Whatever you may think of me, I'm no traitor, not to the causes that matter. Is that why you're here then, tracking them?"

Neri took a breath to answer but Niall cut her off.

"Why else? We can't risk her taking things back to waiting ears. But you go off and roam or whatever. Leave what matters to those of us willing to actually do something about it."

For one brief moment, Neri saw a flash of Finn without his mask in the wide, pained eyes. Then the expression shuttered and he laughed.

"I'll do that." He headed toward the bar but turned back in the doorway. Neri could hear silence on the other side. "You watch your backs now."

He disappeared, no doubt to avoid another bruised cheek. Niall started after him but Neri grabbed one of his fists and pulled.

"Not worth causing a scene," she muttered, glancing meaningfully at Tongue.

Niall exhaled, lowering his shoulders and uncurling his fists.

"I have tomorrow off," Tongue insisted. "Aelon and his friends are leading the rest in the afternoon, but perhaps you'd rather go to the site in the morning and wait there for the procession instead of here? I can lead you and I have friends I can meet after."

Niall rubbed his mouth and sighed. "That might be for the best. Thanks."

"Great! I'll come knock for you tomorrow morning. Oh, wait, I need to show you to your room don't I? Okay. Follow me."

Neri tried not to giggle as Niall gave her a weary look and guided her up a staircase after Tongue. The rest of the inn was in silence and Neri thought longingly of the bed that would no doubt be waiting for her behind one of the many doors they passed.

"As soon as we get our room, we'll bathe your head and make sure it doesn't need stitching," Niall murmured, leaning close. "Then I'm putting you to bed."

Neri glanced at him but he didn't seem to get his own innuendo. Jumping on the opportunity to tease him, she grinned.

"Putting me to bed or taking me? There's a world of difference, Niall."

"I love it when you use my name." He grinned. "It makes me feel like I'm yours somehow."

Feeling a heady buzz of euphoria roll through her veins, Neri let that suggestion slide as Tongue threw open a door and stood back with a flourish. She stepped inside but Niall lingered in the doorway.

"Can you send up food, drink and some clean cloth for a cut?" he asked.

"Absolutely! I'll be straight back. It's pie tonight, Aelon's best."

Tongue scurried out of sight and Niall swung the door shut with a ragged groan of relief.

Neri dropped her pack by the bed. A quick hand test of the mattress proved it thick and comfortable, and she sank onto it with a relieved sigh.

"I think this will do us nicely."

Niall smiled and she saw the weariness in his eyes but he hovered, evidently not willing to settle until the supplies were delivered. Neri considered taking off her boots but she could see a second door that would likely lead to a washing room. She'd wait until Niall was done fussing before taking anything off.

Niall opened his mouth to say something but hesitated, then Tongue burst in without knocking and set a tray down on the corner table.

"Two extra-large helpings of pie." He ignored Niall's irritated glare. "An entire sacking pouch of wine and some clean cloth, plus some ointment which is yours for nothing. I'll knock for you tomorrow, not too early though given how late you've arrived."

Neri managed to thank him as he flurried out again, but she giggled when Niall saw fit to grab a chair and wedge it under the door handle. Seeing her expression, he grinned.

"It's a trick I learnt from you. I came to talk to you one night early on at the sanctuary but couldn't get the door open. I knew remembering that would come in useful."

She smiled as he drank from the pouch before handing it to her.

"Drink some of that while I sort your wound out. It may hurt a bit but it's dried up nicely so the ointment should seal the rest of it up. I should have patched it the moment we get to Mik's but there was so much going on, forgive me."

With a fresh cloth in hand, he wiped it in the peppery smelling ointment and started dabbing.

"I quite like having you play healer," she said.

Niall scoffed and put the ointment on the floor. "I'm no healer. But even I know you need to rest and so do I. Tomorrow will be long and we don't have a room guaranteed tomorrow night either, so we may have to ride back to Mik's after the festival."

He stood up to tidy the things onto the table and passed her one of the bowls of pie. They ate without speaking, both ravenous despite eating well at Mik's. Only once the food was eaten and a large part of the spiced wine gone did they face the bed situation. Or rather Neri faced it without much concern, but as she settled back on her cushion she found Niall hovering nearby with a bashful look on his face.

"It's a small room and it's going to get stuffy with both of us, even with the window. I don't usually get comfortable sleeping in clothes."

He avoided her eyes, choosing to focus on her fingers instead. His coyness sounded genuine enough, but she remembered him dead to the realm earlier at Mik's. That tiny fact gave her the confidence to do what she probably wouldn't have done in any other situation. She reached down and undid the ties of her shorts.

That got his attention.

Smirking at him, she stood up and slid them all the way off. With her flimsy under-shorts on that barely covered the tops of her thighs, she settled back on the bed with one eyebrow raised.

"You want me to cover my eyes?" she asked, amused. "It's not like you to be shy."

Although she'd doubted his motives earlier and been wary of him at the start of knowing him, she'd never been all that shy a person. She wasn't in any way innocent in the ways of intimacy either. Now that Niall had kissed her and not yet given her reason to doubt him, she found it easy enough to be daring.

Almost as if he didn't want to be the to back out of a challenge, Niall's expression hardened, his mouth pressing thin with determination. He pulled his shirt off in one swift move, dropping it on top of her shorts. Neri wriggled underneath the thin blanket but stared with unreserved interest as he undid the ties of his trousers and dropped them to the ground.

She squeaked and attempted to cover her eyes, yelping when she touched the cut on her head. She hadn't thought to contend with the possibility of Niall going without any kind of under-shorts of his own.

Keeping her eyes closed, Neri held her breath as the bed creaked. She detected the heat his body threw toward her but he settled onto the narrow bed beside her and made no move for contact.

Perturbed by the sense of awkwardness, she began to giggle. It started as gentle shaking with her managing to hold in the sound. Then as the thought of them spending the future together, both avoiding each other's nakedness when deep down they both wanted it, she snorted and started to chuckle.

"Are you laughing at me or just in general?" He didn't sound impressed.

She choked back as much of the giggling as she could and supported herself on her elbow to face him, amused that he was under the blanket with the edge of it pulled right up to his chin.

"I'm sorry, it's just ridiculous. We've both been dancing around teasing and taunting each other, and now suddenly we're acting like… like…"

She struggled for a good analogy and failed.

"…like a newly united pair unlearned in the ways of intimacy?"

She nodded and breathed a sigh of relief when he started to chuckle too. Weirdness abated, she settled her cheek on his shoulder and her hand on his chest over the blanket. Niall murmured a gentle rumble of contentment and almost immediately his breathing deepened.

Unable to sleep that quickly, Neri wriggled a bit to get comfortable. In her absent-minded fidgeting, her knee brushed up Niall's thigh and glanced off his hip bone, coming to rest right over the centre. Without drawing a single breath, she waited. She couldn't tell if his breathing was suddenly lighter or if she was simply paranoid from the sheer anxiety of touching him so thoroughly.

After several agonising moments, she allowed her body to relax against him once more. Her leg remaining where it was didn't have to be a bad thing. She tried to remember what she'd been thinking of before moving.

"Is this your way of telling me you want me to kiss you again?"

Niall's voice was little more than a mumble but his tone all husky with sleep and his suggestive choice of wording set a buzz of desire ricocheting through her.

"Accidental placement actually." She grinned. "Is that your way of telling me you want to kiss me again?"

He stiffened against her and she opened her eyes to find dark, hooded pools still dredged with sleep gleaming at her.

"Maybe I won't tell you either way."

She grinned at his playfulness. For all his teasing, he wasn't going to risk pushing her into anything she didn't want to do. The moves were hers to make, the freedom hers to explore or walk away from.

Rolling onto her knees and straddling his taut stomach, she pulled her hair free of the braid and let it dangle loose over her shoulders. With one agile flick of her leg, she arced off the bed and walked a few paces away.

"In that case, maybe I don't want to play anymore."

She kept her back to him and her insides roiled with the quiver of anticipation as she heard the bed creak. She never could hear his footsteps.

The first sign she had that he was behind her were his teeth, gentle but firm, biting the tender flesh of her neck. Before she could react, Niall gathered her against him tightly from behind.

"Are you sure this what you want?" he asked. "Because my nerves have been pure chaos ever since you walked into my life. Wanting you has been torture."

The caress of his breath, warm against her ear, and his fingertips now softly gliding over the ticklish skin on her ribs gave her no room for doubt. She pulled her top over her head and discarded it on the floor, her undershorts too, then arched until her head touched his shoulder and her hips slid back against him.

"Are you done asking stupid questions?"

She squeaked as Niall grabbed her firm around the waist and pulled her off her feet to heap her on the bed. He towered over her, the predatory glint in his dark eyes dancing in the firelight setting a swirling sensation deep into the pit of her stomach.

She watched as his gaze dragged with aching dedication over her bare skin, down, then up again until it came to rest on her face. He leaned forward and the chaotic yearning doing backflips inside her clawed any scant remains of innocence to shreds, casting a wicked smile over her lips.

When his mouth landed on hers, it was just once and feather light. The second kiss landed on her cheek, then with surprising restraint he traced a soft path across down to her chest. Unwilling to be quite so restrained, Neri moaned in frustration and writhed beneath him.

She raised her arms to pull his head down, or up or something that would end the torment but Niall grabbed her wrists easily in one hand and secured them tight above her head. Tiny begging whimpers strayed from her mouth, her cheeks flushing with a burning temptation to slap at him for teasing her.

Soft, warm heat enveloped her skin and she whined as she felt the first firm lap of his tongue against the peak of her chest. Her hips undulated restlessly and Niall's mocking chuckle fired frustration through her once more.

"You really can't hold out much more can you?"

A growl leapt from her throat and turned to a heated gasp as his knee connected light between her legs, holding pressure there as his tongue lashed with sudden, deft strokes against her skin. Holding the swaying momentum of her hips against his lower thigh, her ache grew.

His knee moved away and her attention was drawn by the nimble sweep of his lips against her mouth, his tongue delving inside. She struggled to free her arms from his grasp but he had his entire shoulder stiffened to keep her confined.

Soft wisps of caressing danced across her thigh, up and down never quite reaching the place she needed them to. His fingers travelled over her hip bones, across the low dip of her stomach and back down, never once making the right connection.

Maddened with unfulfilled longing, the rhythmic thump of desire surging through her, Neri hardly noticed the emotional tears leaking between her closed lids. Whether Niall saw and relented or simply decided he was tired of tormenting her, his skilled fingers finally landed between her legs, sliding in.

Her eyes snapped open in time to see Niall watching her with a strain of vindictive pride curling across his lips. Withdrawing his fingers, he returned to trailing them in feather light streaks across her thighs and stomach.

Neri struggled past her lust-fuelled haze, indignation pulling on her eyelids. He stared down at her, the dark predatory eyes glinting with self-assured taunting. He looked like he wanted to hunt her, to own her, and Neri knew that this act had become a mere formality. She'd given herself to him completely many days before. The torrent of sexual urges stemmed to a low, thrumming rumble and she smiled lazily at him.

It distracted him enough that she could whip her wrists free of his fingers. They landed firm on the curved muscle of his broad shoulders and she dug her nails into the flushed skin to punish him.

"What are you planning on doing now then?" he asked.

His cocky smile quirked as he baited her. Still looking up at him with a glimmer of fake innocence, Neri brought the top of her foot up, gliding the sole over the back of his calf and up the inside of his thigh. She stopped just shy of touching him, intrigue mingling with anticipation. Unable to bring her eyes up to meet his, she stared down instead as her foot skimmed across the soft skin.

Her toes curled momentarily over him and then she eased her leg up along the defined line of his hip. The tip of her tongue eased out to rest between her lips and excited apprehension seeped through her as she glanced up to look at his face.

Niall's hands grasped tight around her waist, pulling her lower beneath his body as she giggled from the exhilaration. Strong arms folded her against him, the coarse hairs on his chest scratching against the sensitive skin of hers and forcing a strangled moan to her lips.

"May all the realm gift me, I want you," he muttered.

The words were almost lost as his mouth roved over her lips and her cheeks, across her tender skin, teeth occasionally nipping as he rubbed against her. Neri tried to wrap her legs around his waist, hoping to anchor him somehow, but Niall shook his head.

"It will hurt the first time. I can't hurt you."

Neri huffed and rolled her eyes. He'd never once considered that she might not be an innocent. Tempted to taunt him, to see if mention of folk from the past made him jealous, she pushed the thought aside. Once again she attempted to grasp him with her legs, snarling when he sat up and pressed them down against the bed.

Neri closed her eyes as his fingertips caressed her thighs once more. This time he yielded in sympathy and she groaned in relief as his fingers dipped inside her.

His free hand slid over her chest, manipulating the swells to respond to his touch. She arched off the bed, so receptive to him, and the keening ache of need spilled through the weaknesses in her self-control.

Neri whimpered as he slid his body over her, positioning between her thighs and capturing her lips with his. His fingers wove through her hair, the other curving under her shoulders to pull her against him.

She turned her head away to give him access to the sensitive hollows of her neck as he slid inside, and she squeezed her inner muscles to experiment. Niall's guttural groan tingled over her, bubbling down and igniting a fire in her belly. His subtle movements tortured her, even worse when his strokes became deeper but slower.

"*Vahda*," she cursed. "I'm not made of glass, Niall!"

He stilled for a moment, driving back into her with one demanding plunge that forced her eyelids wide open, her mouth forming an O of shock. His skilled fingers roamed her body, moulding against her and enraging the tender skin. She bucked her hips against his, the tips of her nails toying over his chest, twirling through the hair and tweaking the dark pink peaks.

The deluge of tingling fire creeping deep into her being exploded, her skin flaring hot and her muscles clamping tight as she whined and panted.

Even as the afterglow settled countless moments later,

gentle tremors of the previous intensity remained, and she couldn't help but pull Niall's mouth to hers with fierce passion.

His motions became erratic and his groans became short and laboured. She trailed kisses over his neck and smiled when she heard the low, short roar of satisfaction as he flung himself deep inside her and held there.

She couldn't help a tiny giggle of release when his arms began to shake from holding himself up and his body collapsed in a heap on top of her. Aware he was still inside, she flexed her muscles and giggled again when he groaned and lifted his head. The after-effects and exertion of exercise brought a calm wave of languor and she realised her eyes were closing already.

Niall took pity on her and wriggled until they were holding each other. She could still see his eyes as she fought sleep, the dark brown almost dominating the black orb of his pupils.

"You look dopey as a dormouse." He chuckled.

A tendril of love licked at her as he laid a gentle kiss on her shoulder. When he opened his mouth, she shushed him.

"Sleep now, it's almost daylight."

The suns wouldn't rise for a while yet but she wanted them both to rest. Niall rolled off her and gathered her against his chest instead, dropping lazy kisses in her hair and over her cheeks as her eyelids fluttered, the realisation settling firm into the deepest part of her.

I'll follow him anywhere now.

CHAPTER NINETEEN

Neri woke with a deeply anchored sense of satisfaction. Feeling heat and softness beneath her cheek, she allowed herself to drift along in the thrums of happiness as recollections of the previous night replayed through her mind.

The memories were so real that she felt sensations drifting once again across her chest, arousal rolling through her stomach and kindling a smouldering heat down below.

A moment or two later she realised the feelings were being caused by Niall's hand as it wandered idly over her skin. Humming her approval, she pushed her body against his side. The movement caused a rough ache between her legs and the sense of heaviness in the pit of her stomach from their exertions.

"Morning, you made quite a performance last night, I was impressed." He grinned down at her.

She smiled back with wicked suggestion as his fingers caught her chin and lifted her head. As she shifted further, attempting to roll her lower half on top of him, she could feel him pressing hard against her hip.

He watched her, not saying a word, merely drinking in the sight of her. Neri kept her eyes glued to his as she casually rubbed her hip against his. His lips curved, a glimmer of naughty suggestion lighting on his face.

A loud smash rose up from somewhere outside, startling them both. A rousing cheer roared up moments later as folk jeered over whatever had broken. Neri took a deep breath and succumbed to helpless giggles, her head sinking onto Niall's ribcage.

"Come on we'd better get up." Niall groaned. "As much as I'd like to spend the rest of my days in the realm here in this bed with you, we'll probably get walked in on if we wait much longer."

Neri pouted and pushed herself off of him.

"Just don't make me wait as long as you did last time," she teased.

Finding her clothes and pulling them on, she sorted herself out in the tiny washing room and splashed herself with water from the small wooden bowl provided. She would find time as soon as she could to bathe properly and glanced with a grimace at the hard, cracked skin on the heels and big toes of both her feet.

She pulled her hair into a simple knot and walked out to the room to find Niall fully dressed and seated on the bed. When he held his arms out, she crossed the room and sank onto his lap, resting her head on his shoulder.

"Whatever happens from here on out, you'll always be mine and I will always be yours," he said. "I know I'm supposed to take it slowly, impress you and show I can provide for you, and we've not ever talked about a union or that far into the future. But until you tell me otherwise, you're mine."

Neri nodded, clutching at his arm and smiling with contentment.

"If you say so. Does that make you mine too?"

"Of course. I'll always be honest and faithful to you. I'll tell you when you're being ridiculous. I'll laugh at you when you do silly things. But I'll always protect you, put you first and make sure you're happy and comfortable."

It was as sweet a declaration as anyone could have hoped for. She wasn't entirely sure about the laughing at her part, but there was something very Niall about it so she let it slide. She would probably laugh at him too when he inevitably did something ridiculous.

They both jumped as three loud knocks rained on the door. Neri stood and grabbed her pack while Niall went to the door with a discontented grumble.

"The time is upon us, friends!" Tongue sounded extra loud and extra springy. "No sense wasting the day!"

Neri smiled to herself as she reached Niall's side and he instantly tucked his arm around her shoulders. Tongue was already off down the hall and didn't notice the protective gesture, but Neri couldn't help feeling glad for it all the same.

They followed Tongue outside into the already burning morning heat and set off down the lane.

"No horses?" Neri muttered.

Niall shook his head. "Safer for them here. If anything happens to us, they'll be fed and cared for well enough."

He gave her a reassuring smile but she couldn't shake that idea once he'd said it, that they might not make it back to the horses at all. The barman had mentioned being careful of folk and the Governance might know where Tallow Grange was and what it was going to be used for, so their lack of presence was another potential worry.

"We're so lucky the time is upon us!" Tongue called back. "It's a bit of a walk but you can relax safely at the other end."

Neri's managed a weak smile at his lively enthusiasm, but Niall's eyes were hooded with wary assessment. It seemed as though even the harmless boy offering to guide them was considered a threat. She turned her mind to scanning their surroundings as they joined a dirt track running alongside a yellowing field, but the area was deserted.

Neri settled her pace to match Niall's, listening to Tongue's unending stream of chatter about the local life. He enthused about Aelon, who apparently took him in and gave him board and food in exchange for his services. Neri thought of Hamlin then and sadness hit her. Tongue talked on regardless, and she tuned out when he started explaining exactly how to change the mead barrels.

They walked past a field full of flowers, the splash of red and green second only to the vast glimmering silver jewel of a lake against the horizon. Neri wanted to stop and soak in the view, just for a few minutes before the inevitable chaos of the festival descended, but Niall had her powering along at his side. Even with the suns attempting to roast her skin, she felt a strange sense of acceptance. Whatever came next, she and Niall would face it together.

The suns beat down as they climbed a sandy path that turned to parched earth rutted with rocks. The hill quickly levelled out into a clifftop and Neri squinted up at the sky. The day would start to wane soon, and if the celebrations started at night they could be walking for a good few hours yet.

She hoped Tongue would give them some further insight into the festival, but he'd finally fallen silent as they veered into the slightly cooler canopy of a forest. Neri breathed a sigh of relief, grateful for the shade. She burned with a thousand questions but didn't like to ask a single one in case it somehow turned the situation sour.

It's just another step along the path. Find the festival where nothing magic will happen, Niall will be disappointed, then we can go back to the sanctuary. Will the others even be there still now that Eva and Matty have escaped?

Tongue forged on, pointing out specific landmarks such as an oddly shaped tree, a bush that looked like a woman's face, and finally a fallen log with what looked like giant bite marks in it.

"Just through there is the clearing and down the hill you'll know what to do. This bit will be a thorough-fare soon so I'd find a denser place to wait."

Niall nodded and grudgingly held out his hand. Tongue glowed with incandescent delight and gripped Niall's elbow with his fingers, Niall copying the move with smooth, practised ease.

Tongue waved and bowed low with a sweet attempt at gallantry, then dashed off through the trees with a happy bounce in his steps. Niall turned to her and grinned to see her astonished expression.

"I take it that's a secret shade handshake?" she asked.

Niall wound his arms around her waist and stared at her with undisguised fondness.

"If you like. We have manners in the west, and those who know enough will remember them."

He led her a little way through the woods and found them a fallen tree with an elevated branch to sit on. Neri lowered her pack and settled it on the wide trunk beside her.

"What will happen exactly?" she asked. When Niall glanced at her with doubt splashed across his face, she rolled her eyes. "I think it's a bit late for me to be getting squeamish about magic and monsters now."

He took her hand and fidgeted with her fingers for a moment.

"There will be drinking, singing and dancing. Then when the time is right they'll light the big tallow statue and set a fire around its base."

Neri remembered celebration fire nights from her youth, the dancing flames and the scent of burning wood joining the loud pops and crackles. A memory rose unbidden, the recollection of her childish dreams about a bird rising from the fire and carrying her away somewhere in its talons. She shook her head to clear the relics of times long past.

"Sounds like fun."

Niall chuckled. "Don't tell me I don't know how to show a girl a good time. Once the fire is lit, everyone will chant, and a shimmer is supposed to open. If what Mik's book said is true, the firebird is supposed to appear. Anyone who wishes to cross through to whatever lays on the other side can. Mik said there hasn't been any record of a shimmer conjured on purpose in centuries, and nobody in living memory seen a firebird, not in the east anyway. I suppose everyone hopes each celebration will be 'the one'."

Neri squeezed his fingers and tried to remain objective.

"So why is the Governance worried about this particular one? Or do they go addle-brained over every festival? I guess that's easily believable."

Niall nodded. "I wondered why, but I think they might know something more about your family than you do, given that they kept your drawings. It's all adding together with startling clarity. You drew Jakiris yet you've never been there, I saw that drawing. You talk about firebirds and draw pictures of them. You carve on candles. Your mama sent you to Hamlin, who had an affinity with fire in his gift, enough to warm and to light a wick sometimes."

Neri bit her lip. "It sounds like clarity when you say it like that. But none of this was anything before I ended up with you. Maybe the firebird is using me to get to you."

Niall uttered a harsh bark of disbelief as his eyes caught hers.

"That's a funny one. No, whatever the truth is, we're only here because this gathering could be our chance to hear new stories and find out where to go next."

Deciding to leave question time there for a while, Neri stretched and tried to get more comfortable. The suns were fast disappearing between the trees, leaving them immersed in a strange half-world of greenery and paling light.

"Would you choose to go there, to the west, if you could?" She had to ask. "If the choice was an easy one?"

Niall smiled and curved his arm around her, pulling her close.

"The choice has never been less simple than now. We'll just have to decide together when the time comes, if it ever does."

Warmth tingled Neri's skin from head to toe, a glow that had nothing to do with the waning suns.

"What if there was a shimmer though, and it dumped us somewhere completely random?"

Niall settled her head onto his shoulder with a soft press of his fingertips.

"Then we're somewhere random or exactly where we started. Either way, we'll be together."

She left him in contemplative silence for a while and watched the trees taking the form of shadows as the light faded.

"Hamlin used to know my guardian from when I was a child over there." Niall's voice startled her away from her thoughts. "Apparently he told Hamlin that I would cross the veil and find him. I never realised they were in communication, or found out how it was even possible, but Hamlin left me a message explaining. I found it when I went back to the shop. They both knew but didn't bother to tell any of it to me. But Ma, Moonshine and the others, they're the only real family I've ever known."

Neri looked at him, wondering for a moment what kind of life he must have led before she met him.

"I was lucky to have my family, even though it didn't last," she murmured. "I know that. But as you say, you've got everyone at the sanctuary now. And I think so have I."

Niall hugged her close and said no more as night fell, leaving them with only the stars for guidance. Neri yawned and brought her fingers up to rub her eyes. Tiny fireflies of light flitted through the trees in front of them, hundreds all swaying back and forth. She nudged Niall and pointed. His lips right by her ear nearly made her jump.

"That's the procession. We need to go and slip alongside it."

He jumped off the enormous tree trunk and helped her to the ground.

"Here, wear my cloak," he insisted, fitting it around her shoulders and securing the tie at her throat. "It might get chilly and everyone will know you're mine."

Neri smiled, letting him fuss.

"Nervous?"

He shrugged. "Me? Never. Come on."

Glad of his arm secure around her waist, Neri pulled her pack over one shoulder and followed him toward the lights. They mesmerised her, as if the stars that danced in the sky had fallen to earth and collected together in one forest.

As they crept closer, she realised the lights weren't dancing but moving between the trees in a line. Uncountable numbers of folk walked along in twos and threes, all sporting some kind of pack or small cart. Not a word was spoken by anyone and she bit her lip as Niall guided them into a gap fit for two. He fumbled in his pack as they walked and brought out two candles. The man next to him held out his candle without averting his gaze from the path ahead.

Niall lit both candles from the man's flame and handed one to Neri, once again securing her against him as they fell into a three-legged walk. The folk a few paces in front of them were breaking clear of the trees and the front of the procession had already descended the hill and were heading toward a dark patch of the woods ahead. The candles lit up the forest but a block of what should have been more trees was simply darkness.

Neri settled closer to Niall's side. They followed the others down the hill and even when they drew on level ground, only a short distance from the tree line, she still couldn't make out what the dark nothingness was.

Step after step, she focused on the simple motion of walking forward. The darkness would soon be right in front of them. Niall tensed and her chest clenched with a spike of anxiety. Trusting him to guide her, she stepped forward and shut her eyes, wrinkling her nose and holding her breath.

Niall's grip tightened as he drew her to a halt. Opening one eye, then the other, Neri's bottom lip dropped.

The clearing in the trees looked reminiscent of the sanctuary garden after Moonshine's ministrations with the candles. Balls of amber light hung high in the trees now swaying gently in a soft breeze. Niall steered her out of the procession that was breaking up and led her toward the edge of the wide glade. In the middle towering over everything else was an enormous tallow candle.

Niall didn't take any notice of it as he snuffed out the flame of his candle, choosing instead to search the surrounding trees. When he dipped away from her, Neri blew out her own candle and kept her eyes firmly fixed on his movements. He'd brought her to this gathering and he wasn't going to do a disappearing act now. He returned a few moments later with two supple branches and held one out to her with an impish smile.

"Keep it for later. Before they start the actual ceremony, everyone puts down a natural offering."

She took the stick and folded her arms across her chest as she looked around. Folk seemed to be settling down on various patches of grass and Niall placed his pack down where they stood.

"Here's as good a place as any," he said.

Neri watched him take out a blanket and lay it on the ground. Before she could sit down, he held his hand up to halt her. He pulled out bread, two apples, a wax paper wrap of cheese and a muslin bag which he opened to show her held ripe red berries. He then pulled out the box of blade-metal that Mik had given him.

"It's an ice box of sorts," he explained. "It's kept the food cool. It'll have water in it now as well to wash our hands in. Mik manages to keep ice somehow, although he won't tell anyone where."

He sounded pretty impressed with the idea and Neri opened her mouth to agree, but once again he held up his hand for attention. He drew a small pouch out of the pack and pulled the stopper out with his teeth.

She had to smile. His charming enthusiasm for the picnic in such odd surroundings brought a flutter to her chest. She sat down and leaned her back against a tree trunk, taking a swig from the pouch when he offered it.

"What now then?" she asked.

Niall was busy mumbling curses under his breath at the blunt blade he'd brought to cut the cheese, which was obstinately hard. He didn't respond until the cheese had succumbed to his will and a small wooden plate was piled high with food.

Neri grabbed a chunk of honeyed bread and folded it around a wedge of cheese. Niall started battling with an apple next and she reached forward as soon as the first slice fell, grabbing it and ramming it into her sandwich. She ate hungrily with no other thought than her empty stomach.

Groaning afterwards, she sucked the crumbs from her fingertips and looked up to see Niall watching her. He had a suggestive smile on his face and her insides fluttered in response. He piled together a sandwich for himself but kept his gaze on her the whole time. Realising she'd had at least six hearty swigs of the spiced wine in the pouch and had eaten very little, she held it out to him. He took it and drank deeply.

"So, what now?" she repeated her earlier question.

Niall stoppered the pouch and dropped it onto the blanket. When he reached for her hand and inched close enough for her to feel his body heat, she stared right into his eyes. A thudding noise sounded out from a group of folk starting to play drums, fiddles and flutes nearby. Neri didn't dare drag her gaze away from Niall's for a moment.

"We wait," Niall murmured over the music, his tone low and heavy with emotion.

She moved closer, only an inch away. "And while we're waiting?"

His lips tasted of wine, the brush of his mouth soft and warm against her own. His arms anchored around her, pulling her even closer as his touch incinerated any hope of rational thought. When he released her, she had to fight every intention to pull him closer again. He smiled, a wicked glimmer of intent flickering in his dark eyes.

Neri cocked her head as the drums started to pick up a rolling rhythm with a startling familiarity that burrowed right down to the essence of her being. She frowned, her head beginning to nod in time to the tune.

"That's a sign to watch the dancing." Niall didn't notice her sudden distractedness. "Folk dance as others drop their offerings and they prepare the fire."

Gentle strains of melody filtered over the drumming. The music swelled as a young woman stepped forward first with bold confidence. She spread her arms wide as if about to take a bow, then she whirled around and around on the tips of her toes, ebony hair flying out behind her. Others came forward, their heads bobbing to the beat and their eyes following the girl's movements, looking for a moment to join in.

One by one folk fell into the line, performing the same twirls and swooping in and out of each other with amazing precision. Neri realised Niall was nudging her. She leaned closer to him, excitement tapping its toes through her chest.

"I know this dance."

CHAPTER TWENTY

Neri saw the doubt in Niall's eyes but she was resolved. The dance the others were doing belonged to her family. Her gramma and her mama would spend ages teaching her the steps, the three of them weaving in and out of chairs and piles of books they set out. None of the other children at the settlement had known it or been taught it, and back then it had seemed like just another family secret. Now everything she'd been told about the west being unreachable seemed to fade away.

She rose to her feet and walked forward. Niall's voice echoed behind her, hissing at her to come back, but she ignored him. Bewitched by the low thrumming of the drums, the swell of the strings and the lively, hopping flutter of the flute, Neri approached the candle.

Gasps rose up from the crowd before she could join them. Discord strummed through the air. Everyone around her wore similar panicked expressions, then she realised they weren't dancing. They were scattering.

A flame arched through the air.

The candle of tallow towered above her, the wick

catching fire as she scanned the crowd, her gut twisting and her blood thundering with fear.

"The Governance are coming!" Someone hollered above the din.

Moments passed in complete stillness.

Then chaos exploded.

Folk grabbed what they could and dashed in all directions, bodies bounding into each other in one heaving mass of limbs. Neri turned to find Niall but strong hands grasped her elbows, pinching at the skin. The bony, cold fingers told her it wasn't Niall and she kicked back, leaving a satisfying crack echoing behind her.

The fingers around her arms fell away. She regained her balance and cannoned forward. A loud thud behind her turned into scuffling. She whirled around to find Niall with someone pinned to the grass beneath him. His knee was pressed down hard on their stomach, one hand holding theirs above their head. In his other hand he held a blade to the person's throat.

A lot of folk had vanished already. Someone shouted about the defences not holding much longer. Neri hadn't seen any obvious defences on the way in but the Governance weren't visible yet, the crowd around her still darting panic-stricken into each other.

As she reached Niall's side, her shock intensified.

Eva lay with gleeful malice shining in her green eyes, Niall pinning her with a blade pressing against her neck and tangling with her red curls.

"You won't make it out," Eva hissed. "The Governance has the place surrounded and they're taking captives. Amis is looking forward to seeing your lovely girlfriend again too. He has a special place reserved for her."

Whether the giggle in her voice or fire dancing in her eyes made Eva look addle-brained, or whether she truly was, Neri didn't care. Her ears latched onto one thing.

"That *scum* is still alive?"

She should have been relieved. She wasn't a killer after all. But thoughts of Emelyn's frightened face and what Amis was clearly capable of chased relief far, far away. She thought of all her friends back at the sanctuary and her blood burned to icy fire inside her.

Eva turned her head in Neri's direction and Niall's blade cut a cobweb-thin line of red across her throat, but she didn't seem to notice.

"He is very much alive. He'll be happy to know that you ended up here."

"You don't care about what he did to Emelyn then?" she asked.

Niall glanced up at her then, warning in his eyes.

"Neri, don't. That's not your story to tell."

Their exchange was enough to mar the smile on Eva's curled lips. Her eyes flickered just once.

"That's in the past. Matty might not understand he's on the wrong side but I do. Once I've turned you over to them, they'll reward me and he'll see that we can have a proper life without hiding and sneaking around all the time."

"Where is Matty then?" Neri demanded, desperate to buy Niall time.

Eva grunted, struggling against Niall's hold.

"You think he'd be able to face a fight? He's all things

good and kind. I don't want him to have to see this side of me."

Niall dropped the blade and forced his hand over Eva's mouth, snarling down at her. Neri glanced around, panic flaring even brighter as she realised the area was deserted and screams echoed nearby. Someone in their rush had dropped fire by the candle and flames were beginning to lick at the offerings around the base.

"They're slaughtering folk," Niall shouted. "There's no discrimination, they cull everyone. Last time I saw them fight, they took down three of their own by mistake. Is that really the side you want to be on?"

Even now he was giving her a chance to repent. Neri bit her lip, knowing they had to move. She opened her mouth to say as much.

The feral glint flashed in Eva's eyes as she lunged against Niall's hold. He yelped and removed his hand from her mouth as she bit him.

With an almighty heave, Eva forced Niall sideways and rolled so she landed on top of him. Neri dashed forward, but they were grappling with each other so quick that she couldn't see any way to help.

Niall's palm braced against Eva's cheek as her nails clawed against him. Neri looked around for a branch or a remnant from someone's picnic, anything that could knock Eva back.

A familiar face flew out of the trees, the fire light glinting on something in the man's hand. Neri lifted her arms in a feeble attempt to defend herself, but Finn wasn't stopping.

"They're here," he bellowed. "Get out now, all of you! They're slaughtering everyone."

He lifted one arm as he dashed past. The blade he held left his hand and landed right by Neri's feet. She swept down to pick it up as Eva managed to get free of Niall and draw a glinting weapon of her own.

Neri twisted in time for the long, thin blade to score a thick gash down her upper arm and reeled back. Niall dashed for Eva but she ducked and he came flying toward Neri instead. He had Finn's blade from her fingers in one deft flick and bodily shoved her behind him. Both Eva and Niall attacked at the same time, barely missing each other.

Niall lunged again. Eva's blade moved quicker, so fast Neri hardly saw it. The cold, ghostly chill of dread hit her lungs as Niall's blood bubbled through his shirt. It was too high up his shoulder to be his heart, but Neri knew nothing about the inside workings of folk, not like her gramma used to.

Niall slumped to his knees, his eyes finding hers. Although clouded with pain, there was a glimmer of his usual confident grin. He fell sideways, hooking his leg around Eva's and dashing her to the floor. She wasn't expecting it and the blade soared from her grip. Seeing a chance, Neri glanced once more at Niall and allowed her fury free reign.

Eva was on all fours when Neri reached her. Grabbing the woman by her hair, Neri wrapped her fingers around the back of her neck. She kicked at Eva's thigh, bringing the woman down to her front. With a snarl, she put the heel of her foot on the back of Eva's neck.

The fury urged her to do something savage, something Eva had earned with her betrayal, but her limbs wouldn't move.

So much pain already. Her anger ebbed, but she couldn't let Eva go safely either.

Niall shuffled to a random blanket someone had left. He used it to staunch the flow of blood, but his eyes looked hazy and unfocused already.

Neri heard a stick crack and she reached out even as Eva slammed a short, solid length of branch against the side of her head. She toppled away from Eva and hit the ground with a grunt. The move jarred her back and she winced as she tried to struggle up.

The dark gleam in Eva's eyes as the fire leapt higher and higher around the candle set lose a river of defeat flowing.

Stupid, stupid, stupid, the word danced an agonizing chant through her head.

She hadn't been vigilant enough. She should have just knocked Eva out cold in one quick swoop.

Keeping Eva in sight, she checked on Niall again. He looked like he was trying to focus on her as his hand holding the blanket sagged. With a strangled sob, Neri dashed toward him but Eva blocked her. She blinked away the tears of pain as she searched the ground for one of the knives. She couldn't get to one quickly without being seen. Inching forward, she kept her eyes trained on Eva.

Voices hollered behind them and Eva's smile widened.

"Here he comes," she hissed. "I'll be rewarded for this."

Neri side-stepped as if she was trying to reach Niall, her

focus on something beside him. He hadn't noticed the fire climbing over the branches beside him, but Neri had. She swerved Eva in one quick dash, her breathing ragged and her limbs weak. She ducked down to grab one of the larger branches and almost stumbled to the ground.

She righted herself and whirled around to face Eva, who laughed.

"You're going to hurt me with a flaming stick?" she snorted.

Neri tensed as Niall closed his eyes beside her. His head lolled, his fingers slipping away from the rag he held to his stab wound.

The fury roared. Heat exploded over Neri's skin, through her muscles, incinerating her bones. She would not lose another one. She refused. Vengeful rage lit in her soul, even as real flames flared at the end of the branch.

Eva screamed as a lash of fire from the candle exploded. Sparks surrounded her, dancing around her as her clothes began to smoke a moment before her t-shirt burst into flame.

Not from the candle, from my branch. No time. Niall comes first.

Neri ignored the realisation that the branch had lit itself on fire and kept it in her hand. She dropped to one knee beside Niall, aware of Eva still trying to put out the flames now attacking her.

Struggling with the jarring pain in her body and the gash to her arm, Neri assessed Niall's wound. She would need to bind it but the screaming among the trees was dying down, giving way to ominous shouting.

She ignored the sound of Eva thudding to the ground to roll out the fire and eyed her pack nearby.

"Niall, please say you're still with me."

He opened his eyes at the sound of her frantic pleading, foggy but alive. Shaking with pure relief, Neri lifted his hand that covered his wound.

"I'm going to wrap it as best I can," she promised. "Then we really need to get out of here. If we can make it back to the inn the long way, we might still be able to get to the horses."

She winced at the puckered abrasion on his skin but set about tearing part of his shirt free. With the wound fully revealed, she wrapped a makeshift sling that covered it and also held his arm in place.

"I traded the horses for our room at the inn," he muttered. "The coin was for the food and wine and ointment. Wanted you to have at least one good memory of me."

Undeterred, Neri helped him to his feet and shouldered her pack, even though the rising hysteria screamed at her to shake him until his bones rattled for being so careless with their faster route home.

"Can you walk?" she asked.

Niall nodded and winced in one spasming movement. Neri eyed Eva, still rolling on the floor with the fire mostly out. There didn't seem to be any sign of serious skin damage, but Neri forced the relief aside. They couldn't linger.

She supported Niall with her shoulder under his armpit on his good side, and together they set off into the woods.

"We'll find a simple place to rest tonight," she babbled. "I'll find some water somewhere to cleanse your wound, then we'll find someone who can sew it up. If not, I can do it."

She had no idea how to sew up skin, not sure whether the long or loop stitch would be more appropriate, or where she'd find a needle and thread.

I was never prepared for any of this. All the talk of magic and firebirds and cursed forests, but nobody taught me anything useful.

A little way into the trees, she slowed their pace enough to deaden the sound of their steps.

"Where are they?"

She recognised that voice, not sure if to be relieved that she wasn't a murderer or petrified that the danger had increased tenfold. Against all her judgements and sanity, she twisted herself and Niall around. The clearing was barely visible between the trees now, but she could make out small dark figures moving.

"They escaped," Eva's voice reached her next.

Amis tutted. "I gave you a chance, Eva. We promised you many things, despite you not giving up the location of the enemy. Now you let the girl who almost killed me slip through your fingers."

Neri sagged under Niall's weight.

She hasn't betrayed the others totally yet. Ma, Moonshine and Emelyn are safe still.

"I almost had them but she set me on fire!"

"She did? Or you fell? This place is ablaze as it is, an easy mistake to make."

"She did!" Eva sounded frantic now. "She had a stick and the fire pulsed right out of it and set my clothes alight."

Neri shook her head. *It was the fire.* The memory tugged at her, the recollection of anger becoming flame and pulsing out of her fingertips. *I can't wield fire, that's madness.*

"Then she is more dangerous than we ever thought possible. And you know far too much already."

Neri flinched as she saw the hint of someone raising an arm. She didn't need to stay to know what came next. She'd seen it happen before.

Panic roared at her to do something, intervene, save the girl who'd tried to betray them all. But one look at Niall hanging from her shoulder, barely conscious, and any moment to act was gone as a soft slicing sound filled the air.

Neri held in the panicked whimper, her chest heaving with unshed sobs and exhaustion. Eva was gone now and she didn't have much hope of outrunning the Governance either, but for Niall's sake she had to try.

The trees blurred into one long carousel and Neri sagged under the combined weight of two backpacks and Niall's lolling body. The moments all passed into one long agonising method of step, step, ask if Niall was still ok, step, step, look around, step, step. Finally as the suns began to lighten the horizon, she found a clear spring gushing through the trees.

"We'll rest here for a bit. I'll clean your wound and put a new bandage on it."

She scooped water onto the wound and used one of the

less bloodied knives to tear up blankets. Unsure of whether she should let Niall doze or not after he'd lost blood, she worked as quickly as she could. Every few seconds she glanced around, until she noticed a glowing light seemed to be rising too fast to be the dawn. With more haste than was sensible, she rewrapped Niall's shoulder and threw everything else into the pack.

The light approached them, a single blaze creeping through the trees. Thoughts of the flaming bird filled her head but she shook them aside and leaned close to Niall's ear.

"There's a light coming this way," she whispered. "Can you stand?"

Niall's nodded and struggled to get to his feet. Panic tearing at her chest, Neri helped him up then gripped her blade tight. The tree hid them from the direct view, but she would have to be quick if she intended to use the element of surprise.

"Who's there, I can defend myself," a male voice called out.

Niall's head lifted.

"Trust him," he mumbled. "No other choice."

Neri leaned closer to ask what he was talking about and a moment later he scared the life out of her. He staggered away, clearing the edge of the tree with his hand holding his bad shoulder. She reached out but grabbed at air before stumbling frantically after him. Finn stood before them with a flaming club in one hand and a long blade in the other. He eyed them warily and then lowered his weapons.

"You look awful." He nodded at Niall. "Well, come on,

they'll be combing these woods for days. I can get us to a hidden cluster of rock where I can patch you up better."

Niall lurched toward him, intent on following, but Neri stood her ground, holding him back.

"How can we trust you?" she asked.

Finn turned and surprised Neri with a broad smile.

"You can't. But for what it's worth I saw you about to join the dance as if you were one of us. I promise, no tricks, just healing."

It could be a total lie, but Niall was still bleeding and Neri stood there out of options. She nodded and shuffled forward.

"Is it far?"

"About a half hour as the firebird flies."

He flicked an irritating grin at her before setting off. The words jarred in Neri's mind but she shook her head against the doubts. If he could fix Niall's shoulder, she would happily ignore all of the nonsense. With Niall growing ever heavier against her, they started to follow Finn.

Because it is nonsense, all of it. It has to be. No shimmer opened up and nothing magical appeared. There was that stuff with the fire and Eva, but I must have imagined it. There's no all-powerful magic and no mysterious pathway to the west.

She knew herself well enough to recognise the pathetic attempt at a lie. She hadn't imagined the burning in her fingers as the branch had burst into flame but pretending otherwise soothed a tiny part of her panic, enough to keep her moving forward.

Soon, exhaustion dragged at her every limb. She no

longer cared if magic fire and other parts of the land existed. Only Niall's situation stopped her from giving up and collapsing right there in the undergrowth.

Once they cleared the trees it became easier for her to support him, even though her muscles were screaming and the gash on her arm throbbed against the fresh air trying to dry it. Neri almost cried with relief when Finn pointed out an outcropping of rock.

He led them around the edge and into a large cleft. A ledge had been hewn into one side and Neri guessed it was used as a temporary sleeping place by seasoned travellers to shelter from more aggressive weather.

"Now let's not bother with the pleasantries," Finn said. "I'm going to help and in return you can do something for me."

Neri halted in the entrance to the cleft, her knees shaking from the effort of holding herself and Niall up.

"What is it you need me to do?" she asked.

Unwilling to accept until she knew what the trade was, she clutched Niall to her side. Finn shrugged out of his own pack and strapped his blade to it.

"I need information."

Neri took a ragged breath and nodded. "We'd better do that quickly first. I may not be able to answer."

Shadows flickered but Neri focused on keeping Niall upright as his head dipped. Finn set his torch into a nook so it illuminated the rocks and nodded to the ledge.

"Slump him on that. If you don't want to tell me what I need to know, or can't, then you can pick him up again."

Even though she probably wouldn't have the strength to

pick him up again, Neri lowered Niall down with gentle hands and shrugged her pack off. Despite not wanting to let her guard down, she had to ease some of her muscles or she wouldn't be much use if they did have to set off again straight away. She rolled her shoulders and squeaked when the pang of pain shot through her chest.

Finn pulled a large wrap of fabric out of his pack, unfolding it beside Niall to reveal several small pots and strips of clean cloth. Neri's temptation to do whatever it took for those healing contents intensified and she dropped to kneel beside the ledge.

"Are the others safe?" Finn asked.

He didn't look up, his focus fixed on un-wrapping a small needle-blade from its wrapping.

"They were when we left the day before yesterday, yes."

A thin length of thread unravelled in his steady fingers.

"Do you know anything about the realm or the Governance, or your part in the whole situation, that you've not told us?"

The thread slid through the eye of the needle-blade. Neri looked at him and slowly shook her head.

"No, I've kept nothing back and you all know way more than I do. You all believe more than I do, or so I thought. I can't remember how much I've told you but Niall knows all of it."

Except the whole wielding fire thing, but that can't be real. It can't be.

The lid came off a pot and a hideously bitter scent wafted out which Neri recognised as the same salve her gramma had sworn by for deeper wounds.

"Last question, and humour me with a serious answer please. Why are you here, putting up with all of this? You've said you have no idea about any of it so you could have just moved on, found somewhere else safe to hide. You didn't have to save Emelyn. You didn't have to follow him looking for ways west."

She skipped over the memory that they hadn't exactly been keen to let her leave the sanctuary at first, Niall especially. She knew there was only one real reason for her doing what she did, other than escaping Amis who gave her no choice. It sounded like a cheat answer, but she gave Finn the truth all the same.

"Because I love him. First it was because Emelyn had been kind to me and that's why I agreed to help. Then the Governance were after me and I had to find out why. But yeah, after we rescued her, pretty much that."

Finn smirked, as if that was the least surprising thing she could have said, even though the enormity of that truth was crashing around her.

"I can tell a lot about a person," Finn explained. "But to do that I need to hear them speak. I can tell if they're lying, and I can tell if they're being honest, but I thought you'd be a bit too vague. Luckily your reactions speak volumes."

Finn held out his hand, his eyes bright with some unknown emotion. Neri reached out, guessing they were calling a truce. She flinched as another hand appeared to take Finn's before she could.

"And she's still mine," Niall grumbled.

Neri twisted around to look at him, horror-laced

embarrassment burning over her face. He lay awake on the ledge, and he was smiling his lazy cat-got-the-cream smile at her.

"You love me? Honestly never thought I'd hear you say it."

Neri's chest fizzed with giddy relief at the sound of his sluggish voice. She flushed and resisted the urge to shove him for scaring her. She tried to be tough and not balk at Finn threading the needle into Niall's skin, but she winced anyway and turned her head to the side. Niall squeezed her hand tight, almost crushing the bone, but he didn't make a sound. After a few long moments, Finn wrapped a large length of cloth across the wound and shuffled back.

"There, good as new. No more fighting for a while though."

He stood up with a grunt and turned his attention to the gash on Neri's arm without asking. She stood obediently throughout the sting of the ointment, glad she didn't need stitching up as well.

"We won't be able to stay here long," Finn sighed. "As soon as it's light, you should move on."

Neri nodded. She had no idea what Niall would want to do now but getting back to the sanctuary somehow was the best option. Before that, he would need to sleep while she kept watch. As the silence lengthened, she glanced up to find Finn regarding her with his head tilted and his eyes full of shrewd contemplation.

"I knew it would come one day," he said. "We've all heard the fables but some of us believe more than others. Then, there are some of us that *know*. I expected more of a warrior to be honest, but I reckon you'll soon learn."

Neri looked back down at Niall, assuming Finn was talking some kind of cryptic westerly nonsense to him about the festival.

"You, Neri, the firebird came for you."

CHAPTER TWENTY ONE

Neri stared in bewilderment as Finn rolled his eyes.

"I know what you think you are," he said. "But it seems you're as much one of us as anyone else. Half-eastern maybe but the firebird still came for you."

Neri felt Niall clutch her hand tight and whipped round when she felt him trying to sit up.

"I'm fine." He shushed her. "I want to hear this."

His voice was faint but his good arm wrapped around her with some hint of its previous protective strength. She took comfort from that and eyed Finn warily.

"That's all I know," he shrugged. "Several folk saw it fly overhead tonight just before those *mekhan* attacked us. Emelyn mentioned that a kyne appeared to you at Moonshine's before I left the sanctuary as well. The firebird gifts kynes as a symbol of protection, so it's pretty clear that this all has something to do with you."

Neri frowned and wrapped her arm on top of Niall's. She hadn't seen any firebird at the festival, just a flaming arrow someone had shot before the Governance had arrived.

Or what I thought was an arrow. Did the Governance arrive before or after? Does it even matter?

Finn sighed. "I also know it has visited you before and brought you a shimmer. I almost thought you'd conjured it but then you just stood there staring at it."

Neri recalled the still pond at the sanctuary suddenly full of rushing water, and the instinct she'd had to believe what she saw rattling deep in her bones. She could remember well the curling ball of light forming feathers in the dark on the walk to rescue Emelyn, and the abrupt, momentary change from summer to autumn between the trees.

"You saw what happened the night before we went into the Governance stronghold, didn't you?" she asked.

Finn nodded and settled back against the wall.

"I still wasn't sure if we could trust you so I went my own way instead. I wasn't much further behind you, but folk rarely ever look that far back when they're so focused on moving forward. I figured that there should be someone left to raise the alarm if it all went wrong." He chuckled, his chin dipping as he nodded in Niall's direction. "Besides, he was obviously smitten straight off and Eva hadn't been herself for a while, so for all I knew I was the only one thinking straight."

Niall snorted, the sound bouncing off the rock. Neri tried not to smile but Finn just raised his eyes skywards and ignored him. Neri didn't know whether she could believe any of it, but she had to keep in mind that Finn had fixed Niall's wound.

"I saw you leave the camp," Finn continued. "Thought

you were off to warn them but then I saw the flames. I still couldn't be sure about your intentions though. Wouldn't be the first time the opposing side have had the upper hand with the natural land and their gifts. Anyway, I went straight back to the sanctuary after that. Eva followed and you lot shortly after. The rest as you know it, is history."

Ignoring the mention of shimmers and lands beyond, Neri frowned at him. In the flicker of firelight she couldn't read his expression, the impassive face no doubt a well-practiced mask, but the words sounded earnest enough.

"I don't understand," Neri mumbled.

But I'm beginning to.

Niall inched closer, his fingers threading through hers.

"Don't you see? Your drawings, your family token, the dance, these all say the same thing. Your family must have been from the west. The firebird even left you a kyne, proof that something about you is linked to the west and possibly the forest in between."

Neri shook her head but even she couldn't deny it. All the pieces of her past and the last few days merged into a huge flashing sign that pointed toward her true reality.

"Mik said that the only way through a shimmer by intent was by the bird coming to a summing ceremony," Niall added gently. "But I don't think that's true. I don't think it's a ceremony or a candle that calls it. I think it's a person."

He stopped when he noticed her breath coming in uneven pants, her eyes darting wild. The sheer enormity of it crashed down, that her family may have been raising her for a future they didn't tell her about, that their history led somewhere else entirely. She pressed her hand to her stomach as if that could quell the roiling queasiness inside.

"Why would the firebird choose me? My family has no great lineage, none I know of."

Niall shifted with a pained grunt. "You do attract a lot of crawbirds."

"I feed them, why wouldn't they?"

"Sometimes the land chooses based on merit not on heritage." Finn sighed, drawing her attention back to him. "We're out of time. You should leave before they catch up but whatever you decide, this is where we part ways."

"Why on earth wouldn't you tell us this before?" Niall hissed.

Finn shrugged. "There are those who are supposed to know, and others who need to discover. I could hardly blurt any of this out when I came across you at the inn yesterday in front of everyone. She's already got a big enough target painted on her as it is. Also, I really don't like you." A simmering smile flickered across his face. "But now that Neri's become interesting, I reckon *she* should know."

"We'll have a look around then," Niall insisted, his voice stronger already. "I'd say thank you but I don't like you either."

He released his arms from around Neri's waist and she sensed his intention to get on his feet in case danger came knocking. She hopped up and held out her hand to heave him up before reaching for her pack and swallowing a groan as she heaved it onto her back.

"We're going straight back to the sanctuary," she insisted. "Or Mik's. You need to heal properly before travelling anywhere."

Niall grimaced. "You don't know where we are, do you?"

She waited, her gaze narrowing from a combination of irritation and exhaustion. Finn grinned wider, his gaze bouncing back and forth between them.

"This is the border forest," Niall finished. "We're here to find a way through."

Neri processed that as calmly as she could with her mind a mess and her insides threatening to revolt.

She considered it.

"No."

Niall groaned. "Yes, we have to."

"No."

He wrapped his hand around hers but she held firm, refusing to let him move her forward.

"Neri..." He sighed. "We'll argue on the way, don't worry."

She could accept that only because they needed to get away before the Governance found them. He started walking toward the gap in the rock but a strain of pity held her back. Finn had thrown her a blade to fight Eva and had given her information about the firebird, which was really for Niall's benefit.

She looked back and caught Finn's eye.

"Thanks."

He shrugged a wordless acceptance, for once devoid of any arrogance, and Neri let Niall drag her back into the woods.

Soft dawn light was already rising, dappling through the

trees and casting a mottled reflection of different colours on the ground. They would need to move on to somewhere more permanent before the Governance found them, then strike out for the nearest settlement and potentially 'borrow' a couple of horses.

The trees threw the morning light into shadows and Neri watched the display expand into a slow kaleidoscope dancing across the undergrowth. With Niall moving at a slow shuffle, Neri kept her head up with great difficulty to check for potential enemies.

A shine flickered ahead, catching her eye as the smoothly waving lines and bright, fiery colours triggered a sense of being watched. A strong scent of tart berries filled her nose as the colours merged, yellows and reds and oranges becoming whole and glowing fiery gold as they took a familiar shape.

Neri stared up, her mouth dropping open.

It can't be.

The flickering form of the firebird caught the morning sunslight as it stood in front of them with its wings aloft, tall enough to settle its beak over their heads.

Neri's pulse began to pound. Finn had said it couldn't be a coincidence that these things had happened so far to her. Now she had to believe he was right.

They were all right, all along.

"Niall, look," she whispered.

He nodded, his eyes already fixed with absolute wonderous joy on the creature before them.

A whirl of air gusted past them and Neri took a step forward. Leaves crackled under her feet as Niall sniffed, and Neri recognised the tangy scent of autumn berries, shivering as a sudden bite of crisp wind nipped at her cheeks. The sky that had been lightening above them turned inky, dotted with flickers of dancing stars.

Neri gasped as the bird's delicate head turned toward her. One liquid black eye, rather similar to Niall's when he was angry, winked at her.

"Did you just see that?" she whispered.

Niall nodded. "This must be it. I can't even believe my eyes, but this has to be what we've been looking for."

The ethereal creature stretched its wings and a harmonious, low stream of melody wavered through the air. The notes tugged at Neri's heart, coaxing her forward. Before she could close her eyes, the haunting lament began to fade. The flames guttered, the feathers turning grey.

"No!" Neri cried.

Instinct flared and she shrugged off her pack, digging around inside for the kyne with the bright orange feather inside. She threw it down, the glass shattering on a conveniently placed rock, and ignored the shards of regret at destroying such a gift. She forced her fingers down through the mess until she felt the softness she needed. With the feather in hand, she held it out toward the bird as though she alone could save it. Niall's arm wrapped firm around her waist.

"Close your eyes and believe."

His lips wisped close to her ear but his voice sounded far away as a wind began to howl around them.

Caught firm in Niall's unyielding grip, she stumbled forward.

Inches away the firebird burned to ash.

The charred grey flakes drifted in the wind and Neri closed her eyes tight.

Please, let this work just this once, for him.

Her hand seared with burning pain, but the moment she stopped yelping a bitter wind raced against her, chilling her right down to her bones.

She opened her eyes to starlit twilight and towering pale-trunked trees.

Through the autumnal gloom she could make out drifts of ash still floating away on the wind, breaking up to nothing.

She stared at the avenue of enormous trees that ran either side of the wide dirt path she stood on, forming dark towering shadows that seemed to reach right up to the swirling stars.

She wrapped her arms tight around her chest to fight against the cold, the absence of one thing in particular driving a stabbing panic into her chest.

"Niall?"

She almost couldn't bear to call for him. Wherever she was, it wasn't the heat season of the east. If Niall had disappeared, or if he somehow wasn't with her anymore...

She surveyed the surroundings she'd been thrust into, trying to find him as her eyes adjusted to the darkness.

Even as the panic seared through her, Neri could see the light beginning to dawn above. The trees loomed, the silvery trunks beginning to pick up a sleepy morning hue. The foliage high above turned from a dark blanketed mass, catching enough rays to show leaves of the darkest red.

"Niall, if you're there, I'm going to say this even though I'm really struggling with it right now." Neri could hear the touch of hysteria climbing in her voice. "Are we somehow in the west? Are you here?"

Several moments passed as the wind whipped against her and she shrank into Niall's cloak still draped around her shoulders, fighting the overwhelming urge to sink to the grass underfoot and wail.

Further ahead between the trees she could make out a cliff edge, and beyond that the land stretched on toward the horizon. A stunning vista lay far below, a sprawling golden-green expanse dotted with bodies of silver water. They reflected the growing light source above and Neri forced herself to look up at same two suns rising fast over the trees. Even with the reassurance that the suns were the same, panic thundered through her until her body quaked with fear.

She scanned the forest of half-life shadows yet again for any sign of Niall. She couldn't see him anywhere but somehow the scent of him seemed infused with the air around her. He'd made it through with her, that she was sure of, clinging onto her in the wind before the shimmer had vanished. Now he was nowhere to be seen.

She faced the sprawling landscape ahead once more, the undeniable truth laid out before her. Her family had been tangled up in some kind of magic existence and now she was standing in the part of the realm they had been hiding from her all her life.

No Niall. No family or friends, and nobody I know who can explain what's happened to me. She took a shaky breath. *First step, find out what happened to Niall and where I actually am.*

Making a plan, even a rough one with no specifics, gave her trembling mind something to hang onto. It was either that or burst into screaming tears and never stop. She was sure Niall had made it here with her, wherever here was, and if- *when* she found him, he would have some serious explaining to do.

"I've been on my own before," she muttered to herself. "I can do it again."

With that sombre thought fixed in her head and only a pack of meagre belongings, Neri lifted her chin and took her first step into the west.

ACKNOWLEDGEMENTS

This book has been at least two decades in the rewriting, so thank you to everyone who encouraged me to keep writing, to my family and also my writing family as always, your support means everything to me.

Special thanks go to Aerin Apeltun for reading at least three versions of this book and never once hitting me over the head with it…

Also to Estelle Tudor, Anna Britton, Sally Doherty, Marisa Noelle, Emma Finlayson-Palmer, Katina Wright, Debbie Roxburgh, writing Twitter, everyone at #ukteenchat, the WriteMentor crew, all the libraries and shops who will take a chance on this series and give this indie author a chance to reach more readers, and finally to the readers who will find these books in the future:

THANK YOU!

ABOUT THE AUTHOR

While always convinced that there has to be something out there beyond the everyday, Emma focuses on weaving magic realms with words (the real world can wait a while). The idea of other worlds fascinates her and she's determined to find her own entrance to an alternate realm one day.

Raised in London, she now lives on the UK south coast with her husband and a very lazy black Labrador who occasionally condescends to take her out for a walk.

Aside from creative writing studies, an addiction to cake and spending far too much time procrastinating on social media, Emma is still waiting for the arrival of her unicorn. Or a tank, she's not fussy.

For the latest news and updates, check the website or come say hi on social media:

www.emmaebradley.com
@EmmaEBradley

Milton Keynes UK
Ingram Content Group UK Ltd.
UKHW010443220424
441503UK00002B/21